D0057151

"Beautiful, heartbreaking, and ultimately hopeful.
This is a rare gift of a novel."

—ROBYN SCHNEIDER, bestselling author of *The Beginning of Everything*

"*Some Mistakes Were Made* is a gorgeous meditation on shattered dreams and making amends, found family and loyalty, and what it means to sacrifice for the people we love most. Dwyer's debut is brimming with hope and love amidst angst, longing, heartache, and the bittersweetness of growing up. It is tender and romantic, vulnerable and sincere, but it is never ever cheesy. I was rooting for Easton and Ellis from the very first page."

—ASHLEY WOODFOLK, acclaimed author of *When You Were Everything*

"*Some Mistakes Were Made* is the angsty romance of my dreams. I wanted to linger in Kristin Dwyer's beautiful prose forever and savor all the perfect, vivid details. But once I started this special book, I just couldn't put it down!"

—ELISE BRYANT, author of *Happily Ever Afters*

"Gorgeously romantic and compulsively readable. *Some Mistakes Were Made* and these flawed, unforgettable characters wrecked my heart and then repaired it, filling the cracks with hope and possibility. A captivating story of first love, first heartbreak, and the delicate beauty of second chances."

—RACHEL LYNN SOLOMON, author of *Today Tonight Tomorrow*

"Dwyer's debut reaches into the complexities of family and societal pressure and draws out a one-of-a-kind narrative of the pain and passion of reuniting broken bonds. With vivid prose and heart-stopping romance, *Some Mistakes Were Made* is the powerful entry of a gorgeous new voice."

—EMILY WIBBERLEY and AUSTIN SIEGEMUND-BROKA, authors of *Always Never Yours*

SOME MISTAKES WERE MADE

KRISTIN DWYER

An Imprint of HarperCollinsPublishers

For David, who is always thinking of me.

*And absolutely not for Adrienne Young, who said she would
buy 600 copies of this book if I dedicated it to her and burn them.
This book is totally not dedicated to you.*

HarperTeen is an imprint of HarperCollins Publishers.

Some Mistakes Were Made
Copyright © 2022 by Kristin Dwyer
All rights reserved. Printed in Lithuania.
No part of this book may be used or reproduced in any manner whatsoever without
written permission except in the case of brief quotations embodied in critical articles
and reviews. For information address HarperCollins Children's Books, a division of
HarperCollins Publishers, 195 Broadway, New York, NY 10007.
www.epicreads.com
Library of Congress Control Number: 2021945756
ISBN 978-0-06-308853-5
Typography by Corina Lupp
22 23 24 25 26   SB   10 9 8 7 6 5 4 3 2 1
❖
First Edition

1

I'M THINKING ABOUT HIM.

Again.

In this moment that doesn't have room for him. In a place he isn't invited. And I have to be careful because memories are like rain.

A harmless drop here and there fall against my mind, then suddenly, I'm standing beneath a flood.

The top of the mortarboard in my hand is blank. Forest-green satin covers the cap without a single embellishment. Unlike the other hats belonging to the rest of my graduating class. Nothing to reflect the person wearing it. Nothing about its owner.

Would the top of my graduation cap have been empty if he was here?

I push the thought aside and take a deep breath as I move out of the walkway. A group of my fellow graduates pushes past me in the huge stadium, and somehow, I still manage to be in the way. My eyes go to the blue sky above me, already turning pink.

The sunsets here feel different than the ones in the Midwest. Brighter, as if the light is really golden.

"Oh my *god*," one of the girls says in her California lilt. Everyone here talks different. I wish I was home. I wish . . .

Across the green grass of the football field, I see Tucker **Albrey.**

Not the *him* I was wishing for.

He weaves in and out of the chairs as he makes his way toward me. Sunglasses cover his eyes and his blond hair is messy from surfing earlier. Tucker looks like he belongs here. Hands tucked into the pockets of his fitted pants and his button-down open at the collar to reveal a peek at his tan chest. He's effortlessly handsome. Almost as if he's not from the same flat Indiana countryside we both grew up in. Like Southern California is his home.

It's not.

Tucker grins and winks at a group that passes him. They giggle as one of them looks back over her shoulder, and not for the first time I'm grateful he doesn't flirt with me. Tucker's smile is a powerful weapon.

I give him a stern frown that I don't really mean. He's been like this since we were little. Somewhere between sincere and arrogant.

All the Albrey brothers are.

"What?" He lifts his shoulders in a careless shrug.

"My graduation is not a place for you to flirt."

"Ellis Truman." He puts a tanned hand over his heart. "If not now, when? If not me, who?"

I roll my eyes at him. "Look for your next victim elsewhere."

"I am offended at your verbiage." His arm wraps around my shoulders and I feel a deep sense of relief that he's here. At least Tucker is with me. I've imagined this day a hundred times, but it was never like this. I'm grateful that one thing has survived the past year. Tucker.

He holds out his phone in front of us. "Show us your certificate of 'High School Suffering Completion.'"

I do.

"Not in front of your face, stupid."

With a sigh, I pull my diploma down so the camera can see me. Dark hair that's never truly curly and never truly straight, freckles that seem unavoidable in the endless summers here, and washed-out blue eyes.

I don't feel like smiling.

The group of shiny, tan blondes who just passed stands a few feet away. Polished and perfect.

"Now," Tucker says, "all you have to do is look mildly happy."

I give him a wide open-mouthed grin like I'm in the middle of saying *Yay! I'm free!*

3

Tucker snaps the photo and his arm drops as he grumbles, "You are the most difficult. . . . You know girls are supposed to like getting their pictures taken with hot guys?"

I laugh. Tucker is not a hot guy. Not to me, anyway. He's practically my brother. My best and only friend in San Diego.

Before I can respond, a pair of arms wrap around me. "You did it!"

My shoulders go stiff and my body is taut as my aunt Courtney kisses my cheek with a loud smack. When she sees the lipstick there, she tries to wipe at it with a sheepish smile. "Sorry," she mumbles. Most of her time with me is somewhere between being too friendly and too concerned.

I try to feel grateful for what she's done for me this year. But all I can focus on are the things I've lost since coming to California.

Her fingers tuck a strand of brown hair behind her ear and she clears her throat. "You're a *graduate* now." The words are sweet but timid. "How does it feel?"

Like everything else, it feels wrong.

But that's not the answer she's looking for. I pull the corners of my mouth upward. "Fine, I guess."

Her grin only falls a fraction when she looks down at the tassel in my hands. I run my fingers through the synthetic orange and white strings absently.

I hate these colors because they're the wrong ones.

They're supposed to be the blue and silver of Sylvan Lake High.

4

"You can hang it from the rearview mirror when you get a car." My aunt looks back to me, adjusting the sunglasses perched at the edge of her nose. "Maybe the kids don't do that anymore."

As if *I* would know what the kids do. She seems to have missed the part where I have no friends here.

Tucker lets out a groan as he throws an arm around my shoulder. "Do not hang those disgusting colors from anywhere." He takes my cap and holds it up. The dark green catches in the light and shines. "I still would have decorated this stupid hat, though. Dixon drew a penis on my cap in Sharpie last year."

"Tucker," my aunt says, pretending to be scandalized.

He hands it back to me. "To be fair, I drew boobs on the back of his robe when he graduated. He didn't even notice till after the ceremony."

The memory flashes in my mind. Dixon threw Tucker into the lake later that night and gave him a black eye. I can almost smell the summer grass as I remember something else.

Easton under a darkened sky. Looking up at the stars. Feet dangle off the edge of the dock and into the water. Skin so close to mine I can feel its heat.

The memory falls like rain and I close my eyes. It's too sunny for that.

"Are you going to any grad parties?" Aunt Courtney has asked five times already, as if my answer is going to change. "That boy was talking about something happening on the beach?"

5

"A boy?" Tucker leans forward into the space between us. "A cute boy?"

I put my palm gently on his face and push him backward. "I'm not going to a party. I don't even know those people."

My aunt's red lips press into a thin line.

"Are you busy, Tuck?" I ask. "We could go to the beach." My aunt's face is eager, so I add, "A different beach."

I hear the hesitation in his voice before he answers. "Sure."

He's lying about not having plans. Tucker always has somewhere to go.

My phone chimes with an alert. @duckertucker has tagged you in a photo. I open it and see the two of us smiling in front of a blue sky. I'm holding up my diploma and wearing the most unflattering green gown.

But I look happy. More proof social media is a lie.

Three days ago, my feed was filled with pictures just like this from my old high school in Indiana. My former classmates wore blue gowns and smiles. Things I should have been wearing. Pictures that should have belonged to me.

"Dinner?" Aunt Courtney asks.

I envision sitting across from her at a chain restaurant as we eat and she tries to ask me all the things she thinks an adult, a parent, should ask. But she's not my parent. Just my dad's little sister who happened to have the misfortune of being the only grown-up stable enough to take custody of me. Until this past year, I only saw her at Christmas. An aunt you see once a year isn't who you want to celebrate one of the most important mile-stones of your life with. "I'm not that hungry."

"Oh." Her face falls and then recovers quickly, just like my guilt. "Do you want some money?"

"I have some," I tell her. It's another thing I don't let her do for me.

"Okay. Well. Not too late?" she says, but "too late" has no meaning. I haven't stayed out past ten since I came to live with her.

Tucker is still typing in stabbing motions on his phone, and I wonder who he's talking to. I crush the curiosity there because it feels a little too close to hope. "Hey." I bump his hip with mine and he looks up, confused for a second.

"Sorry," he apologizes as he pushes his phone into his pocket. "I was just texting . . ."

I want to ask; it's on the tip of my tongue. They could be simple words. Small ones. But I'm too afraid that they will hold more than a question.

His mother? His family? Easton?

Tucker's eyes change. Pity lines them and I swallow my frustration. I've always attracted sympathy, but it hurts worse coming from Tucker. He's supposed to see me differently. He's supposed to understand.

"Beach?"

I take a deep breath. "Yeah."

It's only two blocks away because in this San Diego beach

7

town, everything is "not far." Aunt Courtney waves goodbye as she walks back to the parking lot and I ignore my relief. It's a shitty thing to feel for someone who has been nothing but kind to me.

I make my way toward the waves while Tucker goes to the ever-present food truck that sells burritos. The sound of the Pacific Ocean is so loud, it's almost silent. A quiet that you step into, like a fog, and at some point, you stop listening to it and start feeling. I dig my feet into the sand and watch as the sun sinks into the black water.

Tucker drops a brown bag full of chips down into the sand between us and I fall next to him. He hands me a burrito. "Al pastor, no rice, no beans. Because you are gross."

I rummage in the bag. "Where's the green salsa?" I ask.

"She said she was out."

I look at him. "You know your voice goes high when you're lying?"

His tone turns mocking as he mimics my own. "Thank you for the burrito, Tucker. You're the best. Thank you for dropping everything to hang out. I'll go get the green salsa myself because I'm not a coward."

My groan is guttural. As if salsa is the most important thing at this moment and I will die without it. "You know she hates me. She always gives you extra salsa."

"Dramatic," he mumbles as he unwraps the foil. "I can't help that Maria loves beautiful things."

8

We hold up the burritos as Tucker takes a picture with the waves as the background. He captions it *celebratory burritos with my girl*. I take a bite that's mostly tortilla and stare out at the horizon as the sound of people playing in the water rises toward us. The sea has already begun to claw its way up the shore.

When the last of the food is gone, Tucker leans back on his elbows, watching the sunset. "So, what now?"

He's not asking about tonight. Or tomorrow. He's asking about what I do now that school is over. Now that I'm eighteen. Now that I'm free.

I've spent the last year of my life waiting. Waiting to finally exhale the breath I've been holding since last summer. Waiting to forget about all the things I don't have. Waiting to forget *him*.

Easton and I were always going to travel after high school. Then, once the world had sunk deep into our bones and we'd left pieces of ourselves strewn across it, we would go to college.

Together.

But instead of researching the full moon festival in Thailand or planning the best ways to get lost in Prague, I spent my senior year trying to figure out who I was when those things disappeared.

Without Easton.

"UCSD." It comes out sounding like jumble of letters, but I want it to feel like optimism. In college I can decide who I want to be. "I'll work this summer and then I'll go to school in the fall."

"That's it?" he asks.

I pick up a handful of sand and let it fall in a stream. "Maybe."

Tucker lets out a low, thoughtful sound. "She's proud of you." I don't ask who he means. That would be a waste of both of our time. He's talking about his mother. "She wanted to be here."

Of course she wanted to be here. But she doesn't get to be. I dig my foot farther into the sand. "It didn't feel like that big of a deal."

Tucker laughs, but it's without humor. "You are the worst goddamn liar."

I feel the need to justify this to him, which also feels annoying. "I did everything she asked. I came to California. I graduated from high school. I applied to college. She wanted to be here for her. Because everything worked out the way *she* wanted it to."

But I'm not sure it worked out the way I wanted.

"Ellis, I know you don't believe that, which is why I'm not burying your dead body in the sand. My mom loves you. She always has."

Maybe she did. Maybe there was a time Sandry Albrey loved me like one of her own, but that was before.

"Did you tell her about UCSD?" I ask.

He opens his mouth to speak. Closes it. Opens it again. "I think it should come from you, right?"

10

He's right, and I hate that the most. I want to tell Sandry. I want to watch her face transform into pride even if it strips me of mine. Because deep down, I was hoping these accomplishments would mean I had earned my place back home. I thought if I was good enough, quiet enough, obedient enough, I would be worth forgiving.

And after I've said good night to Tucker and washed my face and gotten ready for bed early, I lie awake wasting all my sleepless thoughts on telling her about UCSD. But if I'm being honest, it's not her I'm worried about.

It's him.

I'm worried that Easton will find out. Will he be hurt? Will he even care that I'm going?

It doesn't matter. He isn't a part of my plan anymore.

Without the distractions of the day, I feel the weight of the emptiness in my chest. It wraps around me like rope and cuts until I bleed. I pull up Easton's social media. A habit I can't seem to break.

Him. Friends. Smiles. Sara.

Easton Albrey is fine.

He graduated high school surrounded by his family. Had a big party at his house. He got to do all the things people are supposed to do when they say goodbye to high school. It makes me feel like the tide is pulling out from under me. It makes me do something I shouldn't.

I call him.

My fingers dial the number I've had memorized since the day he got it, but I block my own. Most people don't pick up blocked calls, but Easton does, every time.

I hold my breath as I wait for his voice to come on the line.

"Hello?" It's exactly like I remember it. Deep and a little scratched, like he's pushing a feeling back down.

I don't speak.

And then . . . and then I listen to him breathe on the other end of the line. Of the country.

I want to tell him so many things. About my graduation, my dad, his mom, Tucker, the beaches in California. I want to hear the noises he makes when he's pretending to listen to me.

I want to know if it was as easy for him to cut me out of his life as it looked.

But what I want most is to hear him say my name. Just once.

He doesn't, because even though it's what I want, it isn't what I need. Instead, he's silent. He's just there, breathing.

In and out.

Quiet and steady.

It was the one thing he always was and never was at the same time. Easton is a habit I can't break. A feeling I can't let go of. A truth I only admit in my weakest moments.

In the end, it's me who hangs up first.

But not until I'm done crying every last silent tear.

2

Eleven years old

EVERY TIME I HAD been in the back of a cop car it was with Easton Albrey.

Summer had come early to our town, stealing the softness of spring from the night air. It was the kind of heat that could only be chased away from the inside. I had saved enough money from couch cushions and discarded change from Dad's pockets to get an Icee from the Quickstop.

My bare legs swung down from the edge of the school's roof as the world moved underneath my shoes. I could feel the drink painting my tongue and teeth a bright blue as I pressed the cup to the side of my neck.

Easton stood on the sidewalk staring up at me with his head cocked to the side thoughtfully. His brown hair was messy, but it didn't hide the styled cut, and his dark eyes seemed almost black in the light. I wanted to look away, but from here, I was safe to stare.

And he had started it anyway.

Looking at Easton was like looking into a funhouse mirror if it made everything opposite. He was hard; I was soft. He had a big smile that adults liked. Adults never knew what to do with me. His clothes weren't stained and worn. . . .

"How'd you get up there?" he called.

I took a drink from the straw while I found words to say back to him. "Climbed." A stupid answer, but I wasn't sure how to talk to Easton. We had only ever said a handful of words to each other despite being in the same class our whole lives.

His eyes narrowed just a bit. "Are you a good climber?"

I didn't know exactly why he was asking me, but I could guess.

Only a month before I had stood in the candy aisle of the grocery store and thought about stealing.

The packages looked like gifts wrapped under a Christmas tree. Each one shiny and bright, promising something sweet inside. Something I couldn't have.

Everyone had a better lunch than me. Better food at their houses. Better snacks. They could afford candy that looked like presents.

I deserved them, too.

When I reached out to grab the bar, something else caught my eye. Easton stood at the end of the row wearing a heavy coat and a curious look on his face. His dark eyes looked like he could read my thoughts. Like he knew I didn't have the money to pay for the bar.

For a second I thought about taking it, watching his reaction, seeing the shock on his face of someone doing something wrong. But instead, I considered what that would make *me*.

A thief.

I had avoided Easton since that day. I was embarrassed and afraid he would see the girl in the store who thought about taking what she couldn't pay for.

When Easton Albrey asked if I was good climber, I should have said no. I should have ignored him and sat on the roof till the Icee was gone and the night had grown cooler.

But instead, I told him I was.

Something about the way Easton looked at me, so confident even at eleven, made me want to agree to anything he asked. And when he told me that he needed my help, I couldn't stop the way the words expanded inside my heart.

I climbed down from the roof and met him outside the school. The unlocked second-story window led to an office where the principal was holding a comic book hostage.

They had stolen it from him. He had been wronged. You couldn't get into trouble for taking back something that belonged to you.

I believed him.

So when I heard someone shouting at us and Easton told me to run, I could have probably run faster.

But Easton didn't leave me when I tripped outside the fence we had hopped. And when Officer Thomas caught us, out of breath and frustrated that he had to chase us down, Easton tried to take the blame.

"I told her to do it. It's not her fault." He stood in front of me, blocking Officer Thomas's view. His clothes smelled like laundry soap. I wanted to stay hidden behind him.

"East, you know I can't just let you two go."

East, not Easton. Like he knew him.

Easton's shoulders shifted underneath his shirt and he leaned forward. "This is *my* comic."

I'd never heard anyone speak to an adult like that. Another way he was my opposite.

But both of us ended up in the back of the cop car that night. Riding home on hard plastic seats that were unforgiving. And I knew I had become the thing I didn't want to.

Thief.

Easton stared at me in the dark, a frown carving through his face. "Don't worry," he said. "He's just going to call our parents and drive us home."

That's what I was worried about: Easton seeing my house. The cars parked on cinder blocks, the overgrown yard, the paint that peeled and chipped away.

I turned my head to look out the window, watching the lights color our school in a kaleidoscope of blue and red.

Easton's gaze was heavy on the side of my face. "You really are good at that."

16

"At what?" I asked, but I knew what he was talking about. *Stealing.*

"Climbing." He chewed on his lip. His freckles were darker in the dim light.

I could feel the tug of a smile on my mouth. I pointed to a long scar on my knee. "From the fence at the Wilsons' pasture." I moved to the next one, on my right shin. "Hopping the gate to the raceway track."

"What about that one?" he asked, pointing at the long thin mark on my arm.

I paused. "Climbed on the roof of Walmart."

His eyes narrowed, probably sensing my lie, but he didn't correct me. It was better than explaining about the time I had to break into my own house because my mom had forgotten me.

The driver's-side door opened and Officer Thomas slid in with a huff. "Well, I can't get ahold of your parents, Ellis, but I did talk to your mama, Easton. You're in trouble. Again."

Again?

Officer Thomas started the car and let out a long breath like he was exhausted. The school was only a few blocks from the Albreys', and we drove in a weighted silence.

Easton's house was bright, even in the dark. A white porch sat under large windows that didn't have the curtains drawn and inside people moved around living a life I could see only in snapshots. The yellow paint seemed cheerful and giant bushes of gardenias bloomed under the porch. I listened as the tires crunched against the gravel drive and finally slowed to a stop.

A head of blond curls peered out the long window that lined the side of the door. Tucker Albrey. He was only a grade ahead of Easton and me, but he seemed so much older. I'd heard adults call him *precocious*, but I didn't really understand what that meant. Tucker disappeared and I watched through the window as Easton's mother pushed off from the counter with her hands on her hips and eyes filled with fire.

When the front door opened, Easton groaned as his whole family spilled onto the driveway. I felt myself recoil on instinct as two boys rushed to the window. They stood staring into the back seat as if we were an exhibit at the zoo.

"Sandry. Ben." Officer Thomas greeted Mr. and Mrs. Albrey. "I'm here to deliver your delinquent." He said it in a way that made it sound like a joke. "I've gotta take the Truman girl home."

Mrs. Albrey's eyes shot back to the car. "Ellis? Tru's daughter?" Easton's mother said my name as if she knew anything about me. "I didn't realize East was with her."

Officer Thomas nodded and then let out a groan. "She climbs like a spider."

"Did you call Tru?" She crossed her arms like there was a chill in the air despite the heat.

"Can't get ahold of him."

Mrs. Albrey's eyes became slivers as she looked at her son and then at me. Even in the moonlight, she was pretty in a completely different way than my mother.

18

"I can make sure she gets home, Tommy," Mrs. Albrey said, placing a hand on his arm.

"I should really be the one—" Officer Thomas shifted on his feet in the gravel.

"Do you want to deal with Tru? Do you want that headache?"

He chewed on his options. "If I hear you took her anywhere other than home . . ."

"Scout's honor." She held up three long manicured fingers.

The officer gave her a flat stare. "You weren't a scout, Sandry."

Dixon, the oldest Albrey brother, walked over to Easton's window. He slid a thumb across his throat and stuck out his tongue as if he was dead before Tucker shoved him out of the way. Dixon was bigger than Tucker but still he stumbled. Tucker cupped his hands around his face and leaned against the window. When his eyes found mine, his lips curved upward slowly.

Easton's fist came up to the spot where Tucker's face was and hit the glass. Tucker's face transformed into anger as he slapped the place where Easton sat. Dixon pulled Tucker back with a laugh and the two began shoving each other.

My door opened and Officer Thomas ushered me out to stand in front of the grown-ups.

"Hello, Mrs. Albrey." I looked at the ground when I spoke.

Mrs. Albrey smiled warmly at me. "Call me Sandry."

19

I pulled at my old shirt nervously. Here was the moment when she would make a judgment about me. If I would wait on the porch for parents who would never come or be driven home to a dark house.

Both would change the meaning of her smile to pity.

"Her name is Ellis." Behind me, Easton climbed over the seats and out the door.

"Elvis?" Dixon asked. His expression was a confused version of his brother's.

"Quiet," Mrs. Albrey said.

"Ellis," I repeated, trying to make my voice sound sure.

Dixon made a disappointed face at Tucker. "I like Elvis better."

"I bet you do, *Dixy*." Tucker laughed and dodged out of the way when Dixon took a swipe.

"Ellis, honey, are you hungry?" Sandry asked me.

I was, but I was embarrassed to say so.

She seemed to sense it anyway. "Do you like pie? I have some of that."

"Everyone likes pie, Mom," Dixon said.

I followed the Albreys up the porch steps and into their house that smelled like lemons and sugar. The second my feet landed on the plush blue rug I felt like I had entered another world. Giant shoes were piled by the door in a bright foyer with a table full of mail. Just like a movie. A light gray couch had a soft white knit blanket thrown over the back. Books and papers from school were strewn out on the table. At the island in the kitchen, the boys had already dug into a pie, forks scraping against the ceramic. I ran a hand over the cool marble countertop and thought about the chipped laminate at my own house.

Mrs. Albrey shooed the boys away from the pie and sighed. "Animals," she cursed them under her breath. "Ellis, would you like me to cut you a slice?"

Tucker held out a fork to me—a test. It hung in the air, waiting for me to decide what kind of person I would be here. Inside the house with giant shoes and soft blankets.

My fingers wrapped around the silverware and I took a bite from the pie. A spell broke on the boys and they continued eating, metal hitting against metal as they fought for chunks of fruit or bits of buttery crust. On my fourth forkful, I looked up at Easton, who was staring at me. His mouth pulled tight.

I lowered my fork.

"You're different than I thought, Ellis Truman."

I shrugged, but inside I couldn't help but notice that Easton Albrey *thought* about me.

3

THERE ISN'T A DIFFERENCE between a sunrise and a sunset, really.

The same colors paint the sky. The same light struggles against a darkened heaven, frayed and faded. The problem with the sky is that sometimes you can't tell which is the beginning and which is the end.

My apron lies on the table, stained with coffee and milk from my shift as I stare at the housing email from UCSD. I can't tell if it's a sunrise or a sunset.

"Are you off now?"

I jump even though the voice is familiar. Will stands behind me with a name tag still on his chest and a rag in his hand.

"Yeah," I answer, and look at the ocean.

He pulls out the chair next to mine and sits down. "You forgot your tips and I thought you could use a coffee." Will slides a stack of ones toward me and a paper cup with my name scrawled on the side in black Sharpie. He always brings me coffee. "I feel like I haven't seen you in forever. How was graduation? Everything you hoped for?"

It's such a ridiculous statement that I look at him, assuming he's kidding, but like most things Will says, it's sincere.

Easton would find him so annoying.

I run a hand over the back of my neck and tell myself to stop thinking about Easton. "It was nice."

"I saw a picture. You looked really pretty." He doesn't blush when he says it and I wonder what it's like to just say things like that. Without fear. "My family threw this big party at mine. My grandma got drunk and my mom cried. It was *not* everything I hoped for."

"Really?" I ask, mostly because it feels like I should.

He launches into a story and I watch the way his mouth moves, excited over the words. His hand reaches out to adjust the cup in front of me, out of habit, and I imagine those fingers touching me. His mouth against mine. His lips whispering my name.

I wonder if a different me, one who had never met Easton, could love him. Will has stuck around long after everyone else who tried to befriend me gave up. He's good and steady and kind.

He deserves a better friend than me.

Will smiles and I know I've been caught not listening.

"Sorry," I mumble, not really meaning it.

23

He stutters out a breath. "I'm off in an hour if you want to grab something to eat? Tacos maybe?"

"She's got lunch plans. And she likes burritos better." I turn in my chair and see Tucker standing behind me, smiling. He's wearing shorts, flip-flops, and a T-shirt that reveals the tattoos covering his lean arms.

"Tucker." Will greets him with a tight smile.

Tucker holds up his cup of coffee in a salute and pulls out another heavy metal chair. It scrapes the concrete loudly, but he doesn't seem to mind as he slides into the seat.

Will's brows pull together as he watches Tucker get comfortable next to me and realizes our conversation has come to an end. "I'll see you tomorrow?" he asks.

I nod as he stands and goes back inside.

"You're breaking that boy's heart." Tucker turns his head thoughtfully, watching him go. "He's kinda cute and he always has coffee. You could do worse."

"So generous of you," I deadpan. "Did you need something?"

He frowns and it makes me feel more uncomfortable than I thought it could. "I've been texting you."

I haven't even opened my texts. They've been piling and gathering like a collection of worrying messages in bottles. "I've been busy."

He rolls his eyes at me before his face grows serious. "Serious Tucker" makes me nervous. I've only seen him a few times before. Like when we left Indiana for California.

24

"It's almost the Fourth of July."

It's absurd that he thinks I haven't realized what day is coming up. It's not just the Fourth of July. It's Sandry Albrey's birthday. Every year they combine to make a super-holiday.

"Mom is going to be fifty." Tucker runs his hands over the table.

I don't speak. I leave all the things I feel on my tongue.

He takes a white envelope out of his back pocket and slides it across the table. It's so dramatic, and I would tease him about it if I wasn't scared of what is inside. "A graduation present from Dad."

My hands stay firmly knotted in my lap. "What is it?"

"You know damn well it's a plane ticket back home."

"I have a job. I can't just leave town without notice."

"Oh yes. What will happen if you're not here to wipe down these tables?" His sarcasm is as exaggerated as this moment.

"Fuck off," I say with bite, but it's not about his insult. It's about what he's asking me to do. "It's not that easy."

Tucker runs a hand down his face. "Yes, it is." He leans forward and licks his bottom lip before pulling it between his teeth. "I don't ask for a lot, but I need you to do this. Then you can go to UCSD and forget all about us."

As if I could forget about the Albreys. As if Easton will disappear from my mind. But like an addiction, I try to hide it and pretend like I don't care about Tucker's words.

"Ellis, did you hear me?" Tucker repeats himself. "Mom is throwing a big party. The kind where we all dress up and give speeches. Half the town is invited." He knows I heard him. He's just waiting for me to acknowledge it.

"I don't know if they really want me."

Tucker points down to the paper between us. "Yeah, looks like they're still not sure. Maybe you should wait till they offer first class."

Tucker uses my silence as an opportunity to take a picture of our coffees and the ticket and uploads it. I get the alert a second later that I've been tagged in the post with the caption *making plans* and I glower at him. "Why do you hate me?"

"I need proof that we had this conversation to cover my own ass." He gives me a wicked grin. "Besides, you've already basically said yes."

My teeth smash together. "I'm not going." The thought of seeing everyone. Seeing him. My heart flips behind my ribs at the idea and I hate it for being a traitor.

"Ellis. It's been a whole year. Are you just never going to go back? Never going to see anyone from home again?"

"I see you almost every day. We'll be at the same college in the fall."

"This isn't the same." Tucker leans back and studies me. His long fingers brush at the tattoo on his left arm, a nervous habit he shares with his brothers. "Are you scared?"

I laugh, but it's hollow even to my own ears. He's always been good at getting to the parts of me I try to hide. My next words sound needy and I hate it. "Did they say I should come?"

"'They'?" he asks. He wants me to explain because he thinks if I can say Easton's name out loud it will be some kind of breakthrough. "Ellis Truman. Your name is on a plane ticket."

"One your dad bought," I clarify.

"I already told you this the last time we talked about it. Mom has asked you to come home for every major and minor holiday celebrated in America. She wanted to be here for your graduation. Do you really think I could get away with not bringing you back for her birthday?"

I pick at the side of my nail. Graduation is a raw nerve between us. *Selfish and petulant.* That's what Tucker had called me when I told him I didn't want his mom to come. It took weeks for our anger to diminish. Him bringing it up now means that he's decided this is worth the fight.

"I know it looks like she wants me there, but—"

Tucker opens his mouth and shuts it, and then opens it again. "I'm contemplating assaulting you. You are turning me into a bad person."

Tucker would never hurt me.

"I still don't know if I'll be able to make it with work."

He gives me a measured glare and moves a finger down the side of his coffee. "Easton isn't going."

I can't help how fast I look up. I try not to. I've spent a year trying to ignore the swoop in my stomach and the way my head turns when I think I hear his name mentioned, but some things are ingrained into us like breathing. "What do I care if he's there or not?"

"This." He points at me with one finger. "This is the most annoying thing you do."

"What?"

"Out of everything that makes me want to drown you in the ocean, this is the thing that is the worst. Worse than your snoring, or the way you smack your lips when you chew gum, or the way you put on every single perfume at that stupid makeup store. I cannot stand when you pretend like I don't know about you and Easton."

He doesn't, really. No one does. I'm not even sure I understand all the layers and breaths that are Easton and me.

Tucker takes a sip of his coffee and comes away with foam on his top lip. He licks it off like a puppy. "Did Easton text you? Or call?"

"No."

Tucker relaxes like I've just given him great news.

I swallow. My pride mostly. "Is he really not going?" I hope he can't hear the disappointment. I'm not allowed to feel that.

Irritation lines his handsome face. "Of course he's going. It's his mother's fiftieth birthday. And you are, too. Don't be stupid."

"Tucker."

He ignores me and his head cocks to the side. "You really haven't talked to him?"

I lean back in my chair. "Not since I left."

A muscle ticks in his jaw. "You gotta call him, El."

He must see the fear on my face because a second later he has his phone in his hand.

"What are you doing?" My voice is full of panicked edges that I can't seem to hide.

"I'm going to fix this bullshit." He presses three buttons.

Beasty Easty. The name flashes on the screen as he sets it down between us.

"Tucker." The speakerphone rings once. Twice. I can feel my stomach churning with acid.

"No," I say. "Tucker, hang up now."

He ignores me. I tell myself to get up. Walk away.

"Please."

Third ring.

I can't sit here.

Fourth ring.

I need—

"What?" Easton's voice comes through the line deep and laced with gravel.

Tucker's eyes move to his phone as he answers, "Long night?"

I hear the sounds of Easton stretching sleep from his muscles and I remember exactly what that looks like. His long body pulling taut. His chest going wide. "What do you want?"

"How's your trip going?" Tucker looks at me. Waiting to see if I seem surprised.

"Fucker, what do you want?" Easton repeats, using his brother's nickname.

I feel an ache listening to them talk to each other. I've missed this more than I am comfortable admitting.

"Congrats on your award in that poetry magazine." There is a long pause that eats away at time itself until Tucker speaks again. "Dixon call you?"

"About what?"

"About Mom's thing."

"Obviously. I have to be home no later than the third or he will make sure my dick never works again."

I can't help the way my brain immediately jumps to who he's with. Is he with a girl? Is that why he cares about Dixon's threat?

I am so stupid.

"So you'll be there," Tucker clarifies.

"Why are you asking dumb questions? And why isn't this a fucking text message?"

I hear the thing Tucker holds back in his voice and know it's me. "So. We will *all* be there."

"Yeah. Why are you being weird?"

It stings that he hasn't realized what Tucker is talking about. Easton has forgotten me.

"All of us will be there," Tucker says again. *"Ellis, too."*

My name feels like a stone tossed into the air, and the long seconds of silence from Easton on the other end fall on me.

"Cool." One word. It doesn't carry any of the hurt or hope that I want it to. It sounds . . . normal.

Tucker's eyes are on me, watching my reaction. He lets out a humorless laugh. "*Cool.* This isn't going to be awkward at all. So fun."

Easton scoffs and it scratches at the speakers of the phone. "Why would it be awkward? I doubt she'll care if I'm there or not, and I don't care if she is."

"*Easton.*" Tucker is losing his patience.

"What? Don't worry. I won't do anything to ruin Mom's birthday. Ellis and I are fine."

It's the first time I've heard him say my name in almost a year.

Tucker's had enough. "I'm not going to play this game with you, baby brother. I don't care if you and Ellis are fighting—"

"I'm not fighting with your girlfriend, Tuck."

The line is silent and Tucker looks to me again. Sadness is laced across his expression. It's not for me, though. It's for his brother. "She's not my girlfriend, Easton. Stop saying stupid shit."

"Fine." His reply is muffled, but I can't help but hope that it's because he's hurt. "She doesn't need me. She has you. Call it what you want. Ellis is your problem now."

"The arrogance of the two of you." Tucker breathes out his words in frustration. "Dad asked me to make sure Ellis comes. I don't want her worried you're . . . going to be you. So can you please just reach out to her?"

31

Easton is getting annoyed. I can hear it in the growl of his voice when he says, "She's not a flower."

"How the fuck would you know what she is or isn't? You haven't talked to her for a year." The words seep into my skin and lay their truth against my bones. "Just fix it. Make sure that you're not the reason she doesn't come, all right?"

The call ends and I look up at Tucker with my anger and gratitude in equal parts. "I didn't ask for that."

"I know." He takes a final sip of his coffee. "But you're welcome anyway."

I wish it didn't take six days for me to hear something from him.

I wish it didn't mean so much to me when two words show up on my screen.

I wish they didn't feel like a tether that pulls me home.

Just come.

4

Eleven years old

"YOU ARE TROUBLE."

My mother tsked before lighting the cigarette that hung from pursed lips. Her thick green-lacquered nails were chipped, revealing the yellowed beds of a heavy smoker.

Trouble. I added it to the list of words that defined me at eleven years old.

The smoke left her mouth on an exhale, tinting the air in the room with a dusty gray haze in the filtered sunlight and I realized it was just like her words. Poison.

I was already opening a book to escape my mother's lecture when my father came into the living room. "Come on, Anna. Don't be so hard on her. It wasn't a bank heist."

My dad gave me a wink and lifted up the book in my hands to read the title. *Japan.* He nodded his head slowly in approval. Only a month before he'd given me a stack of them. Blue spines with block letters, each with the name of a different country.

"Not this time. But that's how it starts. Lying and stealing."

She let out a disappointed breath full of smoke.

I hadn't stolen. The comic had belonged to Easton. I turned a page in the book to a picture of cherry blossoms that sat next to travel tips for exploring the mountains.

"I don't like her hanging around those people," she added.

My dad's shoulders straightened and his eyes went a little wider.

But my mom was just getting started. "I'm sure you *loved* her getting mixed up with the Albrey boy."

Dad wore the look of someone trying to stop a fight, so I wasn't surprised when he answered her with "I told her not to go over there, Anna."

I pressed my lips together, trying to trap my words. He hadn't said that when he was taking pie from Sandry, or asking after Sandry's mother, or saying we would just *have to* come back and swim at the lake.

"I told Ellis before this, but you know she doesn't listen," he continued.

He had never.

When my mom smiled at him, I knew why he had said it. Her happiness was more important than the truth, and he was using me like cheap polish to cover up the stains of his lie.

I read the words on the page in front of me.

There are two things every traveler should know when they set foot in a new country. How to say hello and thank you in the native tongue.

34

I wondered what the Japanese word for *trouble* was. I wondered if they called their children that. Did they sacrifice them on the altar of their own deceit?

I decided to spend the rest of my day reading through the old stack of travel guides, which was how Easton found me that Sunday afternoon.

Sitting on the porch in a folding chair with the travel book of Costa Rica. Every so often I would move when the lines from the plastic strips on the seat had dug too far into the flesh of my legs, and I'd read about the world's longest zipline that flew past a waterfall.

My mother had left, not bothering to say when she would be back, and my father was out running an errand. I had just gotten to the part about a hostel where you could sleep in hammocks on the beach when I heard someone speak.

"Seriously?"

Easton Albrey stood in his Sunday best on the dirt where a lawn belonged. His tie was loosened and his shoes dusty from the walk up my drive.

"What?" I asked, letting my feet fall down to the ground. I set the book next to my mason jar of purple Kool-Aid.

"You get to sit on your porch and do nothing, on a *Sunday*?" Woven into his shock was an accusation that I didn't fully understand.

I looked toward the road, like my mother was going to pull into the drive any moment. Maybe I was missing something. "I guess so?"

Easton's face crumpled like I had said something rude, and he let out a hard laugh. "Well, not anymore. My mom sent me to get you."

The nerves in my belly churned. "Get me? For what?"

"Church potluck. She couldn't remember if you went to First Covenant, but Pastor was sure you didn't go to Sacrament since . . . you know."

I did know, everyone knew. My mom could be . . . my mom.

The most embarrassing part of us not going to church anymore was that no one asked why we didn't. It was clear that they would prefer for the Trumans to stay home.

"Maybe we're atheists," I said.

He groaned. Even the atheists went to church in our town. "Well today you're going to the potluck."

"That's okay." I picked up my glass and took a long drink.

His nose scrunched up as he watched me. "Purple isn't a flavor."

"It's grape."

"I have never eaten a grape that looked like that." Easton shifted on his feet. "So, will you come?"

"I don't really wanna go to your house."

"You think *I'm* asking you to come to the potluck?"

A sick feeling of embarrassment spread over my ribs. Maybe I was wrong and he didn't want me to come with him.

"I can't come home unless you're with me."

36

"I don't want to go." I was still sure he couldn't make me. Pretty sure.

He took a deep breath. "And I didn't want to walk all the way here before the cakes were set out. But here we are. Now my brothers are going to eat all the good kinds and I'll be left with the gross vanilla one Mrs. Wallmont makes."

I took a breath to stop myself from arguing with him. It would just make him stay longer, and the longer he stayed, the more chance I had of my dad coming home and seeing who was here.

Easton cleared the few steps to me and brushed off the dirt from the porch as he sat down. "Your choices are come with me or I can stay here and spend the day with you."

My face paled at the horror of Easton hanging out on my porch. The questions my dad would have if he came home, the things my mom could say to him.

"You have another one of those books?" Easton leaned back against the old siding.

I stood. *"Fine."*

"You should probably change." Easton looked like he wasn't trying to insult me, but the way his face changed after he spoke, it made me understand he knew he had.

Which felt worse.

I stomped into the house. My room was messy. Clothes, papers, toys I was too old for, cups and plates I hadn't taken to the kitchen, an unmade bed and a picture of a horse that hung in a cheap frame. I searched for the one skirt I owned and a top that wasn't dirty. They'd been shoved to the side of my closet floor, next to an old pair of shoes my mom gave me that pinched my feet. I put them on and wrote a simple note on the back of an envelope for my dad before I walked outside, holding my hands wide.

"That's fine," Easton replied to my silent question.

I met him in the yard and followed him out to the road.

"You don't have to wait and ask anyone if you can leave?" He looked back at my house, unsure.

"No."

He didn't speak again as we walked down the dirt road that led to his house. The graveled asphalt crunched under our shoes as we followed the edge of the road.

Time stopped on Sundays.

There wasn't a single car on the road or person working outside because everyone was at church or a Sunday potluck.

We cut across an empty field and toward a small brown house that I didn't recognize.

"Where are we going?" I asked as I followed him up the drive.

He didn't turn around when he answered. "I just need to get something."

The windows were dark as we walked around to the back porch. No one was home and the house had an odd stillness. A galvanized metal roof hung over a sagging wooden porch with a white deep freezer pushed under a grimy window. Easton opened the lid and began rummaging inside.

"What are you doing?"

He held out two Popsicles in clear wrappers that had an icy freezer burn around them. "This one is purple." Easton held it out to me like a sword. "Here."

"You're stealing Popsicles?"

"No one even eats these. They're for Mr. Conner's grand-kids that never come over. We're doing him a favor."

"You're taking something without asking. That's stealing."

"I'm not stealing," he told me in a serious voice.

I took the pop from him. "So he said you could just take them?"

He shrugged again. This was a test. I had listened to Easton once before and found myself in the back of a police car, which had ended in pie. Easton was asking me to trust him again, but I couldn't help but wonder how many more times would end in something worse.

I took it from him. We sat next to each other on the step unwrapping the treats and quietly eating them.

Easton finally spoke. "You're not really bad."

Now it was my turn to feel confused. "What does that mean?"

"You don't want a Popsicle because it might be stolen, and you went to get my comic with me, but only because I told you it was mine." He shrugged. "You're good."

I wanted to ask who thought I was bad, but was too embarrassed.

He stood and wiped his palms on his pants. "People think I'm good, but I'm not."

The discarded wrapper sat in the place he had just left. I picked it up and placed it in a small trash can next to the freezer.

We walked back across the field and eventually Easton turned down his drive to his home. The two-story yellow house with white trim from the other night. In the light I could see the lake that it sat in front of, making it even more like a picture that came with a frame. Cars in the drive were parked under trees with wide branches and the dirt below us was covered in grass.

Green and mowed.

It was hard to believe this house was only a short walk from mine.

Mrs. Albrey stood on the porch in a powder-blue dress with white flowers talking with another lady. Everything about the Albreys seemed like it was from a magazine. When she saw us, Mrs. Albrey touched the woman's arm and excused herself.

"Ellis, you made it." Her smile made my body feel warm, even if I didn't completely understand why she had asked me over. "Are you hungry? Can we get you a plate?"

I wasn't sure what I should say, so I settled for a kind of shrug and a kind of nod.

"Can I go now?" Easton moaned, and his eyes moved to a

group of kids sitting on the dock.

Mrs. Albrey said, "You can help Ellis."

Easton had had enough of me. That much I could tell. "He doesn't have to, Mrs. Albrey."

She spoke through upturned lips, and it felt forced. "Oh, he most certainly does. But that's sweet of you to say, dear. And call me Sandry. Go and have fun. Make yourself belong."

Make yourself belong. What an odd thing to say. As if people fit into spaces and shapes like puzzles. Mrs. Albrey waved toward the food with a tight gesture.

Easton gave me an exasperated glare and motioned for me to follow.

We walked through a large set of glass doors that stood propped open. Inside on the counter were several casserole dishes. He handed me a plate and made a "hurry up" gesture.

"You don't have to stay with me," I said.

"My mother may look nice, but she will make my life miserable if I leave you."

I spooned a potato dish onto the plate and asked, "Miserable?"

Dixon Albrey stood next to his brother, grin on his face, as he picked food from the table without a plate before putting it in his mouth. "It's true, Elvis," he said between bites.

Easton grabbed a roll. "Peanut butter and jelly sandwiches in my lunch. Forgetting to wash my soccer uniform—"

"Peanut butter and jelly?" I stopped him.

"He hates it," Dixon answered for him.

I shook my head from side to side. "No one hates peanut butter and jelly."

"I do." Easton folded his arms across his body.

"Sounds like you're the problem." I piled broccoli on my plate.

"Oh, he is," Dixon laughed. "When he was eight, he only ate macaroni and cheese. Breakfast, lunch, and dinner."

"Ew." I made a face.

Easton frowned. "I'm not telling you where the dessert is."

I sighed dramatically. "You said all the good stuff would be gone anyway."

Dixon laughed. "You're funny, Elvis."

"I'm not an idiot," Easton mumbled. "I hid some before I left."

"It's probably pumpkin pie," I tossed back to him.

"Why do you think it's pumpkin?" he asked.

"Because pumpkin is the grossest dessert I could think of."

"Can pie be gross?" Dixon mused seriously.

"It's berry," Easton answered. "My favorite."

My lips turned down. "Mine, too."

Easton grinned at me, wide. Some information he had just discovered burned in his gaze. It caught me off guard, and for a moment the air in my lungs stilled. "You don't like me," he said.

"I . . ." There were no words for my feelings about Easton

Albrey. They were undefinable.

"Everyone likes me." He didn't say it with arrogance but like it was a puzzle to solve.

"It's true," Dixon added. He took a bite of bread and studied us. "He's everyone's favorite."

"I'm sure you're nice—" I started.

"I'm all right," Easton interrupted with a shrug. "People always think I'm the same as my brothers."

Assumption was something I could understand. Easton seemed different in this kitchen than the boy who had convinced me to break into the school or the one who stole Popsicles. And yet he also seemed the same.

"It's okay. You don't have to like me."

But he was wrong. I did like Easton. We took our food outside and sat on the dock, eating off paper plates that grew soggy and watching people spread over the yard like inkblots on paper.

"Do you always have this many people over?" I asked.

"Yeah," he answered with a full mouth.

I squished my eyes and tried to imagine all these people in my yard. It was impossible. There was nowhere for them to go. But at the Albreys', life seemed limitless. It burst from the house and overflowed onto soft grass that pushed against the lake. Music and laughter filled the air and the breeze from the water carried it to unknown places.

It was almost like another planet. A world I had never

known. Peaceful and exciting.

Until I heard the shouting.

My mother stood on the side of the house, with hair brassy and ragged at the ends from dye and hairspray. She wore cheap clothes as if they were designer. The pockets of her jeans covered in rhinestones and her black shirt a size too small. For a moment, I was in awe. My mother was a different kind of beautiful than the people around her.

The people around her. I noticed the shocked eyebrows lifted and mouths pulled into tight O shapes. They didn't see Anna Truman the way I did.

Sandry moved across the yard with a singular purpose, her steps sure and heavy.

"Who's that?" Easton asked his brothers.

"Anna, please," I heard Sandry say.

My mother's eyes were hard and her face was red, as if Easton's mother had done something terrible. "You have some nerve."

"Anna, it's just a potluck." Sandry's voice sounded reasonable and measured. And that was a mistake. "She's having fun. Let her stay."

"Right, a potluck." My mom spit the words like poison. "Ellis?" She called my name and I felt myself shrink back.

Everyone, possibly in the whole universe, had stopped to see who was yelling at Sandry Albrey. My mother was making another scene.

44

Sandry was trying to save the situation, which was rapidly unraveling. "Tru wouldn't—"

"Don't you even start with your shit, Sandry. Just because you and Tru used to be close doesn't mean that you can talk to me like that."

I stood. Easton stood with me.

Sandry didn't look hurt or angry, only tired. "Anna, I'm not trying—"

"I don't want you around Ellis." My mother scoffed. "I don't want her to end up brainwashed by your cult."

This was Sandry's breaking point. She stood straight-backed and jaw clenched. "Then maybe next time Tru gets himself into trouble you can bail him out," she said. "You don't want me around your girl? Then stick around long enough to take care of her yourself."

I took a step forward and Easton put his hand on my arm. His face transformed in confusion and I hated how embarrassed it made me feel. I stepped forward again, but Easton didn't let go. It was too late anyway; my mother had seen me. She was marching toward us.

"There you are," she said. "Didn't you hear me calling you?"

I couldn't speak.

"I thought we talked about this."

My silence set a fire in my mother's eyes.

"Come on. Tenny is waiting for you at your grandmother's,"

she said, taking me by the wrist. I knew Tenny wasn't waiting for me; it was a lie she told me to get me to do what she wanted.

Her eyes caught on Easton's hand and I waited for him to pull it back and apologize. Instead, Easton's jaw was tight and his gaze sharp with disapproval and anger.

I had never seen a kid look at any adult like that.

In the end it was me who slipped from Easton's grip and followed my mother out of the yard. When she told me never to speak to those people again, I agreed.

Because when it came down to it, it was best for everyone.

I was trouble, and it followed me everywhere.

5

JUST COME.

I stare at the text message as I lie on my bed. They are the only words between Easton and me. Long ago I deleted the chat log that had years of texts, screenshots, and videos.

I've relegated them to a past I'm not allowed to keep visiting.

Regret sours in my throat as I stare at the blank screen and wonder what he sees on his end. Are the texts still there for him? Does he ever look at them or does it hurt him like it hurts me?

Just come.

"Hey," my aunt says from my open bedroom door. "Your dad called earlier."

I know. He tried to call me first. I have a series of missed collect calls from the prison on my phone in addition to the other texts and notifications I refuse to read.

"He was pretty disappointed that he didn't get to talk with you." She leans against the jamb and for a minute I feel guilty that I ignored the call until I remember that he probably just wanted money for his commissary account.

I sit up and swipe out of the text message.

"Do you think you'll see him when you . . . go back home?" she asks, trying to appear casual. But my aunt knows she's holding a bomb in her hands, making assumptions and talking to me about the Albreys.

I force her to make a decision about our conversation. "Home?"

My aunt chooses bravery. Or stupidity. It seems to be a thin line for Trumans. "I talked to Tucker." Then she adds, "And Sandry."

Betrayal slithers like a snake in my mind before I decide to crush it with my heel. I always forget she grew up with Sandry. I forget that Aunt Courtney was one of the few people to leave our town. Maybe she really is the brave kind of Truman. I'm still deciding what I am.

"I'm not going."

"Ellis." Her voice is filled with edges softened by her pity.

"Would you go see Grandma if you went back?" I mean my words to sound accusatory, but instead they are a question. I find myself curious what she will say.

She works an answer around in her mind, probably wondering how she can tell the truth and still tell me to see my father.

"No, but not because of Grandma. Because the rest of the family . . . it's not healthy for me to talk to them. I can't handle being pulled into their chaos." She looks hurt when she says it. I can feel the regret in her words. Even if she can't talk to her brothers, she still *feels* like she should talk to them. "It's only a few days. You might not get a chance to once school starts."

My aunt takes two steps into my room and sets a red envelope on my bed. I recognize the writing immediately. Sandry.

The door shuts behind her as if that will give me the privacy I need. Instead, I stare at the ceiling, I count my tips and send my dad commissary money, I check Twitter, but eventually, I rip the envelope open and see a card inside.

Glittery letters shout CONGRATS, GRAD. The inside is filled with Sandry's looping handwriting in purple ink. It's so familiar that I feel an ache staring at it. Every space is filled with her scrawl and smashed between the YOU DESERVE IT written in the middle.

Ellis! I'm so proud of you. You did it. Graduated. I wish that I could have seen it, but I understand why you didn't want any of us there. I wish your dad at least could have made it, but I know how proud he is of you. It was important to him, even if he never said. Dixon just moved to the day shift at the police station. He's got himself a new girlfriend—we'll see how long this one lasts. Tucker tells me you're still working at the coffee shop. I keep imagining you standing next to the beach serving drinks in the sun. Sounds so fancy. Like a movie.

You have beaten every odd and now you get to decide who you are. I hope whatever it is that you do, it's what you

want. Not what you think someone else wants you to do. I
know you're angry with me, but all I've ever wanted was for
you to stand on the edge of your life and know that you could
jump into the unknown. I wanted you to be confident and
independent. I wanted you to define yourself. I'm so proud of
you, my girl.

    I love you.

    Sandry

I sit up and take a worn shoebox from under my bed. The green rubber band that keeps the lid on is losing its elasticity, and I push it off with ease. Inside are all the letters Sandry has sent me since I moved. They are filed in chronological order, and even though she's never received a response, they still come every week. I tuck the card into the box and flop back onto my pillows, staring at the ceiling.

"The edge of life" seems like a ridiculous thing for her to say. I have been backing away from it for so many years I don't know what confidence would look like. Standing at the edge of life is for kids who have backpacks filled with parachutes. For people like the Albreys. The fact that Sandry doesn't seem to realize that she took my ability to stand there and not be afraid feels like a grave injustice.

Any confidence I have is something *I've* earned, not her. On my own.

Something niggles at the back of my mind. It always feels

purposeful when she leaves Easton out of her letters. Like he's a wire she's afraid to trip, that would set off an explosion.

I pull up Easton's social media, but I find all the same pictures. A beach. Bright turquoise water. Blue sky.

Mostly.

Easton stands on top of a dark rock, his arms wide like a young king, bare chest and broad shoulders with sun-kissed skin. Dark wavy hair hangs wet, framing his upturned face. His grin is lopsided. The one he wears when he's overly confident of something.

Where is he? There isn't a geo tag, but I see a familiar handle has liked the photo. @sarasmile7360.

My finger hovers over her name a second before I decided not to listen to the voice telling me that I won't like what I see.

Sara is in Mexico. Her first three pictures are on the beach with a bright filter. She has her arms wrapped around Easton's waist in one picture and he looks up in mid-laugh. I stop breathing. He's in Mexico with Sara. He's traveling with her. I keep looking at her pictures as if they will tell me all her secrets. An acceptance letter to NYU. Of course. She has both the money and the grades to go to a school like that. A picture of her in Central Park by a giant fountain. And a smattering of Easton.

For a long moment, I'm not sure what to do. Call Tucker? Call Easton? I don't think my voice would work anyway.

He's traveling. With someone else.

How could this happen? How could he go without me? How could he continue to dream when I couldn't?

I find my cousin's number. A conversation with Tenny which is mostly GIFs and emojis pops up. I type out three simple words.

Ellis:
Hey. Miss me?

Tenny:
I think the answer is obvious. No.

I smile.

Ellis:
I'm thinking about coming home for a bit.

The text reads Read and I worry about what could be going through her head.

Tenny:
For the Albreys' thing? That party?

Ellis:
Yeah.

More silence and then—

Tenny:
Why?

Excellent question. Why? If I was honest, I would say it's because I want to prove Easton wrong. Because I'm weak. But I can't go home for those reasons.

Ellis:
It'll be the last time before school starts.

Tenny:
Do you want to see them?

Yes.

Ellis:
They bought me a ticket. 👻

Tenny:
You don't owe them anything and it's your choice.
Come if you want to.

I imagine her face when she says it. All conviction in her bright eyes. Her wild hair around her like a lion. She has always hated the Albreys. Easton was always too much of something for her. Too loud, too arrogant, too rich. And when he wasn't those things, he was too quiet, too modest, and not rich enough. To Tenny, there is no difference between Easton and his family.

They will never be good enough because they aren't like us. Life isn't hard for them, and our struggle makes us better than them—stronger.

I was secretly hoping she would just tell me not to come home, but that's not Tenny's way. She wants me to make the choice myself.

I don't know how to explain to her that this is my chance to show them how much I've changed in a year, and how much I don't need them.

The conversation with Tucker from earlier comes to my mind. Easton winning an award. I click on the Google app and search for a mention of what he's won, but I can't find anything.

I toggle back to Easton's social media. Nothing about where he's going next year or Sara.

My eyes close and I tell myself for the millionth time college will be different. I'll finally escape this world of in-between where I wait for Easton or my parents or myself.

I'm so sick of waiting to be saved or waiting to find myself because I'm too afraid the person I find will disappoint someone else.

I send a text to Tucker.

Ellis:

I need a ride to the airport.

Tucker:

☺

I'll pick you up at seven. Be ready. I'm not waiting for you.

His response is immediate, as if he knew it was coming. And then it's followed by another.

Tucker:
And because I know you're curious.

He's forwarded a link to a news story saying that a teen from Indiana won the *New York Tribune* national poetry competition with a link to purchase the magazine the poem is in.

Ellis:
What is that?

Tucker:
😆 It's so much fun when you play games.
Speaking of games.
You ready to see Easton?

Ellis:
I plan on telling him you're my new boyfriend.

Tucker:
Ugh. Gross. Stop saying stuff like that. I just ate.

Ellis:
See you at seven, Fucker.

He sends back the middle-finger emoji and I lie on my bed for the rest of the night. I don't sleep. I think about Sara in Easton's pictures. It's hard to not feel like they were inevitable. They've always been on-again, off-again. She is all the things I will never be. Polished, poised, popular.

I briefly drift off, my pathetic thoughts like a lullaby. When I wake, I pack a suitcase and wander to the car idling in my driveway. Exhaust fogs the cool morning air.

My aunt gives me a hug with sleepy eyes. "Excited to go home?" she asks.

My words don't feel like a lie. "It will be good to see everyone one last time."

It's true. It will be good to prove to myself that I don't need them. Or anyone. That I can change and grow and leave behind the parts of me I don't need anymore.

And I don't need the Albreys.

I fall into the passenger seat and Tucker looks over to me with a frown. "Did you have coffee yet?"

I stare out the window instead of responding.

At the airport, Tucker makes me take a picture with him and our luggage. "I need to get the airport in the background," he orders, and then, "Smile."

I obey.

He uploads it instantly with the caption *Heading home. But first, coffee.*

"You sound like a forty-year-old divorcée figuring out social media," I tell him, shoving my phone into my pocket.

"But a hot divorcée, right? With 'don't be mad that your husband wants to smash this' vibes?"

I give him my most annoyed face. "Oh my *god*. You're so embarrassing."

He smiles at me a little too long. A little too soft.

"What?"

"Thank you for doing this," he says seriously. "It's going to be good."

I nod. Wanting to trust his words even when I don't trust anyone else's.

But it's not until he takes my hand that I feel like maybe he's right.

6

Thirteen years old

DIXON WAS LEARNING TO bake.

The countertop where we normally pulled up a barstool and did our homework was covered in flour and chocolate chips. Several sizes of measuring cups were strewn across the kitchen, and a bright red mixer whirled next to an arguing Dixon.

"I already put in three eggs."

Sandry wiped a hand across her forehead, smearing something the color of caramel next to her temple. "Dixy, put in the third egg or the whole thing will fall apart."

"I'm telling you I already did it."

"Sweet boy, look at me. I put out three eggs. Only three. The one in your hand is the third."

Dixon's shoulders slumped and he threw his head back, letting out a low, whiney moan. "Why do I have to do this?"

Easton handed me a bag of chips, his eyes still on his brother and mom. I took a handful and continued to watch our after-noon entertainment.

"Because I told you that I wasn't going to do this for you. You signed up to bring these brownies. *I* didn't agree to make them. I'm already more involved than you promised me I would be. So put the egg in the batter before I put *you* in the batter."

"Mom—"

"Here, Dixon. Let me help." I took the egg from his hand as I leaned over the counter and looked into the mixer. "Let's add this one to be safe. It won't hurt it."

Annoyance crept over Sandry's face as she stepped aside, but I couldn't handle listening to Dixon complain. Easton's eyes narrowed as he watched me crack the egg into the mixture, frustrated that I had ruined his fun.

"Are you sure this isn't going to make it suck?" Dixon asked.

I washed my hands in the sink and picked up a towel to dry them. "I have no idea if it's going to suck, but if it does, the egg wasn't the reason."

"You're going to stay and help me, right?" he asked.

"We have homework," Easton said, hitting my shoulder as I came to stand next to him. "Come on."

He picked up both our book bags and took them into the dining room, dropping them on the table. We took up the seats that we ate our meals in, spreading our work out over the worn wood. The sound of the television in the living room and the argument between Sandry and Dixon was like a soundtrack.

There was always noise at the Albreys'.

Easton pulled out his notebook from his backpack and opened it. On the top of the page was a series of words that he had scribbled. "You have homework in Mr. Graves?"

I nodded.

"Good, you can tell me the answers." He took out a textbook.

"What's that?" I asked.

As if he had just noticed, he moved the notebook toward him and tried to turn the page. But Tucker walked into the room with a smoothie in his hand. "It's his poems."

"Poems?" I repeated.

"Easton writes girly poems."

"Poetry isn't gendered!" Sandry yelled from the other room. "And stop teasing your brother."

Tucker pursed his lips. "It is, and he totally does."

His hands clenched on top of the paper.

"Shut up, Tucker. You still pee the bed."

Tucker's face went white. "I was sick!" He looked at me, serious. "I don't pee the bed."

I held out my hands. The universal sign of surrender. Being in the middle of Tucker and Easton's fights was never a safe place.

"Mom!" Easton yelled.

But Tucker's hand reached across the table and plucked the notebook from under Easton's grip.

"'*Eyes made from fire and words that are knives.*'" Tucker read the words, enunciating each syllable. The chair Easton sat in fell to the ground as he stood. He flailed over the schoolwork and centerpieces as he tried to pull the notebook from his brother.

"Tucker, *stop!*" Easton yelled as he climbed toward him and pulled at Tucker's arms.

"'*Flowers come in different colors just like feelings,*'" Tucker continued, backing up to the wall as Easton finally landed on the ground. I could see him becoming more frantic. His eyes were growing glassy from the angry tears that threatened to escape.

"Tucker," I said, and stood.

And then two things happened at once. Sandry came into the dining room, and Easton balled his fist and hit Tucker right in the stomach.

"Easton!" Sandry yelled as Tucker fell to the ground.

Easton pulled the notebook from his brother's hands, flipping the pages to shut it.

"Damn it!" she continued as she leaned down. "What the hell did you do that for?"

"He was reading my stuff," Easton answered, barely containing his fury.

His stuff. The poems. I didn't know why that was important, but I knew that she did by the way the anger disappeared from her face.

"You still don't get to put your hands on another person." Sandry sighed as she looked at Tucker and then back to us. "Get out of here. Go into another room and wait for me to come get you."

In the next hour everyone's anger would be gone, but in this moment, it burned brightly as Tucker held his stomach and groaned.

Faker.

"Why do *I* have to go?" Easton said, indignant.

"Because Tucker is lying on the ground. So go before you're lying next to him."

In the kitchen, Dixon was pouring dark batter into a greased pan. "If your fight ruined my brownies . . ."

Easton took a finger and swiped it across the top. Dixon's face transformed into frozen shock. It looked delicious, so I grinned and did the same, putting my finger into my mouth.

Betrayal was clear on his face. "You're going to get salmonella and die and I'm gonna read all of your poems at your funeral." He groaned as he tried to smooth out the places our fingers had carved valleys into his creation. "Just go to Elvis's house."

"Ellis," I corrected, more out of habit.

"She doesn't like people to come over," Easton said as he stared down at his notebook. It almost sounded like his words were an afterthought. "Let's just go to my room." His footfalls were filled with frustration as we made our way up the stairs.

With each step, I replayed Easton's words in my head. When

we were quiet in his room I asked, "Why do you think that?"

"Think what?" Easton asked, only half listening. He was shoving his notebook into a drawer.

"About me."

"About *you* what?"

"About my house. Why did you say that to Dixon?"

Easton seemed to understand that something was wrong. His mouth turned down in confusion. "What's happening?"

"Why did you say I don't like people to come over?"

He looked to the doorway, probably for his mother's help, and then turned back to me. "'Cause you don't." His tone implied it was obvious. The same way people spoke to my mother when she was unreasonable and impolite.

My teeth pressed together. "I never said that."

"Well, you never invite me over," Easton said, matching my angry tone, but then he instantly relaxed. "It's okay if you don't want people to come over."

But that wasn't it. He was wrong.

With my hands balled at my sides, I went downstairs with Easton following. Now it was my turn to make angry stomps on the stairs. The dining room was empty, and I shoved my books into my bag.

"El, don't leave. It's not—" Easton started.

But I cut off his words. "Let's go." I held out my hand to him.

"Go where?"

"You're coming over."

He stared at me. Confusion and curiosity fought for a place on his face. I wondered if he was going to say his mother wouldn't let him. I wondered if Sandry *would* let him. I wondered what my mother would say if she saw Easton. She had learned to accept our friendship, but that didn't mean she wanted him in the house.

Easton chewed on the side of his lip before sighing. "All right."

The relief of getting my way was instantly taken over by the weight of what was going to happen.

Easton was coming over.

He grabbed his books and motioned for me to lead the way. We walked in silence, without the usual talk about school or friends. Just the sound of our shoes scraping against the dirt and rocks below our feet. When my house came into view, I noticed the garage was shut and my mother's car was gone. There was no telling if she would be back anytime soon; she had been gone since the day before and her returns were always unpredictable.

The porch had a stack of cinder blocks spotted with black soot where cigarettes had been put out. I opened the door, smelling the musty air and stale Marlboro Reds, wondering if he smelled them, too. Our orange couch had been worn to a dingy brown in the place where my mother sat and smoked. There were beer bottles on end tables and a paper pan with the microwaved meal that was last night's dinner still on the stove.

I looked at Easton as he glanced around the room. "Want some water?" There wasn't anything else to offer.

"I'm good." His hands stayed in his pockets like he was afraid to touch anything as he took in my house.

We weren't just poor, we were dirty, too.

"Where's your mom?" he asked.

"Gone."

"Is she coming back?"

I didn't answer.

"It seems like she's gone a lot," he added.

I lifted a shoulder as we walked back to my room. The faded yellow furniture and the unmade bed seemed different to me now, but Easton's eyes weren't on any of that. He was looking at the walls.

Every free space was filled with pictures of places around the world. I'd cut them from the travel guides that lay on the ground below them. They hung with clear tacks from the dollar store, making the walls almost textured. And next to them were two words in languages that matched the photos.

"Hola. Gracias." He ran a finger against the edge of the paper as he read the words aloud.

"Hello and thank you," I translated for him as my feet pressed into the carpet nervously.

Easton stood in the middle of the room, just staring from picture to picture.

I kicked at a pile of clothes and pushed them under my bed, hoping he couldn't see the underwear near the top. With his hands still in his pockets, he leaned toward a paper with highlighted words on it.

"'The beaches of Thailand.'" Easton said it aloud. "'Sawadee ka.'"

"You would say 'sawadee khap.' You're a boy." I tried not to squirm as he studied the wall. "What are you thinking?" I asked him.

"'Guten Tag,'" he read, and then let out a little laugh before bending down to the books pushed against the wall. "What's with all this?"

I played with the loose string at the hem of my shirt. "I like travel guides."

"Apparently." He took a deep breath and searched for a place to sit. "Why?"

"Because I like knowing that there are places other than here." I slid down to the ground and opened my book. Easton followed and his eyes finally landed on me. I took out my papers. "I like imagining what the people who live in those places are like. How they talk."

"Like 'hello' and 'thank you'?"

"I like words." I scribbled on the side of my paper before adding, "Other than Tenny, you're the first person I've shown this to."

"Why hasn't anyone else been here?" he asked.

"I guess for the same reason you haven't." I looked at my homework, trying to concentrate on math and not on Easton Albrey. I didn't want to be honest. I was embarrassed. Of my house, of my parents, of who I was.

But his attention shouted at me, pulling the numbers from my mind and calling for me to pay attention. "What are you thinking?" I asked again.

His eyes still moved across my room. "Thoughts aren't free."

"What?" I asked.

"You don't just give them away without them costing something," he said, and cleared his throat. "I'm thinking we are the same."

"Oh," I said, like I understood, but I didn't.

"We both like words."

His poetry. I wondered if it was the same for him. If the words made him feel free. "Will you let me read your stuff?"

"Maybe one day."

I pressed the tips of my fingers into the ground until they turned white instead of letting Easton see how much what he said meant to me. "Did you know in ancient China if you wanted to have a job in the government you had to submit poetry with your exam?"

"To get a job?"

I nodded and looked back down at my paper. "Poetry is important." We listened to the sounds of our pens against the paper as we let our thoughts grow.

"I like your room," Easton said eventually.

He liked that I had shown him. He knew it was a big deal even if I was pretending like it wasn't. And that was the scariest thing about Easton.

He always knew what I meant.

7

I HAD EXPECTED INDIANA to feel different. A year can change a place. A person. A town. But as we drive down the streets I've known my whole life, I see that everything is the same. The same brick buildings still line the main thorough-fare. The same two-pump gas station still sits below a sagging sign saying Quickstop. The fields of corn still stretch on forever.

Everything waited for me.

The car winds down the roads as Tucker sends message after message on his phone from the seat next to mine. I try to ignore the way my emotions feel like they're choking me.

When the Uber's tires are on the driveway, Tucker looks up and I watch a smile spread like wax across his face. He's home.

The Albreys' house hasn't changed. Light fades around it as the sun fights to throw its last rays onto the water.

A cop car in the driveway makes me think of the first time I came to the Albreys'. Dixon leans against his police cruiser in his uniform with arms folded.

"Dixy." Tucker unfolds himself from the car and moves to his brother, leaving me to grab our luggage from the trunk. Which is fine. I need the moment to prepare myself anyway.

Dixon holds a hand out to his brother, stopping him from giving an unwanted hug. "Don't start your shit, Fucker."

Tucker doesn't seem upset as he bats his arm away and wraps his brother in an embrace. I hear the hollow pats of back slaps.

"Where's Elvis?"

I shut the trunk with a loud slam and I look up at Dixon.

We haven't really spoken since I left. A few short texts here and there, but nothing . . . nothing like how it was before.

Gone are all the confessions about girls he likes and teasing messages making fun of his brothers. He was collateral damage after I left—a painful reminder of all I had lost when I was sent to San Diego.

I wait to see what kind of welcome I'm going to receive. Is he angry? Disappointed? Have I put too much distance between us? I hold my breath and then—

Dixon's arms are around me and I'm off the ground. My relief is so strong, so intense, that I can feel tears pricking my eyes and nose. I bury my face into his neck, the stiff uniform collar and vest pressing against my soft cheek, but I don't care.

"I missed you," he whispers against my hair.

He means it. I feel it in the way his words land against my heart. No pretense. Nothing added. Just the truth without a single caveat.

When he sets me down, I keep my eyes on the ground and let Dixon carry my luggage up the stairs. I can't help but notice a chunk of wood missing from one of the steps, and remember the time Easton pulled his bike up the porch, clipping the wood.

The whole week can't be like this. Me remembering a million different moments with Easton. I can't.

I won't survive.

Inside, I can smell the roast cooking, and I hear noises from the kitchen. "Mom," Tucker calls. "We made it."

Sandry rounds the corner, her eyes wide and her hair escaping from the ponytail she has pulled over her shoulder. Her smile is forced, nervous. I'm sure it mirrors the one I wore moments ago. She unties her apron and tosses it on the counter as she pulls Tucker into a hug.

"I'm so glad you're here," she says, a little too loud.

Ben Albrey stands and turns his dark eyes to me. I hold my breath as he wraps an arm around my shoulders and kisses the top of my head like a dad would. Except my dad isn't allowed to hug me. Inmates can't touch visitors.

"Welcome home, El," he tells me.

I don't say anything back, but I lean toward him and he keeps his arm over my shoulder for another long moment. It feels a bit like a shield.

Ben has always been like that. The mediator of the family.

Sandry asks Tucker about our flight and the drive from the airport and I can't hear all their words because my ears are ringing. Because I'm worried, because I'm a coward, because I'm angry. Because . . .

Because I badly want Sandry to look at me like she still loves me. And I hate that I need that. I hate that it's a requirement for me to feel like I belong here.

Her hand drops from Tucker, and finally I have her attention.

"Ellis." My name feels reverent.

My lips curl up without my permission. Her arms reach out like she's going to hug me, but instead she places both of her hands over mine.

"I'm glad you came." The words are tight. "Are you hungry?"

It's such a stupid question. It isn't any of the things I want to talk about.

"Starving," Tucker interjects. "I need to eat *now*."

I've eaten here so many times that I have a spot. The chair next to me is empty. It's where Easton would sit. Which is how all of dinner goes. Something is missing. Not just the unspoken words, not just the ghost of who isn't here.

We avoid the subject. Even Tucker, who usually wouldn't miss an opportunity to make an uncomfortable comment between bites of roast chicken and buttered potatoes and a salad made with vegetables from Ben's garden all drizzled in olive oil.

It's a sin for heat to come near these tomatoes.

It was the first tenet of Ben's garden religion.

And in the center of the table is a bowl of red pepper flakes next to the salt and pepper shakers. Because Ben thinks all meals, in general, lack red pepper.

For some stupid reason that bowl makes my throat tighten. It's the realization that I'm really, truly here. Not *home*. But . . .

Tucker asks about Ben's law firm and people from town. About Sandry's party and all the drama that comes with throwing an event for two hundred people. We talk about Dixon's job on patrol. The girls he's dating. And then it moves to Tucker.

"Is there a reason your brother seems to think the two of you aren't speaking to him?" Ben asks suddenly, crossing his arms over his body.

My stomach drops. I'd forgotten how the Albreys never avoid awkward conversations.

"Who knows why he thinks anything, Dad," Tucker says dismissively. "I talk to Easton all the time."

The silence in the room carries a weight that thickens my breaths.

Sandry's lips press together. Her disapproval of our choices— Easton's, Tucker's, mine—is clear on her face. "This is getting ridiculous, Tucker."

"Me? Why me and not him?" Tucker asks. "How come I have to make East feel better because him and Ellis had a fight?" He looks at me, unfairness drawn all over his face. "This is not my fault."

"You're older and more mature," Sandry says. "Allegedly."

Tucker runs a hand down his face. "I hate this family."

"Just fix whatever this is with your brother," she tells him. "Call it a birthday present for me." She's talking to Tucker, but I know the order is for me, too.

"Manual labor for your party is my present," Tucker jokes. "Does no one realize that I'm actually the victim here?"

"You'll be doing more than manual labor; there are a hundred things that need to be done and—"

"Sandry." Ben calms the storm brewing with a hand on hers and we watch Sandry take a deep breath.

She stands, signaling that dinner is over, and I collect the dishes, which had always been my job from before. We fall back into our patterns as if it's muscle memory. Van Morrison plays softly in the background. Sandry sits at the island while Ben refills her wine. Tucker and Dixon load the dishwasher and wipe down the counters. We put away half-used vegetables and spices Sandry had forgotten in her cooking frenzy.

The boys shove and push at each other and it makes something grow inside me. The normalcy of it. Except for the giant Easton-size hole in the room.

Ben sits down next to Sandry and pulls her feet onto his lap. A finger traces her ankle softly.

"When does Easton get here?" Tucker asks. "Still the day before the party?"

"Yeah," Ben answers. "He's cutting it close."

"Typical Easton getting out of all the hard work," Dixon mumbles.

"It's not really his fault. Sara planned the trip." Sandry takes a drink of her wine.

Sara planned it.

I don't know if I feel the betrayal of him planning a trip with someone else, or relief that it wasn't his idea. And I can't tell if I'm happy to have more days without Easton or if I'm disappointed.

Part of me can't wait to show him how I don't need him anymore. And another part of me, the weaker part, just wants to see him.

"Ellis, tell Mom about next year," Tucker presses. He's ready to get rid of this secret that I've asked him to keep.

I've imagined telling Sandry this news a million times. It was always with a letter in my hand and tears in my eyes, but it's been too long. Since I spoke to her, since I found out, since I wanted to tell her.

Sandry looks at me with curiosity in her eyes.

The words form in my mind first before I say them. "I got into UCSD."

"You . . . got into UC San Diego?" She says it slow. Surprised. And then.

Sandry jumps up. Her arms are around me, hugging me tightly as she makes high-pitched noises. I stay still as a stone.

"You got in!" She steps back from me, her joy spilling over

until realization settles. It freezes the happiness in her features. "I'm so proud."

"Thanks," I say, but it feels false. I don't want her to be proud. I don't want her to think I did this for her. "I got some grants and financial aid and scholarships—" I want her to know I've done this on my own. I made college work.

"I am so proud." She says it again and this time I let myself feel the words.

"You and Tucker at the same school." Ben shakes his head, putting a hand on Sandry's shoulder. "That's a nightmare waiting to happen," he teases.

"I can't believe Courtney didn't tell me," she murmurs. "Did you . . ." Sandry clears her throat. "Does your dad know?"

I take a deep breath, but there doesn't seem to be any oxygen in the room. "No. I haven't talked to him."

Her brain works through the timeline of an acceptance letter's arrival and when that would put my last conversation with my father. "He'll be happy for you when you go see him. I know he's missed you."

On my tongue are all the things I want to say to her. He wouldn't miss me if she hadn't sent me to California. College will just be another anecdote that he can tell people so they think he's a good father. That he did his job. "Yeah," I say just to stop her from asking about it.

I need air.

The French doors lead out to the lake behind the house,

and every step against the spongy grass feels grounding. All my memories have seeped into the dirt like rain and I know it could sprout a thousand blades of *me* if it wanted. I've spent so much time staring out at the water I'm not sure where it ends and I begin.

My legs dangle off the edge of the dock and I don't look up when I hear footsteps on the wood. Dixon sits down next to me, his booted feet not hitting the water. He hands me a flask but keeps his eyes ahead.

"Officer Albrey," I tease. "Do the other cops know how you disregard the law?"

"Shut it. I know you and Easton used to drink out here all the time, so just consider it a homecoming ritual."

I take a small sip and focus on the way it burns at my throat.

"Tucker seems happy."

"He is." It's true. Tucker fits in California. No one in his world there asks him to explain himself. Tucker can exist without labels the way he prefers. Sandry has always been big on telling her kids to be anything they want to be. Even if it's undefinable.

"I still don't know why Tucker was the only one you weren't mad at. I . . . asked him about it. Even accused him of talking shit about us to you. About Easton." He seems embarrassed that he had to take it that far.

I feel my own guilt slither around me that I put Tucker at odds with his family.

I look down at the flask when I speak. "Was Tucker hurt?"

Dixon clears his throat. "Yeah. Felt betrayed that we could even think that. You and him have always had a weird friendship."

I lift the flask again, as if it will give me the courage to say his name aloud. "No weirder than Easton and I."

"No," he says, shaking his head. "You and East have always been exactly what you are. It's always made sense."

My fingernail finds a deep groove in the wood and I press into it. "Until it didn't."

"Ah." He takes the flask from me and drinks. "It's going to be that kind of trip."

Tucker finds us and sits on the other side of me, and for the first time in awhile, I feel a sense of peace. It's little, but it's there. I pass the alcohol to Tucker.

He takes a sip and grimaces. "When is this from?"

"Alcohol doesn't go bad." Dixon reaches across me to grab the flask from Tucker.

"I don't think that's true," Tucker says, leaning back on his palms.

We sit in the quiet. I don't want to go into the house. I don't want to go upstairs. I don't want to go to sleep.

Dixon breaks the silence first. "Dylan Kimble just applied for an internship at the station."

I let out a groan.

"*The* Dylan Kimble?" Tucker asks with a laugh. "Does he still hate us?"

Dixon scoffs. "He doesn't hate me. He came in asking for my recommendation and implying heavily that I owed him a favor. Because of the incident."

"'The incident,'" Tucker laughs. "He got what he deserved."

I had a crush on Dylan when I was fourteen. It was mostly the idea of a boyfriend since I barely talked to him. But he had asked me to a party and then kissed Riley Baker, leaving me to walk home. Alone.

My insides squirm with guilt. "Well, he did have to spend the rest of his summer repainting his house."

"It's not our fault that he didn't wash the egg off." Dixon shrugs.

Tucker's grin covers his whole face. "There is probably still toilet paper in those trees."

Dixon high-fives his brother over my head.

Now I smile, remembering the hot summer night. Easton wiping my tears and threatening to kill Dylan. Tucker pulling out the Costco-size eggs and toilet paper. *"You'll feel better if you can throw something."* Dixon, typically the voice of reason, starting the car.

I had felt better when every inch of the yard was covered in two-ply and egg yolk. Not because he would have to clean it all up, but because the boys had wanted to defend me. Even if it was only against a stupid jerk. They were on my side.

And it felt nice.

Tucker yawns and stands. "Tell Dylan you already gave him a favor when you stopped Easton from murdering him."

Dixon helps me to my feet and the three of us head back into the house.

Each step on the staircase feels heavy.

My door is across from Easton's. His room is shut. The *Keep Out* sign we made is gone and I can't stop the way my emotions leap at it. He's removed me from his life.

Inside my room, nothing has changed. Same white furniture. Same bare walls. Same boxes piled in the corner and closet.

I change into my pajamas and go to the bathroom and brush my teeth. Easton's ghost stands next to me, brushing his teeth and smiling at me with a mouth full of toothpaste. I feel his hip as he nudges me out of the way to spit into the sink. I feel him watching me stare at my reflection in this mirror.

"You're always beautiful."

I blush, thinking about the way his voice sounded.

When I'm done, I stand in the doorway of my room and stare at Easton's. It's not a conscious decision when my fingers reach for the handle. It feels colder than it should, and I tell myself whatever is on the other side won't matter. The click of the doorknob is loud in the quiet and the door squeaks.

Easton's room.

A blue plaid comforter covers the bed. He hates it. Says it's boring.

On his mirror are photos of friends, of his brothers, but not a single one of me. The trinkets of our life together are all gone.

Movie ticket stubs and the stupid necklaces we got at a festival. I see the lack of my things in his space. My lotion is gone. My travel books. Me.

Everything but the map that's tacked above his desk.

All the pins of all the places we planned to visit are still stuck in it with bright colors.

"Bolivia? Do they have beaches?"

"They don't need them. They have this food called—"

My nails dig into my palms. He forgot about me. Forgot about our promises.

Tears fall from my eyes, and before I can stop myself I crawl into his bed. Slipping beneath the quilt, I press my face into his pillow and smell his shampoo mixed with the scent that is just his. Earth and salt and citrus. A sob breaks from me because I've missed it so much.

And I fall asleep staring at a map full of broken promises.

8

Thirteen years old

AT SCHOOL IS WHERE I learned that kids don't always mean the things they say.

Junior high was hard for everyone, but for a kid who didn't wear the right clothes or have the right things, it was brutal.

Most of my afternoons and weekends were spent at the Albreys'. No one ever asked me to go home or why I was there or why I was eating their food. But school was different.

At school, Easton had different friends than I did. All of his got out of nice cars in the morning, had food packed or money in their hands for the fancy hot lunches from the restaurants nearby.

Tenny and I rode the bus and got free lunches from the school. It was where we fit, Tenny had told me.

Normally, I sat in the cafeteria with her, but in class, Sara asked why I never sat with Easton at lunch.

She lived three doors down from the Albreys, right on the

lake. Her hair always looked perfect, clothes were always new, and her expression was always friendly.

She always sat with Easton's friends at lunch.

"You're best friends, right?" she asked me. "I see you at his house all the time."

I nodded slowly. I wasn't even sure I was supposed to tell people that.

"Well," she said, smiling at me. "Come sit with us at lunch."

Sandry had told me she would be a perfect friend for me and had tried to set up playdates for us. Something we were too old for and I was too embarrassed to admit I needed.

So, I had agreed, stupidly.

Carter Johnson watched me all the way from the lunch line as I moved with my tray toward their table. He was the kind of boy who only talked to a certain kind of person. I could feel his eyes as I sat down next to Sara. A hush fell over the group as everyone turned toward me. The thing that didn't belong. Even though it was a bright April day, I could feel their cold stares seeping into my skin.

"Ellis is gonna sit with us," Sara said cheerfully. "She's already friends with Easton."

Everyone turned to Easton, who sat at the opposite end of the table. His eyes found mine and quickly looked away. Apparently, that was enough because the table went back to whatever they had been doing before I sat down.

Sara plucked fries off her plate and laughed at something

someone said. Her bright hair was piled on the top of her head and she had enough freckles on her nose to seem adorable without making her childish. She was kind and considerate. The kind of person who always thought before she spoke.

I mostly hated her.

My palms were sweaty as I rubbed them over the tops of my jeans and I tried to pretend like I knew what I should be doing.

When she asked me questions, she made sure to avoid all the things that could embarrass me in a way that only made those things feel more exposed. At the opposite end of the table, Easton looked completely at ease. Except for his fork. It made small circles around the food on his plate.

Easton never considered that I was different from him. Not once. He couldn't fathom that both my parents didn't come home sometimes because one of them chose not to and the other was in jail. He made comments about getting good grades so our parents didn't kill us. My mom didn't even know if I went to school.

And I felt like Easton knew me best because he never considered all that. I wasn't the sum of things I couldn't control. With Easton, I lived outside of it.

"We'll be in high school in a few months," Sara mused. "People are different in high school. Not so close-minded."

I nodded, feeling the lump in my throat. I wasn't sure what words would make me sound grateful, which was what I knew she was waiting for. "I'm excited about homecoming."

Her eyes found mine. "Me too. My sister is a junior. Dresses and dinners and dancing. She wore this disgusting tiara, but somehow it was still pretty."

I thought of wearing a pretty dress. Of wearing a disgusting tiara and being a princess for a moment. And then I thought of a date. Who would I go with? I didn't know any boys but the Albreys. Easton would probably ask another girl. One with shiny hair and a tiara like Sara.

"I have a bunch of dresses my sister doesn't wear anymore if you want to borrow one."

I frowned, confused, before I realized what she was assuming. She thought I was making that face because I was worried about the cost of a dress. "Oh, thanks."

"We're about the same size."

She was doing me a favor. She was being generous. And I could tell it made her feel good to be those things. "That's really nice of you."

And it was. It was also humiliating.

Carter's voice moved down the table even though he had lowered it. "Why is Ellis Truman here anyway?"

All the muscles in my back tensed.

"She's here with Sara," Easton said.

I couldn't even look up at him. I let the silence fall into the cracks of the afternoon air as the hurt settled over me. He stood up and I didn't watch him go.

"I heard her dad is in prison."

I couldn't tell who was speaking because of the ringing in my ears.

"I heard she lives at Easton's and helps around the house."

"So she's like their maid?"

"Probably not," Carter said. "But maybe. It sounds like she's more like their pet."

"Her family—"

"She's my friend." Sara's voice rose above all the others. "I invited her. If you don't want to talk to her, you can leave."

"You gossip like a buncha church ladies," Taylor, a kid I barely knew, said.

Sara's hand covered mine. "Wanna go outside?"

Yes. Of course I wanted to go, but I wouldn't. I shook my head no. I didn't want to go anywhere with her. When I stood up and walked to the trash can, no one stopped me.

That afternoon, I was still embarrassed, but I didn't want to go home. Walking up the porch to the Albreys' didn't feel as humiliating as it should have. Even if I was their pet. Dixon and I sat in front of the television while Sandry hummed around the kitchen.

And then the door opened with a loud commotion. Tucker was in mid-yell. "—so stupid."

"I didn't ask for your opinion, Tucker." Easton was making his way from the door into the kitchen. When his face turned toward mine, I could see what had happened—the red marks—but just as quickly he was looking away. Easton had a busted lip and the beginnings of a bruise on his cheek.

"*You* did this," Tucker said, following him. His shirt was ripped.

"And I didn't ask for your help." Easton moved to the sink and turned on the faucet.

"What is happening?" Sandry asked. "Did you two fight?"

No one spoke until finally Tucker gave his mother an arrogant expression. "Ask Easton."

Sandry was up a second later, grabbing Easton's chin and examining his face. "Did you do this, Tucker?"

"What? No." Tucker appeared surprised that the conversation had turned on him so easily. "Well, not the lip."

She turned Easton's face and he winced. "Explain. Now."

"I got into a fight with Carter."

"Carter Johnson?" Sandry repeated.

I waited for Easton to look up at me, but his eyes stayed down on the ground.

He hissed as Sandry pressed on his lip and then jerked his head from her hand.

"For any reason in particular?" she asked.

Easton's hands stilled under the water and he shrugged.

Tucker smiled. "Tell her, Easton."

I didn't need a crystal ball to predict what happened next. Easton rounded on his brother and grabbed a handful of his shirt, but Sandry was quicker. Before Easton could hit Tucker, she was standing between them.

"Easton Albrey, use your words. I am sick of telling you to stop using your hands. You're acting like Dixon."

"Hey." Dixon looked momentarily wounded.

Sandry ignored him.

Tucker explained. "Easton tackled Carter at practice."

"Tackle soccer?" Dixon asked with a laugh.

"He was talking . . ." When Easton's eyes went to me, I knew what had happened. I felt the acid churn in my stomach.

"So you hit Carter?" Sandry asked again.

"He was talking about Ellis," Tucker said. "And then Taylor Vane said that Easton could at least have defended her at lunch if he cared. So I punched Easton."

Sandry shut her eyes and took a deep breath. "Defend Ellis?"

Easton pulled his bottom lip in and stared down as he ran a finger over the broken skin on his hand. "Carter was being an ass at lunch."

"Language," Sandry corrected. "He was being mean to Ellis at lunch, so you punched him hours later?"

Easton stepped backward out of his mother's reach. "Should I have hit him at lunch instead?"

"Yeah," Tucker added. "You should have."

But when Easton looked at me, I could see the apology there.

"All of you," Sandry started, "go to your rooms. Everyone is grounded."

"Mom," Dixon whined. "I wasn't even there."

"Shut up right now," Sandry said.

Easton threw down the towel in his hand and stomped out of the kitchen, and Dixon laughed as he followed him up the stairs.

I should have followed Easton. I always did. But I was still raw from the sting of lunch.

Tucker winked and nodded once for me to come with him. It was the out I needed. I started toward the stairs after him.

"Ellis." Sandry's voice stopped me. Her eyes crinkled at the corners with concern. "Are you okay?"

I wanted to say yes out loud, but the words stuck and I ended up just nodding.

"Yeah, I thought so." She wiped at the counter and then looked up at me. "I'm sorry Easton was a coward. I remember what that feels like." She set the rag on the edge of the sink and folded it. "Your dad had a hard time remembering we were friends sometimes, too. It never felt good."

"Why would my dad be embarrassed of you?"

She sighed. "Is that what you think? Easton's embarrassed?" She shook her head. "Your dad and I were always different in the wrong directions. Being a kid makes all of those things feel really important. Sometimes it didn't matter, but sometimes it did. You know I grew up in this house?"

I nodded.

"We spent a lot of time together the same way you and the boys do. We turned the boathouse into a clubhouse. We did silly things, but your dad didn't really have the luxury of being a kid. I think he was a little ashamed about it. I pretended to be okay with him ignoring me if other people were around, and I shouldn't have done that. It wasn't until we graduated and I had gone to college that he stopped."

She looked me in my eyes, making sure I understood her completely.

"Don't be okay with him acting that way. Don't pretend."

My words said that I agreed, but I still wasn't sure that I could. She let me go with a squeeze of my arm and I headed up the stairs toward Easton's room out of habit. My hand found Tucker's doorknob instead and I knocked once before pushing it open.

His space was so much messier than Easton's. Clothes thrown everywhere, books, plates with half-eaten food, trash. The source of many fights between him and his mother.

He lay across his bed and motioned for me to flop down next to him. "You're not the only one who had a shit day."

I made a noise. "Why was it bad for you?"

"I had to fistfight my brother for being an idiot—still worth it, by the way. I failed that stupid econ test. And I kissed Gretchen last week and she hasn't stopped asking me when I'm going to ask her out."

"Do you like Gretchen?"

He let out a breath and I understood. The question wasn't important, except it was.

"Sorry," I muttered. And I was. I wanted to be the kind of person who just let Tucker be Tucker. Let him discover what kind of person he was going to be. He seemed to realize that and took my hand, lacing our fingers together.

"You know you're better than Easton's stupid friends, right?" he asked. Or told. I wasn't really sure.

I let the understanding that I loved Tucker Albrey settle inside my heart.

It wasn't the kind of love that gave me butterflies or nerves. I loved Tucker in a way that was deeper. An unbreakable friendship.

"Did you know in Spain they send kids home for lunch?" I asked.

"Is that true?"

"I don't know, but it seems like something they would do."

His hand squeezed mine. "You're reading about Spain now?"

My eyes moved to the ceiling fan, watching it spin slowly, trying to track a single blade.

"It's movie night. Are you staying? It's my dad's turn to pick, so it'll be *The Princess Bride*." Tucker could sense my apprehension. "You should stay."

But I couldn't. An odd sense of vulnerability squirmed in my belly because the boys had defended me. I didn't want to feel like I needed someone, even if it felt good. I needed space to remind myself that I didn't need them.

I walked down the road in the moonlight and I thought of all the words Easton should have said.

Each step I took away from the Albrey house made the full and warm feeling slip away from me as if it was never there. My feet took me the short walk to my grandmother's house. I could see lights on in the living room and I knew, if I wanted to, I could go in and sit on the sofa. My grandmother wouldn't ask what I was doing, only sigh and offer me something to eat. There was comfort in not having to answer questions. Tenny would be there, but she would wonder why I wasn't at the

Albreys', and I didn't feel up to defending myself. Instead, I walked toward the place that was cold and distant. The place where I belonged.

Inside the house, my mom was in the bathroom, mascara in her hand and music blasting through the speakers. She sang along to the song as she opened her lipsticked mouth wide to apply the final touches to her lashes.

"Hey, baby," she said in a cheerful tone when she noticed me. She continued to primp in the mirror. "I didn't know you'd be home tonight."

"It's a school night."

She clicked her tongue. "How'd I get such a responsible daughter?"

I stood taller at the praise even if I didn't believe it.

"I'll be back later." She air-kissed the top of my head and grabbed her cell phone. "Call if you need me."

The door shut behind her. She hadn't asked about my day. She hadn't asked about school or my friends or even where I had been.

I brushed my teeth, washed my face, and put on my sweats. I couldn't lock the door because my mother might not be able to find her keys if she made it back home. So instead, I turned off all the lights as I made my way through the house. Alone.

At the door to my room, I stared at my bed only a few feet from my switch. I didn't often wish that my family was around, except for when I had to turn off the lights.

No one should have to turn the lights off alone.

9

IT TAKES ME A second to realize where I am.

Only one, because the light is different in this room. It filters through white curtains in thick streams of gentle morning sun. I stretch like a cat, feeling its warmth on my face. The sheets that smell like Easton. I turn my face into the pillow and take a deep breath as I pull my limbs back to my body. Everything feels right.

In the place where sleep still fogs my mind, it lets me pretend.

But like all fog, it lifts.

The Albreys' house. Sandry and Ben and Tucker are all here. I don't want to get up, but the thought of someone finding me here has me lifting the blankets and padding down the stairs. Explaining why I slept in Easton's room isn't the way I want to start my day.

My bare feet know all the grooves in the wood. I avoid the plank at the bottom of the step that I know creaks. Even a year can't take the familiar feeling of this house away from me.

In the kitchen I rub my eyes, trying to get rid of the sleep that still clings to me.

That's why I don't realize what I'm looking at until it's too late.

Easton stands in front of the coffee maker. His pajama-clad hip leans against the counter and his ankles are crossed. Dark hair sticks up at odd ends like it does when he wakes up, and some of it falls into his eyes.

He is exactly the same.

And completely different.

I can't breathe. His brown eyes stare back at me and he doesn't move. Doesn't speak. We are frozen.

A thousand things fill my mind as I will myself to do anything—say *anything*. A funny comment about who made the coffee. An angry comment about not expecting him so soon. A simple greeting. *Hello* can't be that hard to say.

But the words that fill my mouth aren't any of those.

I missed you.

Instead of speaking them out loud, I stay quiet.

I watch his throat work, a long tan column that I want to bury my face in.

"Your hair." He points at me with the mug in his hand. His voice is rough and I watch his Adam's apple move as he swallows.

My hair.

Maybe it's longer. Maybe lighter. But I don't even know what to say back. Those are the first words he speaks to me after a year?

Your hair.

I ball my hands at my side as I force myself not to reach out and smooth it. Or touch it. Or acknowledge that his stupid words actually mean more than they should to me. Because the truth is that he's *speaking* to me. And the words don't really matter. It's him that matters.

And I hate myself for it.

His face changes from surprise to something like worry. . . . But I'm mistaken. Easton doesn't worry about me.

"Ellis." It's a whisper.

"Don't." I hate the way I can't hide the pain in that word. I hate that it would be futile to even try. I hate everything about this room. The light is too soft and seems to fill the spaces between him and me. I can see the memory of a smile at the corner of his lips and I want so badly to work at making him show it to me. How alone we are.

I tell myself I hate Easton Albrey, but really, I hate that I don't.

A yawn cracks through the quiet and Dixon comes into the kitchen rubbing his belly underneath his shirt. "Easton? When the hell did you get here?"

I step backward, embarrassed that I was caught, but for what, I don't really know.

"Last night," he answers, never taking his eyes from me. We are in a staring contest, and I refuse to lose.

"You heard Ellis was here and you cut your trip short. Predictable," Dixon teases as he moves across the kitchen.

Easton takes a step away, and as he looks up, his shoulders tense, and I see his ears turn red. "Don't you have a house you're supposed to live at?"

Dixon ignores his brother and asks, "Are you guarding the coffee or can I have some?"

Easton takes a step away and his shoulders tense a moment before arms wrap around my shoulders. A face presses against mine and pushes a kiss against my cheek. It's rough and completely Tucker.

I pull away from the scruff on his chin but he just rubs it against me anyway. It causes me to break eye contact, but when I look back, Easton's jaw is clenched tight.

Tucker follows my eyes and seems to see Easton for the first time. "Baby brother!"

Easton's face never changes. "Fucker."

Tucker moves over to him and pulls him into a headlock, spilling Easton's hot coffee everywhere. Easton yells, but Tucker doesn't care as they begin to wrestle. I move over to the coffee-pot and Dixon hands me a cup he's already poured. "Still take it with enough creamer to give you cancer?"

I force a smirk to my face. "I prefer my coffee to be mostly caffeine and prediabetes." Does my voice sound steady? Nothing feels that way.

"Well, there you go." He takes a sip and motions toward his brothers. "You going to stop your boyfriends from fighting?"

I want to swallow my coffee to give myself something to do, but I can't seem to stomach anything.

Tucker finally lets go and I hand him a coffee cup.

"Thanks," he says and pushes the hair from his face.

Easton's eyes narrow on the cup as Sandry walks into the kitchen with a smile at her youngest son. "Oh, good. You're home."

"You knew he was coming home early?" Dixon asks.

"Yeah." She pours the last of the coffee into her mug. "I texted him and told him Ellis was on her way."

"And *me*." Tucker puts a hand over his heart. "I'm here, too."

Sandry makes a bored face. "I don't think there was any doubt that *you'd* make it on the plane."

"How'd you sleep?" Dixon asks me.

I focus on my coffee. "Good."

"That bed is really comfortable," Sandry says. "I slept on it a few times when Ben's snoring got too loud."

"Ellis wouldn't know because she slept in Easton's room," Tucker adds, his eyes wide over his cup as he takes an exaggerated sip. I wish looks could actually kill, because he would be dead.

The coffeepot in Sandry's hand stills only for a second. "Then where did Easton sleep?"

I wish the floor would open up and let me fall through to the center of the earth.

"I slept on the couch," he says.

My face burns as I think of Easton coming home and seeing me curled up in his bed. All amounts of my pride are destroyed. He knows how weak I am. He knows how foolish—

"You do hog the bed, El," Tucker says.

"I do not." Is my voice high?

Easton scoffs and Dixon looks back and forth between his brothers.

I take a sip of my coffee. It's small, but it gives me something to do.

"Oh good, everyone is up." Ben walks into the kitchen fully dressed in a suit with perfectly styled hair. He kisses Sandry good morning before taking the empty carafe from the maker and glaring at us as if we've betrayed him. "You drank all the coffee?"

Dixon shrugs. "It's not magically refillable."

He sighs heavily and turns toward me. I hold out my cup. "You can have mine," I offer. It's a gesture mostly.

"You have always been my favorite child." He makes a face at the milky color in my cup. "But you drink coffee like a monster."

When I smile at him, he smiles back. These are normal things. Typical things.

"What time will you be home?" Sandry asks as her finger runs up and down the side of her mug. A nervous habit.

"Same time." He sees the concern in Sandry and addresses it before she has a chance to do it herself. "You have all these people here to assist you. Some of them are even competent.

Ellis, would you help Sandry make a list?"

No. "Sure."

Sandry's whole face lights up and I feel guilty that I dread it so much.

"I wanted to go for a walk before," I tell her.

"Sure, yeah. Of course." All her words are too fast. They give away how worried she is that I'll take back my offer, and I stop myself from opening my mouth to make her feel better.

"I'm going to shower," I say, putting my mug in the sink.

"You're not going to finish that?" Ben asks. "I work hard to provide coffee for this ungrateful family. The least you could do is finish it."

I smile. It's the first time someone has spoken to me like there isn't a canyon between us.

Tucker laughs, "Dad sounds like Will."

For a second, I can't remember who Will is. My life in San Diego seems so far away from this kitchen. A smile finds my face at the absurd comment. Ben is nothing like Will. I tip the cup back and finish every drop before setting it in the sink and hold my hands up. "Good enough?" I ask.

He ruffles my hair. "Sure."

When I walk out of the room, I don't look at Easton, even though I can feel his eyes on me. In the bathroom I stare at my reflection for longer than I should, searching for the cracks and breaks in my veneer. My eyes are sad. I hate that they look like that.

In the shower, I try to wash all those things from my face,

from my body. The water is so hot that it reddens my skin.

I turn off the shower, and hear voices outside the door.

". . . whoever that is." I hear half of what Easton has said.

"Get over yourself and just ask if you want to know something," Tucker responds on the other side of the door.

"And watch you and Ellis smirk at each other again?"

I debate staying in the bathroom and hiding until they're gone, but I know they've heard the water turn off. So instead I get dressed, and when I open the door, Tucker and Easton are leaning against the doorjambs across from each other. They look like bucks waiting to lock horns. Easton is wearing a frown, but Tucker . . .

He gives me a wink. "Hey, pretty girl. Care to join us?"

It's obvious what Tucker is doing. He's doesn't want to be the one to have this conversation with Easton. In truth, he doesn't deserve to be stuck in the middle like this. I give him a pleading look, one that says *please don't make me do this.*

Tucker's face softens at my unspoken words. "Come on, El."

"Are you guys going to act like this the whole time?" Easton asks.

Tucker tilts his head to the side. "Probably." His jaw clenches. "He wants to know who Will is."

"Tuck." I say it quietly because even as I speak his name, I know he's not going to stop until one of us breaks and acknowledges the other.

Easton rolls his eyes, but his jaw clenches. "Do it where the rest of us don't have to watch."

"Watch what, East?" He's goading him. "Why can't we act this way? Didn't you want to ask about Will?"

I swallow, heavy. "Tucker, knock it off." I push back into my room and drop my pajamas near my luggage and pull the towel from my hair.

"I don't care about whoever the fuck that is, but I don't want to see all your inside jokes." Easton takes a step forward.

"Why? Jealous?"

Easton steps close to his brother and I can feel the anger tighten in the air, ready to snap.

Tucker lets out a frustrated laugh. "Holy fucking hell, Easton. Just *talk* to her." His jaw clenches as he closes the distance between him and Easton. "You are the dumbest smart person."

I press myself against the wall.

Easton glances at me and then back at Tucker. "Before she was your girlfriend—"

"Do you hear yourself?" Tucker steps back toward the stairs as if he could escape this situation. "Shut up and stop trying to deflect your shit onto everyone else. She's not my *girlfriend*. Don't even joke about that."

Easton doesn't look at me while the silence stretches. It feels sharp between my ribs.

Tucker takes a breath and his fury transforms to hurt. "Stop putting me in between the two of you. I'm sick of being a casualty of your war."

We watch his back as it disappears down the stairs and it's only Easton and me standing in the hallway. Finally, my eyes lift to meet Easton's.

I can't read them. I don't see anger or pain or a smug "*I knew it*" glare. They're black. Empty. Like nothing.

"Just . . . don't ruin this for Mom," Easton says. "Whatever your reason—don't."

Don't. It's the same thing I had told him only an hour ago. I lick my dry lips and he tracks the movement. "You lost the right to ask anything of me when I left for California."

I set my shoulders back, ready for the fight I know is coming, but Easton nods. And when his door is shut, I'm left in the hall, holding a towel and dripping water from my still wet hair onto my shirt and the carpet beneath me.

I stay there till the water on me turns cold and everyone except me has moved on.

10

Fifteen years old

THE FLU HAD BEEN the last straw for Sandry.

On the floor of our dirty bathroom, shivering from fever, I tried to tell myself I didn't have to call anyone. I didn't need anyone. I would be fine.

But my mother was gone again without a word of when she was coming back and my dad was in jail. He had been before, but this was the first time I truly *needed* a parent. I could make sure I got to school and feed myself, but . . . this.

Easton had come looking for me after I stopped responding to his texts. He pulled me up from the linoleum floor and deposited me on the couch with a blanket and a glass of water.

"You look horrible."

I didn't have the energy to yell at him or feel embarrassed.

The next time I opened my eyes Sandry stood over me with a tight jaw as she tried to remain calm. Her eyes moved around the house and she pulled her jacket tighter. Maybe I had forgotten to turn on the heat.

"Where's your mother?"

My eyes squinted. It took me a moment to understand why she was asking. Moms were supposed to take care of kids when they got sick. I hadn't seen mine in weeks, and her inconsistency was more normal to me than a mom who took care of an ill child.

Sandry wrapped a blanket around my shoulders and walked me to the car as she softly patted my back. I stayed on their couch, while the boys pretended to be annoyed I was there but jumped up to refill my water any time it was empty.

I told them not to, but Sandry just shrugged and said it was what people did.

When I was little my dad would let me stay home from school. I would come out of my room and tell him that I didn't feel well. My face would screw up into what I thought someone in pain should look like and I'd shuffle toward him sitting at the dining table. His morning cigarette would dangle in his hand as he watched the news quietly in the corner.

"Hm," he'd say while he held out a hand for me to press my forehead into. "Doesn't feel like a fever. Is it your stomach? Or your heart?"

I'd pretend to consider his question before I answered, "I think it's my heart."

"Well," he'd sigh. "You know the drill."

The smile on my face was unavoidable, even as I tried to hide it. Sitting on the couch, my dad would tuck a blanket around me and turn on cartoons. Breakfast would be brought to me on a plate, faces cut into bread and fruit for eyes. Lunch was always ice cream; it was the cure for all ailments. He would sit with me, laughing at the show, or patting my leg at emotional parts.

And as I sat at the Albreys' I realized I wasn't just sick in my body, but my heart, too. I missed my dad. Sandry brought me food and gave me medicine, and even though I appreciated it, I couldn't help but wish it were ice cream.

The next week Sandry marched me upstairs.

It was only a bed in the mostly empty room across from Easton's.

"I know it's not much," Sandry said, smoothing her hands nervously over the throw in her arms. She had folded and unfolded it twice in the time since we walked into the room. "I figured it was time anyway. The couch is uncomfortable."

It was only a bed.

Brand-new. Not secondhand like all the furniture in my house. It was clean, pristine, and even with bedsheets clearly laundered; I could tell those were new, too.

"I know you said you didn't need anywhere to stay . . ." Her words all seemed to dissolve at the ends. They lacked all the confidence that Sandry usually had when she spoke. "It's just that if you do need a place, I want you to know this is it. Right here. It's for more than just tonight. I don't ever want you to be sick and alone again."

I nodded because that's what she wanted me to do. I said thank you because it was what she was waiting for. I smiled because it was the easiest way to end this.

It was only a bed, but it made me feel as if they had given me something more. Something I had to live up to. That I owed them something.

How's your heart now?

It was grateful and I despised it.

"Your dad has a hearing on Tuesday, so we will know more about what's happening then. Just." She cleared her throat and set the blanket on the edge of the bed. "This will always be your home. I want you to remember that."

My home. It sounded so strange.

And even though living with the Albreys was temporary, I felt like a traitor for wanting it. Like I was choosing sides. "Am I not going to be able to live at my house anymore?"

"No. No." More rushed words. "I mean . . ." She took a deep breath. "We both know how often your mom is home, and I want you to know that this space is always here. Use it or don't, but just know it's here."

Officially, my mother lived at our house, and people didn't ask questions about who was taking care of a child after a certain age. I still attended school and I wasn't abused, so the state didn't seem to care if I had a parent at home or not.

But Sandry did.

When she shut the door behind her, leaving me in *my room,* I felt all the air leave.

I was supposed to love this bed, this space, this family, but loving it felt like a betrayal to everything else in my life. I couldn't see a way to do both.

After dinner, after the dishes were done and the family slept, I stood waiting for permission from my heart to lie down on *my* bed.

In the hallway, I could see the light from Easton's room. I stood at the door that was open a crack. Easton sat on the bed with his elbows on his knees, focused on the television in front of him. Furiously, he stabbed at the controller of the video game he was playing with his thumbs.

"You coming in?" Easton asked without taking his eyes off the game.

I pushed the door the rest of the way open and stood at the threshold, still not sure if I should.

"How long have you been trying to get out of there?"

He always knew what I was thinking without me having to say it. I found it annoying. "Not long." Two hours.

"I was wondering what took you so long." He was still staring at the screen.

"I didn't know if you had practice in the morning."

Easton just shrugged as if his five a.m. soccer practice didn't matter. His eyes tracked me as I sat down on the bed and leaned back against the wall, propping my legs out in front of me.

He went back to his game without saying anything. As if this was normal, and I guess it was to him. Just the two of us doing nothing but sitting in the quiet. I read about Guatemala's volcanoes while he shot at fake soldiers. Easton always understood I didn't want to talk about the hard things. The feelings that got caught in my throat and strangled my mind as I tried to put words to the sea of emotions that lived under my skin.

After a little bit, he put down his game and opened a journal. This was the quiet version of Easton. The one who didn't feel like he needed to smile, or argue, or have a clever answer. This version had relaxed shoulders and hushed laughs. This version of him was rare and special.

"Will you tell me if this is bad?" He held out his journal to me.

Others crowd into spaces that were promised for me and my argument is the sound of fear.

I didn't understand it, but I still thought it was pretty. "I like it."

"You like it?"

I shrugged. "I like the words." That wasn't it. "I like your words."

I liked that he shared them with me. He looked back down at his journal as if he was holding something sacred, and I knew he had done more than just share words with me.

He asked me about nothing and everything. About my parents, about my favorite color, about boys at school. Reading bits and pieces of his poetry to me. Some were horrible. Some were wonderful. Eventually, the night turned late. Easton and

I scavenged ice cream from the kitchen and sat cross-legged on his bed eating from the same bowl as we talked.

That was the first time I fell asleep in Easton's room. It was ironic that it took me actually having a place to sleep to start sharing a bed with him. I woke up with a blanket over me and Easton away at practice. The light in the room was hazy but also made me feel like an intruder as I pushed the covers off. I wiped the sleep from my face and opened the door to the hallway and crawled into the bed in my room.

Easton never mentioned it and I never brought it up.

But it happened again the next night and the night after that.

On the sixth night, I got up to go to my own room.

Easton looked confused. "Where are you going?" he asked me.

I tried to appear casual, like he was asking me an absurd question as I stood at the door with my hand on the knob. "My room."

"Why?" Easton looked genuinely baffled, and I hated how much I loved it.

"Because," I started, searching for an excuse, but he would see right through it. "You can't keep sharing a bed with me."

"Why not?" he asked, adjusting a pillow behind his head with one hand. His bicep flexed. "And what does that have to do with you sleeping in there?"

He'd said "in there." Not "your room."

"It's big enough for both of us." Easton said it almost mid-yawn.

"I can't . . ."

I could. I could continue to sleep next to Easton Albrey and it wouldn't be a big deal. That was the whole problem. Because he made everything easy, even sleeping next to him. But Easton didn't know the truth I kept hidden.

It would be a big deal to me.

"Easton, we can't keep sleeping in the same bed. That's stupid. What if your mom comes in here?"

"My mom knows you sleep in here."

My face heated. "No, she doesn't."

"Yes, she does." He repeated all the words with exaggeration, like I was ridiculous, not him. "Besides, I like listening to you snore. It's like a white noise machine."

"I do not snore."

He smiled in a way he knew I had a hard time saying no to.

"Fine." I crawled into the bed and scooted up against the wall, pressing my body as far away from him as possible.

Easton turned off the light with a loud click, and as my eyes adjusted in the dark, I watched him pull off his shirt and the moonlight shine against his skin. His breathing was the only sound in the room as he slid next to me. This was different than all the other times because this time was intentional. I tucked a hand under my pillow as he laid down next to me and stared at his profile. Could he hear the way my pulse beat? Had talking about this ruined everything?

Easton didn't normally sleep like this—with his shoulders flat on the bed, his face turned up to the ceiling. Typically, he laid out and spread across the mattress, or on his side curled up like a cat. Not . . . tense and proper.

"Is this weird?" I asked in a whisper.

He kept his eyes closed. "It's only weird if you keep asking that."

I focused on his torso as it rose and fell, rose and fell, rose and fell.

"Stop staring at me and close your eyes." I had no idea how he knew I was staring at him. Like knowing I needed him to tell me to stay. He always knew.

"Thank you," I whispered.

His breathing stopped. One. Two. Three. Four. "You can always sleep here."

It was moments like this I wondered what he would do if he found out my secret. The one I never dared utter to anyone because the cost was too high. I could never tell anyone that I was falling in love with Easton Albrey because it would cost me his family, and a room I didn't want.

But mostly, it would cost me Easton.

And no matter how hard I tried to stop myself, I couldn't seem to prevent my feelings, because this is where I wanted to be.

Next to Easton. Watching his chest rise and my heart fall.

No matter the danger.

11

OBLIGATION WEARS ON ME as I lie on the floor of my room.

I feel obligated to help Sandry plan the party. I feel obligated to go see my dad.

I feel obligated to try to reach my mom even though I know I won't find her.

The urge to be a good daughter overrides the fact that she's a bad mother. And if I'm honest with myself there is always the hope that this time she will stay. She will be good. She will want a daughter.

My fingers tighten on the phone that sits on my stomach. My earbuds have music up at the highest volume as I try to talk myself out of sending the text I know I need to. A groan escapes me as I open my contacts and find the name I'm looking for. *Uncle Rick.* He's not my real uncle, but he's my cousin Tenny's, and he's been around long enough to be considered family. If anyone will know how to get ahold of my mother, it's him.

> **Ellis:**
> Hey, Uncle Rick. Have you seen my mom recently?

The text back is almost immediate. I imagine his meaty thumbs stabbing at the screen and his double chin as he stares down at his phone. For a second I miss him and the sound of his deep voice.

> **Uncle Rick:**
> Hey, El Bell. I haven't seen her since Thanksgiving, I think.

Of course. Who knows where she is or if she'll even come back to town this time. But I've fulfilled my obligation.

> **Ellis:**
> If you see her in the next few days can you
> tell her I'm in town?

> **Uncle Rick:**
> Yep. You coming by? I'm sure your aunt Minnie wouldn't
> mind seeing you.

Aunt Minnie, Tenny's mom. She's worked in the kitchen of the Tavern for as long as I can remember. I feel instantly guilty

113

that I haven't even thought about her. Another person I feel obligation to.

Ellis:

I'll try.

I press the edge of my phone to my forehead and let out a breath. I tried. No one can say I didn't. I refuse to feel guilty at the relief I feel that she's still gone. Nothing good comes out of seeing her.

I push down the rejection that tints my relief.

A loud knock has me pulling out my earbuds. "Yeah?"

Tucker opens the door and sticks his head inside. "Mom's waiting for you. I'm going to run into town and . . ."

"And look for James Nash?" Two years ago Tucker declared that James was his soul mate. James was still deciding.

He gives me a wink. "This town has really missed me," he says, then disappears.

I find Sandry in the spot I expected her to occupy. She sits on a barstool at the kitchen island with a pad of paper in front of her and a frown carving across her face.

All decisions in the Albrey house are made at the kitchen island. The big ones and the small ones.

Dixon applying to the sheriff's academy. Tucker telling his parents he wanted to go to school in California. Easton admitting he didn't want to be a lawyer. The call from the doctors about Ben's mother and what they should do next. And the plans for every Fourth of July party Sandry has ever thrown.

On a good day, I think about the very first time I met the Albreys. The day I ate pie straight from the pan. I like to think I was a decision, too. Important.

On a bad day, I remember that I was standing here when they sent me to California.

Most of my memories involve finding one abandoned earring sitting on the counter like treasure as Sandry pressed the phone to her ear. Because this is how Sandry is, completely immersed in whatever she's doing. Earrings abandoned, meals forgotten, conversations spoken in half thoughts.

I take the stool next to hers.

Sandry massages her temples as she leans across the kitchen island. "I just can't think in a straight line." She grabs an unopened envelope and a purple pen. A pen I recognize. She lists off things under her breath as she writes them down. "Flowers, caterer, tables, lights, generator, dance floor . . . Oh, god. Did I order the cake?"

I wait for her to search her mind.

"Shit. Yes. I . . . I think I did." She scribbles on her paper. "Check with bakery."

"Plates, napkins, stemware?" I ask, trying to think of all the other things not yet down. The sooner the list is made, the sooner I can leave.

"The caterer will have those. Except for dessert. *Damn it.*"
She writes *plates* down and puts a star by it.

"Music."

She looks at me like I've just said the most horrifying thing
ever. "Music?"

Easton walks into the kitchen and kisses his mother's cheek.
My stomach tightens and I don't miss the way Sandry sits up
a little straighter. We are all remembering the last time we all
stood at the kitchen island.

I will not be embarrassed.

"I can make a playlist," he tells her, keeping his gaze from
mine. I watch as his ink-stained fingers grab a banana and begin
to peel it.

He must have been writing.

She smiles gratefully at her son the way only a proud
mother can. "None of the garbage Tucker listens to, though,
please."

"He doesn't listen to new wave anymore, so I think we're
safe," I add, and then realize what I've said.

I meet Easton's eyes. I wait for him to say something about
the conversation earlier this morning. But he only takes a breath
and tells his mother, "Yeah, it's all nineties rap now. He keeps
sending me songs to listen to. Don't worry, I won't put that in
the rotation."

"Well," Sandry considers. "Maybe some Dre."

He opens the fridge and laughs. It skitters across my frayed feelings and I want to hold onto it.

"Music . . . Easton." She writes it down and considers the list. "You still want to wear your suit from graduation?"

He makes a noise that sounds like a yes. His dad does it, too. A habit Ben says he picked up from his mother. I try to erase that information about him from my mind.

Sandry asks me, "Do you have something to wear?"

I nod. "My blue dress." Sandry swallows and I don't look at Easton. It was the dress I wore to his award ceremony for best in teen poetry, for my birthday, for more than a few special occasions. I try to break the tension by saying, "It still fits."

She seems a little disappointed. "And shoes? Jewelry?"

My mind flashes back to the one piece of jewelry that isn't costume or plastic. A necklace Sandry gave me on my sixteenth birthday. I can't remember the last time I wore it, but I know I didn't take it to California. "I have that, too."

She hums an understanding noise. "Dixon is giving a speech. Can you help him with that?"

"Easton is the one who's good with words," I deflect.

"They'll just fight, and you'll make sure he doesn't tell any embarrassing stories."

I don't want to do her another favor. I count to three before I say, "Sure."

"I need to get Ben a new shirt and I could probably use a new pair of earrings. Do you want to run to the mall with me? We could grab you a dress."

The idea of going anywhere with Sandry is still too much. So I lie. "I have plans today."

"Oh." She smiles, but it's too bright. "That's okay!" The cheerfulness in her voice feels false. "Can I get you anything? Maybe grab you something else to wear? Shoes?"

She's trying so hard. The cowardly part of me just wants to clear the air and forgive her. But I'm reminded that Sandry sent me away and there would be nothing to forgive if she really meant the things she said.

When she leaves, it's just Easton and me.

"Plans?"

"I told Uncle Rick I would come by, and I need to go see Tenny." I wonder if he can still see my lies or if that has changed, too.

The muscle in his jaw tightens and I wait for the inevitable. "Uncle Rick." He repeats his name slowly. "You're going to his house?"

For a second I want to say yes. He knows sometimes Rick sells pills and sometimes more. But my head shakes, no. "Probably to the restaurant. Tenny's working there now."

"Have you talked to her?" he asks.

"Of course. She's my cousin."

He stares at me and I see a million memories and arguments finding him. I know what comes next, so I decide to speak first.

"How was your trip? Mexico?"

His eyes are on mine, searching. I stare back into the warm brown of his irises and remember when they felt like a place I

118

knew. When I could read all his thoughts. But now he looks hurt, and that isn't right. Because Easton can't be hurt.

"How was your graduation?" he counters. "I saw . . . pictures."

The problem with knowing him so well is knowing when he's baiting me. I let out a heavy breath and lift my eyebrows in a challenge. It's more bravado than I actually feel.

And then.

He looks exhausted. "Why are you here?" he asks.

The band around my chest tightens. *Because I wanted to see you one last time. Because I can't stay away. Because I'd hoped you would still love me. Because I'd hoped that I could stop loving you.* "Tucker asked me."

"So you're here for him?"

His phone chirps on the counter before I can answer and I look down. A bad habit. I see Sara's name light up against his screen. He puts it in his pocket without checking it. I'm ready to make a snide comment, but Easton's quicker.

"Please." The word is firm. "Please just pretend that you're here for my mom. At least when she can see. This week means a lot to her. And I know that . . ." He shakes his head. "You mean a lot to her. So. For her. Or for whatever makes you feel better. Can you just do that?"

I am so tired. Tired of pretending to want to be here. Tired when I think about how much more pretending I need to do. Tired of being angry.

I nod because I don't have the energy to do anything more

119

than that and let a single word slip past my lips. "Okay," I tell him.

His face should be victorious. He's won.

Instead, he looks as defeated as I feel.

I go up to my room and decide against staring at the ceiling. I search for the necklace that Sandry gave me. Under the bed, in the boxes stacked in the corner of the closet, in the dresser. The top drawer of the nightstand is empty except for a box of tissues and a journal. Shoved between them is a folded piece of paper, and I instantly know what it is.

My hands shake a bit as I unfold it and read the words I already have memorized.

Her smile isn't the same as others.
In the corners you can see the pain that never really leaves.
At the seam you can see all the things she doesn't say.
On the bow you can see a heart that never forgets.
Her smile isn't like others because she isn't like others.
Deep crevices in her heart that you can't seem to crawl your
way out of.
Lungs filled with sky.
Feet that don't belong on the ground.
Hands that reach for things that you want to give her. Badly

The words trail off the page; the poem is unfinished because he abandoned it on the kitchen table and I stole it. He said he

120

wasn't going to submit it to a contest anyway. He thought it sounded cliche. Which made me glad. Even now, I think the poem is good. Not just because it's about me. I remember reading the words and wondering how he saw me the way he did.

Now I read the words and wonder if I was ever the girl in this poem.

12

Fifteen (and a half) years old

I WAS GOING TO learn how to drive whether I wanted to or not.

Four months earlier they had given me a room. Now they were giving me driving lessons. I wondered when I would stop receiving things I hadn't asked for.

The afternoon light shined off the silver hood and through the front windshield of Sandry's car. I had sat in it more times than I could count. The back seat, the front seat, the one time Tucker accidentally locked me in the trunk for three solid, terrifying minutes.

But I had never sat in the driver's seat.

My hands tightened on the wheel and I took a deep breath as I kept my feet firmly on the floor mat. "Are you sure?" I asked Dixon for the millionth time.

He ran a hand over his forehead and motioned out the window to the empty dirt field. "Elvis, do you see another car anywhere? Or a building? Or literally anything else you could hit?"

I turned toward the passenger side where he sat. "I don't know, because I don't know what could jump out and kill me when I'm *driving!*"

"Oh my god," Tucker groaned from the back. "Easton drives. If that idiot can operate a motor vehicle—"

But a second later Tucker was fighting off Easton behind me and throwing a series of punches.

The car shook as the weight from the back seat shifted.

"Hey. *Hey!*" Dixon shouted as he twisted toward them. His arms flailed as he tried to reach for his brothers.

I ducked my head to avoid a stray foot or elbow. "Stop!" I yelled, and like someone had hit pause, they all froze and turned toward the front seat. "We're going to crash!"

Dixon fell back into his chair and gave me a patient face. "You know the car can't move until it's started, right?"

I hadn't realized it wasn't on, but I didn't mention that. Instead, I unbuckled my seat belt. "I'm not doing this." My hand fumbled with the button. "It's stupid, anyway."

It came free and I reached for the handle of the door.

"Ellis." Dixon used my real name. He never did that. "Do not get out of this car. You are learning how to drive. Today."

At twenty years old, he thought he was so smart. I made a frustrated noise. "I'm *never* getting my license. I can't pay for the driver's ed classes, so it doesn't matter if I can drive or not—"

"Yes, it does," he corrected. "It's a basic life skill."

"No, it isn't. Lots of people don't drive."

"Lots of people aren't my sister," Dixon said. Like he always did. Completely confident.

I ignored the way that simple declaration made me feel special. Like I belonged to someone other than my last name. Like I belonged to him. "I'm not really your sister."

He pushed gently against the side of my head. "Don't say stupid stuff."

Tucker leaned forward and wrapped his arms around Dixon's headrest. "Can you two please save your Hallmark Channel moment for later? I have shit to do today and I need you to learn how to drive so Dixon—"

Dixon reached back to hit his brother. "You are the—"

I turned the engine over.

Oh shit.

"Oh shit is right." Tucker laughed.

Had I said that out loud?

My hands felt sweaty against the dark plastic of the steering wheel, but I had already set this lesson into motion. There was no turning back. I was going to learn how to operate a gillion tons of steel and glass. Not that I wanted to.

"Check your mirrors," Dixon instructed.

I checked the ones on the side and then I moved the rearview. Easton's reflection was caught there and my eyes met his. He gave me a wide smile and I felt myself echoing it. I couldn't tell if my heart was beating harder because of him, or because of the car.

Easton's expression transformed into a challenging look. "Let's see if you're any better than me."

"I'm better at everything," I said with a cocky grin. I wasn't. Easton was good even when he wasn't. I had to study to get a B, whereas he didn't even have to think about the test and he would get an A.

He silently mouthed, "You're going to crash." With his smirk still wide.

I rolled my eyes but, oddly, his teasing made me feel better. More relaxed.

Dixon began his instruction. "Foot on the brake?"

I nodded.

"Take the car out of park and move the stick down to D."

"That's what she said," Tucker added to no one in particular. A second later I heard the sound of a punch.

"Now press your foot on the gas," Dixon continued.

I lifted my foot and pressed it against the gas.

The car lurched forward and I hit the brake.

Dixon's hands went out on the dashboard, Tucker let out a surprised yell, and Easton cackled. But the car kept lurching and stopping and lurching and stopping. "Ellis, brake. Brake. Hit the brakes!"

"I am!" I shouted, looking at the wheel. I was missing something.

"We're going to die!" Easton said between his laughter.

I didn't know what I was doing wrong, but I knew the car wasn't in my control anymore. It was possessed.

"Ellis! Hit the fucking brake with one foot, you psycho!" Tucker had leaned into the front seat and was pointing to my feet.

"I am!" Tears were falling down my face.

"Drive with one foot!" Tucker repeated the instruction I didn't understand.

"Lean back, asshole!" Dixon was shouting at his brother.

From the back seat Easton pushed toward us. "Shut up, you're making it worse!"

But Tucker didn't stop. "She's driving—"

Dixon put his hand on Tucker's head and pushed him back.

"Listen to me!" Tucker said, pointing at the pedals as the car continued to heave. "Both feet!"

Dixon paused. "What?"

"She's driving with both feet, jackass!" Tucker announced.

Dixon looked down at my feet and then back up at me. "Elvis, take your foot off the gas."

I did and the car came to a sudden stop.

Precious relief flooded me, until I realized that Easton was holding his stomach, laughing. Dixon ran both hands down his face and looked up at the roof.

"When driving—" He let out a breath from his nose. "When you drive, you only do it with your right foot. Never both feet."

My mouth pressed tightly closed and I nodded my head. A shaky breath left me and I wiped at the tears falling.

"Are you crying?" Dixon asked gently.

"No," I answered through obvious sniffles.

Easton leaned forward and made an annoyed sound. "I told you, you're not allowed to cry. You make a weird face when you cry."

"I'm not crying!" It was a wet noise. A cry. I found his face in the rearview mirror again.

"It's okay, El." Easton's voice was kind. Too kind. "I promise to give you rides until we're eighty and they take my license from me."

My eyes tapered and my mouth fell open in shocked anger. I shut it and ground my teeth together. With *one* foot, I hit the gas.

"Hey!" Dixon said, excited. "You're doing it!"

And I was. I drove all over the field until I was sure that I *could* drive.

Dixon and I switched seats to go home, and when I caught a glimpse of Easton's face, I could see the small satisfied upturn of his lips.

I had learned how to drive and I was proud.

But that feeling faded as we pulled into the driveway of the Albreys' house.

My dad's car sat on the gravel. A faded paint job next to Ben's sleek black foreign car. It had been only five months since he went to prison, and there were supposed to be another three months left on his sentence. He stood on the porch with a smile that was a little too bright and a fresh haircut that left the skin on his neck pink. Cheap clothes that still had the creases from the packaging on them. My dad was home.

It took me twice as long as it should have to pull the handle of the door and get out. When I did, my father was standing in front of me a second later.

"El!" He wrapped his arms around me. "I missed you."

My arms went around him on reflex but I couldn't speak. All the words caught in my throat because I could only think about him taking me away.

He was going to take me from the busy mornings of doing nothing and the loudest quiet filled with thoughts and people. And afternoons where people shouted at each other with love.

If he was out of prison, I would have to go back with him.

"What were you doing?" he asked me.

Before I could answer with something evasive Dixon spoke. "We were teaching her how to drive."

My father's brows dipped low. "Drive?" He took a breath. "You should have learned with a stick. That's how I did. Don't worry, I'll teach you."

I didn't know what to say. There were a hundred things I wanted to learn from him. But.

"Oh lord," Sandry said with a groan. "It took you three full months and two clutches to learn how to drive a stick, Tru.

128

Spare the girl that heartache and let the boys teach her."

He smiled at Sandry but she didn't return it.

"You staying for dinner?" Ben asked.

Over my father's shoulder I watched Easton shift from foot to foot and cross his arms over his chest.

"Sure," my dad said. "Don't really know what's at the house."

Inside, we began the routine of setting the table. Ben uncorking the wine for the adults, Tucker setting the plates, Easton with the silverware, Dixon filling up a pitcher with ice water. And me putting out the cups. We did it without instruction, because these were our jobs. The ones that meant we were a part of this family. That we belonged here.

I hadn't thought it was weird until I watched my father notice. His shoulders were pulled back and his jaw set in a firm line.

"You know, actually," my dad said. "I think Ellis and I better get going. We've got a lot to do."

A stone sank inside my stomach.

Easton opened his mouth, but Sandry's hand landed on his shoulder. "Are you sure, Tru? We have enough for you."

She didn't say enough for me, because that was a given.

My dad's gaze was direct when he answered her. "Yeah. I'm sure. Ellis, get your things. I'll wait outside."

I didn't look at Sandry. I knew the face she was making and I could hear her words in my head without her having to actually say them. This wasn't a battle she could fight for me. My feet felt like lead as I walked up the stairs to Easton's room and grabbed the few items that were mine. I put them into a bag and tried not to wonder when I would be here next.

"You can't go," Easton said as I grabbed my toothbrush from the counter.

It was so simple for him. "He's my dad, East. I have to go home."

"Why? He's just going to end up back in prison."

"It's not like it happens all the time. It's only happened twice."

"Four," he corrected. "Four times."

"Those were for probation violations." This was hard enough without Easton making judgments. Maybe it was naive to hope that this would be the last time, but what choice did I have? "I don't want your opinions about my dad."

I brushed past him, but he grabbed my wrist. "I can tell my dad to not let you go. Or my mom."

His voice was gentle. He'd fight this fight for me if I asked him.

"I'm not really your sister, Easton."

He didn't frown or look at me hurt or confused. He looked infuriated. "I *never* said you were."

I pulled my hand from his wrist and made my way down the stairs.

At the bottom, Sandry stood by the door, her hands

wringing as she made small talk with my dad. "So, you'll be back at work?"

He was about to answer when he saw me. "Ready?" His smile was sunny.

I nodded.

Sandry kissed my cheek. "See you soon," she whispered into my ear as she let me go.

I tried to ignore the panic that felt like claws in my chest.

The door opened and my father walked toward the car. "I think we should stop by the store and grab some ice cream. We can get a movie and celebrate—"

Each step I took felt like it was pulling all the air from my lungs. "Dad."

"What do you want to do tomorrow? Maybe head to the river?"

"Dad." I swallowed, mostly my own dread, and stopped in front of his car with my feet planted on the ground.

"Huh?" he said. "What's up, sugar?" His face was open. Optimistic. I knew as soon as I spoke that look would disappear. "I'm not going home."

It took him a moment to understand the words. He didn't say anything as he waited for me to continue.

"I . . . I'm not going. I . . . I don't want to."

My father shook his head, heavy, as if it would change my mind. "That's not your home, Ellis. Not there." He sounded like Tenny. Like my grandmother.

131

Like my mother.

Reminding me that the people inside those walls had no real loyalty to me. That I was only there because they had decided to let me stay, and as soon as they decided that I wasn't welcome, I would be gone.

He jabbed an angry finger at the car. "You're *my* daughter. Get in."

But I couldn't. I couldn't get in the car just because his pride was hurt. "It's not fair for you to ask me to go home, when you and Mom both don't live there. Not really."

"Ellis, what are you saying? *I* live there."

"Sometimes, sure. But sometimes you don't. Sometimes you're in jail, or when you're not you're at work." I swallowed. "I don't want to go. I want to stay here, with the Albreys."

His mouth opened and closed, and he shook his head as if he could shake off the hurt. "You're a Truman."

Our last name was something my uncles and cousins pretended to say with pride. It was meant to make us feel like we belonged, but really it was only used to guilt us into obligation. The truth was, the family that shared my name hadn't let me stay. My grandmother's house was full and Tenny didn't have room to share what little she had. They kept telling me the Albreys wouldn't always want me, but the Albreys were the only ones who had never turned me away. "Dad."

My dad let out a deep sigh as his jaw tightened. "I'm sorry I can't give you what they can."

He didn't sound sorry. He sounded bitter.

"I don't want to go to sleep alone," I told him, truthfully.

He nodded. "Fine. *Fine.*" He got into his car. With the window down he leaned toward me. "When you get sick of pretending, you can always come back where you belong."

13

THE LAUGHING IS WHAT pulls my attention from my phone as I scroll through different travel accounts on Instagram.

I look up to see Easton and Dixon shoving each other on the dock while Tucker treads water a few feet away. The game they play where they try to throw the other off-balance is one I recognize.

Easton pushes Dixon with his flat palms and Dixon stumbles backward with his hands flailing. Easton's arms go up into the air victoriously. The scene is familiar and foreign all at the same time. I have a hundred recollections just like this one. I can see the hole at the bottom of Easton's trunks from when he fell off the boat two summers ago, but I barely recognize the muscular body that wears them. His hair is wet and sticks up at odd angles, but it's longer than I've ever seen it.

Easton's arms cross over his stomach and his head falls back as he laughs at his brother.

Emotion beats erratically against my ribs before my brain can stop it. For a second I pretend that he is *just* a boy. One who didn't tell me to leave. One who I don't hate.

And now I'm irritated. There is nothing special about Easton Albrey. Nothing.

The back door opens and Dixon stands there, pulling my attention from Easton.

"Elvis," he calls, and I curse myself for jumping at the noise. "Grab me a beer?"

"I'll grab you a pop." I slide off the stool and open the fridge. "You need professional help."

When I hand him the can, he gives me a wink. "For a Coors Light? There's barely any alcohol in it. Stop being mopey and come swim."

The faces smiling and splashing outside used to make me want to join. "That's okay," I tell him.

"Sure. If you want to be a coward because you're afraid of some boy, stay inside."

He takes off back down the small path to the dock. Dixon shoves Easton like a linebacker and both of them fall into the water.

Easton comes up and shakes the water from his hair, light scattering from the drops. Dixon treads water as he opens his beer and takes a drink like the lake rat he is.

. . . Easton isn't some boy.

I'm being a coward.

Upstairs I change into the suit that I bought for the ocean. It's a black two-piece that dips low and is definitely not the high-necked one-piece I've worn here in the past. I bought it for all those reasons. It made me feel beautiful and strong, but now I'm second-guessing it. Maybe I should find my one-piece and . . .

"What the fuck is wrong with you?" I whisper, staring at my reflection. I set my shoulders back and force myself to be proud of the parts of me that I want to cover up. Grabbing a towel from the closet, I make my way toward the glass door, and before I can talk myself out of it, I pull it open.

Gravel path under my feet, summer sun on my skin, the smell of the lake in the air. This is every good memory I have. This is my childhood.

Dixon is the first one to see me standing on the dock. "What happened to you?" he asks with surprise.

I don't slump my shoulders, even though I want to. I don't dive into the water to hide, even though I want to. I don't run inside . . . even though—

"She looks amazing," Tucker says. "Don't be jealous 'cause you're not as pretty." He gives me a wink.

I refuse to look at Easton, even though I feel his eyes on me.

"I'm just teasing you," Dixon says with a smile. "What I meant to say is you're pretty."

"Are you hitting on me?" I tease him to break the tension but save Dixon from having to respond and jump into the water.

It's still freezing, but I stay under just a moment longer than

136

I should, letting the air burn in my lungs and the quiet of the water sing back to the ache in my heart.

When my head breaks the surface, Easton is eyeing me carefully.

"What?" I ask, wiping at the hair in my face.

"You hold your breath when you're upset." He says it like a fact. Like the sky is blue and the grass is green and life always comes to an end.

But the part that irritates me the most is that he's right. "Yeah."

"Oh, look at that, Dixon." Tucker laughs and we all follow his eyes toward the dock three houses away.

Katie O'Donnell was an institution at the Albrey house. Dark hair, golden skin, always in a bikini and sunglasses as she pretended to ignore the boys in the lake. Many summers had been spent with the boys staring at her as she lounged on her lawn working on her tan. She was only five years older than Dixon, but when you're sixteen that's a lifetime.

"Like clockwork," I tell Dixon, and his cheeks color.

"I didn't even know she was back," Dixon grumbles and dips his head farther down in the water.

"Back?" Tucker asks. "Did she go somewhere?"

"She moved." It was all he said, and . . . something was off.

"Did you . . ." I start, still putting my thoughts together. But those two words are enough for Dixon to panic. "Oh, you and Katie O'Donnell?"

"Keep your voice down," he hisses at me.

But I laugh as Tucker becomes relentless in his teasing. "You hooked up with Hot Katie?"

When I glance up, Easton's eyes are still on me, and just like that, the tightness is back in my body.

Rivulets of water run down his face, and he blows air from his lips. I've seen him like this so many times, but for some reason, this time feels like the first. I watch his shoulders move as he treads water.

"Wanna race?" he asks.

I don't want to race. At all. Racing is normal. Racing is what we did almost every day of every summer. On a good day, on a bad, on a Tuesday. It was a constant like Easton was a constant.

I wanna stay here and tease Dixon. "Sure."

He smiles at me like he's won something. "One, two, go!"

I push out at the water, my body taking over and muscle memory directing me toward the wooden post in the lake. In and out, in and out, in and out. I push myself farther and farther.

Easton's arms are carving through the lake and I catch him stealing looks at me. His smile lights his whole face and I feel myself mirror his.

I pull up and breathe. Simple.

And then my hands reach the post. My fingers touch the soft wood that splinters. "El & East" is carved at the top, and I reach out, running my fingers against the indent of my name.

Easton breaks the water gently and sees my hand but doesn't comment. We hold onto the post, catching our breath.

"You won," he says.

I haven't beaten Easton since we were thirteen. In swimming. In anything.

"You let me," I say, and I'm surprised by my own jovial tone.

"Maybe." He smiles. His perfect lips curve upward and his eyes crinkle at the corners.

It stops time.

"You let me." I say it again. Quiet and soft.

"I . . ." He stops and runs a hand over his face, trying to get rid of the water there. We aren't talking about the race. "I don't know what you want me to say to you."

His attitude and his tone remind me that I'm angry.

"You could just repeat everything you've said to me this past year." I smile. "Nothing."

"Ellis." The way he says my name. Soft and gentle. It makes my rage burn brighter.

I open my mouth to say the one word I know I shouldn't. Even thinking it hurts. *Why.* I feel it cutting its way up my throat with jagged edges. Instead, I shut my mouth.

We let the silence fall into the cracks of the afternoon air.

Easton stares back at the house. "You told me not to call you." He won't look at me, and it gives me a small amount of satisfaction that this is hard for him, too. "And I didn't. I had to hear about you from *Tucker*."

"What did you want from me? Did you want an update about how awesome San Diego was? Or, like, how *totally* cool the beach was?"

Now his eyes turn to me, and I wish they hadn't. "I wanted to hear your voice."

The words sink into me like a blade. To the hilt. I want to pull them from me, but I know they will only cause me to bleed out right here.

"I wanted to know that you were okay and all I got was *Tucker* telling me you weren't ready to talk."

"I was busy, Easton," I say. The lie is easy. I put up my armor and let the words protect me. "I was starting a new school and I got new friends. You were in the past." I make the last word into a bullet that I etch Easton's name onto before I fire it into him. I tell myself he deserves this. "It's fine. Let's just forget about all of it."

"Forget about it?"

My fingers dig into the post. "It's easier."

"Ellis."

"It's done. I moved on. You should, too." I push off from the wooden beam and swim back to the dock, pulling myself up.

My feet dangle as I lean back on my hands. Tucker hangs off, his big arms folded on the wood to anchor him.

I don't watch as Easton pulls himself up and stands. I tilt my head toward the sunshine with my eyes closed.

"Where are you going?" Dixon asks.

"Inside," he says over his shoulder as he stalks up to the house.

I wait until my body is warm from the heat and light before I head back. I wrap a towel around me as I walk up each of the stairs. Easton's face plays over and over in my mind as I hear myself say *"it's done."* What a liar I've become.

My door is slightly open and when I push through, I see it. A black dress hangs off the curtain rod against the window. Its edges glow in the afternoon sun and I feel my throat tighten.

The fabric is soft and simple and the lines are classic. It's beautiful. Mature. Nothing like my blue dress, which now feels juvenile. And there's a note sitting next to it on the nightstand.

This will look great with the necklace.

It's so simple. So Sandry. She doesn't even think about being generous because ultimately it doesn't cost her anything.

But all I can do is stare at a dress that my mother would have never bought me even if she could.

And that is why tears are falling down my cheeks. Not because of Sandry's kindness, but because of all the people who are supposed to be kind and aren't.

14

Sixteen years old

NOTHING WAS DIFFERENT.

I still had the same full cheeks. Same freckles dotting my nose and the top of my forehead. I was exactly the same as I was yesterday. But on this day, I was sixteen.

Today was a milestone.

"You going to stare at yourself all night?" Easton leaned against the doorjamb to the bathroom with his arms crossed over him and a smile tugging at the corner of his mouth. He had been sixteen for three and a half months already. He drove. He swore more. He had even drunk a beer with Dixon.

"I was just . . ."

"Trying to see if today had turned you into a woman?" He asked it seriously.

I hit him in the shoulder but he caught my arm before I could pull it back. "You still look like you, El."

I frowned. I wanted today to be a change. I wanted it to matter.

But I had spent the morning with my dad eating canned cinnamon rolls for breakfast, and Tenny had brought me flowers. Which was nice, but like every other birthday. Nothing special for sixteen.

"I don't want to look the same." I pulled my hand back and pushed out of the bathroom.

"What's wrong with how you look?" Easton said, following me.

I resented that Easton couldn't read my mind this one time. I resented that he wanted me to *say* it. "You wouldn't get it."

"Okay, El."

We walked out to the darkened patio and I pushed open the doors. The soft bistro lights came on, revealing a table covered in flowers and food. A banner overhead said "Happy Birthday" in white and gold letters and Sandry and Ben rounded the corner carrying a chocolate cake covered with strawberries and sixteen lit candles.

Sandry began singing off-key, and when the boys joined in I smiled.

"Make a wish," she said, holding the cake out to me. The soft light made her cheeks glow pink and her irises sparkle.

I closed my eyes and pursed my lips to make my wish.

But when I blew out the candles, I couldn't think of anything I wanted.

I had everything here.

"I think the dessert is supposed to be after dinner," I told her.

Sandry winked at me. "You know we eat dessert first on birthdays."

It was a silly tradition that Sandry had always done since I started celebrating birthdays with the Albreys.

We sat and ate cake before Ben unveiled a platter of steak sandwiches. He usually made them on the last day of summer, but had made an exception because they were my favorite.

Dixon kept checking his phone during dinner until Sandry threw a strawberry at him.

"What?" He picked it up from his shirt and popped it into his mouth.

"What is on your phone, son?" she asked.

His ears turned pink. "I'm texting."

"A girl?" Tucker asked with a shit-eating grin.

"That's none of your business."

"Well, since you're done with this portion of the evening, why don't you go first with your gift."

Dixon made a face at his mother and then handed me a small wrapped present. "It's a book."

"She only reads the ones with guys without shirts on the cover," Easton teased.

I hit him with the package.

Dixon winked at me. "I think you'll like it. It's about a shepherd who travels all over the world."

"Now tell her the three things," Sandry ordered.

Dixon groaned. "We still have to do that?"

Sandry only smiled. "Who she was. Who she is. Who she will be."

"Fine. Last year, you refused to put the cap on the toothpaste in the bathroom after you used it. Now you are squeezing the tube from the middle. In the future, I hope you will be the kind of person who will do neither."

"Dixy!"

"What, Mom? I gave her the book and wrote something nice on the inside."

I ran my hand over the wrapping paper and smiled. "Thanks, Dixon."

"You're welcome, Elvis."

"I'll go," Tucker said. "I bought you tickets to that movie as a present. And last year you were obsessed with floating in the lake to prepare for floating in the Dead Sea. Now you're not as good at floating or swimming. I think it's the boobs. I hope this next year you'll continue to grow—"

"Okay!" Sandry said, interrupting.

I threw a another strawberry at him but he caught it with his mouth and winked.

"Easton?"

"My present is upstairs."

I smiled and wondered what he could have hidden in his room.

"And?"

"You used to wear those stupid-looking boots with the heels. Now you wear those stupid sandals, even with socks. I hope this year you buy real shoes."

Sandry's lips flattened into a thin line, but she didn't push. "My turn, then."

She slid a small box toward me, and when I opened it, the most beautiful pendant on a silver chain shined up at me. The center was a round opal that caught the low light, like a rainbow had been trapped inside the white stone. The silver filigreed edges made it seem old and expensive.

It was beautiful.

"I got this on my sixteenth birthday. My mom got it on hers and her mom . . . My great-grandmother said a handsome man that she had refused to marry had given it to her. I want you to have it."

"Sandry." It was too much.

"I was saving it for my daughter, but I only ended up with these." She motioned to the boys, who didn't seem the slightest bit upset about her comment.

"I can't. What about . . . a daughter-in-law or . . ."

"The boys will pick a daughter-in-law, if I even get one. I pick you. You're the closest thing I have to a daughter."

"Dixon's pretty close to a daughter," Tucker corrected.

"I think your gendered titles are stupid anyway," Dixon said as he lifted a shoulder.

Sandry cleared her throat to say her three things.

"You used to be a stranger. Now you're family. And in the future, I hope you will always feel like your place is here."

I took the necklace out and put it on. It felt heavy against my chest, which was appropriate. I wanted to be worthy of that weight.

Eventually, Easton tilted his head toward the stairs and I followed him into his room. He opened his bedside table and handed me a small box of colored pins in blue and red and green.

"Pins?"

His grin got wider. "Yep."

Easton reached under his bed and took out a poster tube, pulling the plastic off. As he unraveled it, the picture became clearer.

A map of the world.

"What . . ."

"You keep talking about all the places you want to go." He shrugged like this was the easiest thing. Dreaming of places. "I figured if we got this, we might actually start making plans."

For him it was so simple. He wanted to go. There weren't a hundred thousand things keeping him in place. He had no fear.

It just was.

"Easton." I couldn't keep the emotion from my voice.

His eyes moved to my mouth as I said his name and I watched him swallow. Quickly, he turned and tacked the poster to the wall of his bedroom. "It's not that big a deal, El. It's a map."

I decided to let him out of the moment by making a joke. "What if I don't want to go with you?"

"Of course you want to go with me," he said over his shoulder. "Who else would remind you that you hate heights and can't stand tomatoes?" He searched through his nightstand for a moment before pulling out a small notebook with flowers on it. "You could keep a journal of all the places you want to go and the things you want to do."

I ran my hand over the cover and flipped through the blank pages.

"It's stupid, probably. You don't—"

"It's amazing." I kissed his cheek. Light and fast and unable to stop myself.

Easton stepped back and sat on the edge of the bed looking at the wall. I sat next to him, so close that our legs were touching. My fingers fiddled with the cardboard box of pins as I stared up at the world.

"What are you thinking?" I asked him.

"Thoughts aren't free," he replied automatically.

"It's my birthday."

He sighed but gave in. "It doesn't seem as big," he said. "The world."

I stared at the "not as big" world. It seemed enormous and endless and—

It seemed like I could reach out and touch all the places my heart wanted to see. I wanted to sink my feet into land that I had only heard of. I wondered what it would feel like to be in them. Was *I* the same in those places, or could I be different?

Could I be new?

"East or west?" Easton asked as he leaned back.

I stood. My hand moved over Europe. So many places and things I wanted to see. Moved down to Africa and over to South America and then Asia.

I put a red pin in Tokyo.

And a red pin in Berlin.

And a red pin in Cape Town.

And in Rio de Janeiro.

And in Athens.

And in New Delhi.

When I turned around Easton was staring at me. His brows were pinched and his tongue ran against his bottom lip.

"Before you only dreamed of going places." His eyes moved down to the floor and back to me. "Now you're making plans."

He smiled softly and I felt it in every part of my body. Easton was saying my three things. Not the silly ones he had said at the table, but these that were just for us. The ones that meant something.

"Next you'll be standing in those places."

I looked back at the poster with Easton watching me put the pins it. "Who knows when I'll actually be able to go."

He let out a breath. "Let's go when we graduate."

I rolled my eyes. "Sure."

Easton sat up. "I'm serious."

"I don't have any money. I don't have a passport. I don't—"

"We could save. And stay in hostels and eat cheap food and call my mom and beg for money for croissants stuffed with chocolate in France."

The way he spoke it made me believe it. I worked hard to stamp out that hope. "Easton."

"I'm serious, El. Let's go before we go to college."

"It's not practical. And your mom would lose her shit if we didn't go to college."

"We would still go, just after. Old people say all the time that they wished they'd traveled when they were young. Let's go on an adventure. Let's see the world and meet interesting people and eat weird food and live a life that's bigger than this house and a lake and your parents and my parents."

Easton wanted to see the world and fall in love with it. And I wanted to see the world to know that my life wasn't small. I wanted to feel like I didn't have to stay where we were. I didn't have to take care of my dad or wait for my mom. And I wanted to go with Easton, but I was worried that he would realize that while he was falling in love with the world, I had fallen in love with him. "But . . ."

His face changed into something sad and it broke my heart not knowing what had done it. "Just—just let me believe that you'll do this with me. That you'll go and we . . ."

"What about Tucker or someone else?"

"There isn't anyone else. I don't want to see anything without you."

"Easton."

"Do you want to go?"

I closed my eyes and I said the one thing I knew better than to say. The one thing that would make me hope. "Yes," I whispered.

When I opened my eyes, he was smiling. "Then we'll go and come back totally different people. I promise."

And Easton always kept his promises.

15

THE FAMILIAR SOUNDS OF a summer night at the Albreys' house float in the air as we sit around the fire pit by the shore of the lake. Soft lights line the dock and a dusty sky hangs overhead. The Adirondack chairs here are worn smooth from so many seasons in the sun. I pull up my legs onto the seat and drape the blanket farther over them.

This is something I know how to do. I listen to Ben and Sandry ask questions while they sip wine. The boys tell stories. Water quietly laps at the shore. My role here is defined, and because it doesn't require anything from me, I let my ever-present anger slip down and dissolve into the content feeling that floats in the air.

Tucker tells the story about learning how to surf. Easton's eyes are on me and I have to remind myself to act normal.

But what is normal for Easton and me?

"It's so much harder than you think it's going to be," Tucker says.

I laugh. "He's a horrible student."

Sandry takes a sip of her wine and I see her look at Easton.

"I was distracted by the guy teaching us," Tucker continues. "He had that wet suit pulled down—"

"Don't blame the teacher." Dixon stops him. "You've never been athletic. Neither has Ellis. It's not a bad thing."

"Uh, bullshit. I made the all-star team when we were kids," Tucker tells his brothers.

"Because Matt Brody broke his ankle," Sandry adds.

Tucker shakes his head. "A win is a win, Mother. Ellis surfs now, too."

Everyone's eyes swing to me.

"She's good," Tucker adds. "Better than me, actually. Her aunt gave her a surfboard and everything."

"Better than you is not a high bar," Dixon says.

"It was just her old board, and I think I've used it twice," I explain. "Too much work for ten seconds of payoff."

Easton is silent, and I want to know what he's thinking. My self-control is herculean.

"That's not what it's about," Tucker argues. "It's about how peaceful counting the sets are and connecting with the water."

"Or being eaten by a shark." I take a sip of my tea.

Tucker rolls his eyes. "One documentary about sharks and she refuses to get back in the ocean."

I finally meet Easton's eyes. His gaze burns, so I look away. "I'll get in, I just don't want to bob on the surface like bait."

"I didn't know your aunt surfed," Sandry says offhandedly.

"I still picture Courtney as the little girl chasing after your dad."

"I've always wanted to surf," Dixon says.

"When you come out to California, I'll teach you," I tell Dixon.

"I probably already know how to do it since I've seen so many movies," Dixon tells us seriously. "If Tucker can do it, I'm sure I can."

"Oh." I take a drink. "Okay."

But Dixon just takes a sip of his beer. "You'll see when I get there," he mumbles against the mouth of the longneck.

"Ah, the unearned confidence of an Albrey. Must be genetic." Tucker pats Dixon's leg. "At least you're not as bad as Easton."

"What does that mean?" Easton asks.

Tucker smiles. "Remember in sixth grade when Easton wrote a letter to the school board asking to have his science grade removed from his transcripts?"

Easton groans. "Mrs. Crosby."

"Oh, good god. I thought that would never end," Sandry adds.

"She was the one who didn't teach science right," Easton protests.

"You wrote a letter to the school district." Dixon is laughing so hard he can barely get out his next words. "They said if you would have turned that in instead of your science paper, they would have given you an A."

154

Easton seems like he's going to argue but Sandry cuts him off. "I can't talk about this again." And we let our laughter float away like sparks from the fire, up to the sky.

"What other secrets do you have, Ellis?" It's Easton who asks, and I stare down at the fire instead of him.

I want to tell them about my job and the backpackers I met who travel the world. The time a kid taught me to find tiny hermit crabs on the beach. The one time I thought I might be a person who *runs* and then threw up half a mile from home.

But Easton doesn't deserve those things. So I tell him what social media has already said.

"I work at a coffee shop."

Tucker looks at me, a little disappointed, and I feel shame heat my cheeks.

I ignore it.

"Did you make any friends? Anyone other than Tucker?" Dixon asks.

"Sure."

"There is a guy at the coffee shop that thinks our Ellis is his soul mate. He's asked her out on at least a hundred dates." Tucker laughs and Dixon gives him a sharp glare.

Sandry and Ben shift uncomfortably.

Tucker sits up straighter. "But Ellis doesn't date."

It still isn't the right thing to say, and I scramble for a way to look less pathetic.

"Right," Easton begins, and I can hear the edge in his

voice. "Why would she need to date when she has you."

Tucker pulls his bottom lip into his teeth and worries at it. He knows a fight is coming. "Well, probably because I'm not her boyfriend, like I've said a hundred times already."

But Easton isn't deterred. "The picture of you two. At Christmas."

The mistletoe one. The Christmas party at the coffee shop, our lips pursed in a kiss and his arm wrapped around my shoulder. It was cute and I knew that it would be the final straw with Easton—I knew he would assume the worst—so I let Tucker post it.

Ben's hand tightens on Sandry's as they glance back and forth at us.

"And the picture after that was of me and the girl I was dating," Tucker tries to justify.

Easton's whole demeanor changes. His shoulders stiffen and then he's standing. Everything in me tells me to go after him, but I can't chase a boy who doesn't want me.

I'm not that girl.

Instead, Tucker stands and follows his brother.

When they're out of earshot, Dixon looks at me. "I'm sorry. I didn't think . . ."

"It's okay. It's about him and Tucker anyway. Not really about me."

Dixon laughs. "Everything with Easton is about you, Ellis."

As the fire dies so does the group. First is Dixon; he gets hungry. Then it's Sandry and Ben.

And finally, as the last log turns from red to ash, I get up. In the house, Tucker stands in the kitchen, with a glass at the water dispenser and a weary set to his shoulders. "Hey," I greet him. "You okay?"

He sees me and nods. "Just a . . . a hard conversation."

"With East?"

"Yeah."

"I'm sorry—"

"It's not really your fault. We have our own shit. He didn't want to punch me, so that was a good sign." He takes a long drink. "But I wanted to punch him, so that was a bad one."

I move toward him and wrap my arms around his waist and press my cheek into his back. He pats at my hand as I feel him relax into my hug. I hope it helps.

"Go to bed, El. We can talk in the morning."

I unwrap myself from him and quietly pad up the steps until I reach the bathroom door. The knob doesn't move as I try to turn it, but a second later the door opens and Easton stands in front of me.

His eyes move to my bedroom. "Getting ready for bed?"

That's obviously what I'm doing, so I don't respond and try to push past him, but he doesn't move. I end up standing in the doorway with him, our backs pushed against the frame.

From here, he's the same. He smells the same. Same Easton. His chest moves slowly as he breathes, and I know how soft his arms feel around me.

"You're going to finally sleep in your own room?"

157

I bite into my embarrassment and turn it into anger. "Whatever you're thinking, it's wrong. You know I don't like sleeping in that room. I never have—"

"Because you liked sleeping with me." Easton says it like a challenge.

"I *liked* your *room*." I scoff. "That room smells like cardboard. People don't live in there. It's . . . weird."

"If you want to sleep in my room all you have to do is ask." He lifts a brow, and I'm reminded of all the times Easton spoke to me like this and I felt like the sun was rising inside me.

"I don't want to sleep anywhere near you, Easton. That's what you wanted, right? It's why I went to California? Let's keep doing that, okay?"

"That's not why you went to California."

"Who cares—"

"I do." He cuts me off. "I care."

His eyes look down to me and I want to stay here forever.

"What are you thinking?" he asks me.

I raise my eyebrows and repeat back to him the thing he always told me. "Thoughts aren't free."

But he doesn't respond, he only watches my face as if he could read them there.

"Whatever," I say, and push off the doorjamb.

I don't want to be here anymore. His hand reaches out and brushes against my arm. And I can't. I leave and instead of going back to my room, I go to the front door.

The summer air hugs me and I walk down dark roads without sidewalks and flat land that challenges the stars as both stretch out before me. When I was little I would walk and time the sound of my steps to the beats of my heart. It seems a habit I haven't outgrown. The sky here is the same one in California, but I feel like all these stars know me. They watched me as I grew tall enough to try to reach them. And they saw every single one of my heartbreaks bleed against the dirt here.

And then.

I'm standing in front of my house. Moonlight makes it feel like a tomb. Not a single light is on because nothing lives here. Not even the bare tree in the yard despite it being summer. Even the grass that has yellowed and died. Nothing.

I could go in. I know my dad left a key under the mat for my mother.

Just in case she decided to come home.

"Are you waiting for something?"

I'm not even surprised to hear Easton behind me. And for a brief second, I think I might have imagined him there. Like my subconscious is actually his voice.

"No."

He stands next to me. With his hands in his pockets, he stares at the carcass of a home. "Are you going to see him?"

Him. Even here Easton doesn't want to say my dad's name.

My eyes move to the garage, where he spent most of his time. There was so much that was wrong about my father, but . . . his love for me wasn't. It's hard to separate that. To not feel guilty for wanting the love of someone flawed in the worst kinds of ways. I used to feel that way about my mother until she left for long enough that those feelings festered into hatred.

And just because I miss him doesn't mean I want to see him. That pain isn't erased with a visit to the prison.

"You should," he tells me.

The second time my dad went to prison I was thirteen, and every time that I was supposed to see him, I caught a cold. It was Easton who dragged me to those visits, even when I cried the whole car ride. He held my hand the entire time and when I got out of the visitors' room, he was there, smiling and holding two Icees and pretending everything was normal.

"You're right," I lie. I have no intention of seeing my dad. "I'll ask Tenny to go with me."

He looks hurt for a second, and then his face flashes back to passivity. "I'll go with you, El." He says it like he doesn't care either way, but I know it's a lie.

"I don't want that anymore, Easton." I turn away from him and I walk inside the house that's more like a grave.

And let all the things that Easton and I need to say die.

16

Sixteen years old

A FEW WEEKS AFTER my sixteenth birthday, Tenny declared
I had spent enough time at the Albreys' and not enough time at
Uncle Rick's Tavern.

Like most things, it was said with sharp-toothed words and
softened by her love.

When I was younger, I spent most of my time in the sticky
booths and on the dirty floors of the pub, playing with Tenny
and Wyatt, Uncle Rick's son. My mother would drop me off
and Uncle Rick would complain about not running a daycare,
but he always let me stay. We were kept just in sight but not
underfoot.

Old men sat bent over barstools drinking flat beer and
taking shots between pints. Greasy food was made under suspicious conditions. Hazy light filtered in from filmy windows.

Tenny's mom had set up a television in the corner that played
cartoons we could barely hear over the jukebox that blasted Dolly
Parton and Hank Williams Jr. As we grew older, the cartoons

changed to older shows and eventually the TV was put away.

By the time I was sixteen, I hadn't set foot in the bar in more days than I could count. But as soon as we walked through the heavy wooden door, all my childhood memories came back to me like ghosts.

"Well, well, well," Uncle Rick said from behind the bar. "Looks like trouble has finally returned."

I stiffened at the words, even though I knew he didn't mean them. To him, they were endearing. There was an expectation of who I was here.

Anna and Tru's girl. Minnie's niece. Tenny's cousin. A Truman.

I was never just Ellis.

They were proud of the girl they knew—the *real* me—and I couldn't find the words to tell them the idea of being known in that way wasn't comforting. It was suffocating. But Tenny had decided that I couldn't truly celebrate my birthday until I had done it at the Tavern.

"You get hungry, girl?" he asked.

I shook my head. "No, it's—"

"I know what it is," he told me seriously. "It's Saturday."

I smiled, knowing he was teasing me. "No—"

"It's not Sunday."

"It's—"

"It's your birthday. A big one," he cut me off. "Do you think we forgot?"

I had, but I shook my head, no.

And that was the thing about being known like this. Sometimes it felt good. It felt like being seen. In that moment, I was happy I had come to the Tavern so Uncle Rick could tell me he had remembered my birthday. The "big one."

Wyatt slid into the booth next to Tenny and set down a basket of fries with a candle propped in the center. It was a tradition that had started when Wyatt was nine and said he hated cake.

"Happy birthday," they said in unison.

I blew out the candle but decided to save my wish.

Tenny, Wyatt, and I sat together eating fries and telling stories as we waited for the Tavern to change.

Eventually the lights dimmed and neon signs painted everything in a rainbow of artificial colors. The music slowly got louder as the people coming and going changed into heavier makeup and darker stares. Tenny's mom came out from the back to tell me stories about Tenny and me that I had heard hundreds of times. And to remind me that she missed seeing my face. Wyatt took glasses to the back, cleaned up spills off the filthy floors, and wiped down every imaginable surface except for the booth in the back where Tenny and I sat laughing and remembering all the silly things we had done within these walls.

"Remember when that biker was about to punch that guy in the face and you yelled that he was being too loud?" I asked her with a laugh.

"He was," she said with a shrug, but the corner of her mouth tilted upward. "I was trying to do my homework."

I shook my head. "Our lives are not normal."

Something hardened in her face and I wanted to take my words back. I wasn't sure when I lost the right to joke about it, but I had.

"*Our* lives are fine." She took a drink. "Better than whatever the fuck 'normal' is."

A million words bubbled in my throat. *I didn't mean it like that. I think it's great. I'm still one of you. I'm sorry.*

Instead, I changed the subject and asked about the old car her mom bought and how she was going to fix it up.

"It's not nice like the Albreys' or whatever, but I like it. I'm excited."

The little comments hurt the most. Each one was a shovel that dug into the dirt between us, creating a canyon. Self-preservation. I knew that was what she was doing, but it still hurt.

It was just after nine when my mother walked in.

Her hair was done and so sprayed that it was immovable, her clothes tight and dark with a low-cut top. And her makeup was thick.

"I want to go," I told Tenny and Wyatt.

"Go where?" she asked with irritation bleeding through. "Wyatt and I have to stay till close to clean up."

I cleared my throat. "My mom is here."

Tenny's face changed from confusion to curiosity as she

searched the bar, and when she finally saw my mother, I recognized the pity in her eyes. Even from where I sat my mother was a mess.

"I need to go."

"We can't leave," Tenny said, but her frustration was gone.

"Just stay over here and ignore her." Wyatt threw an arm over my shoulders. At that exact moment, my mother shouted from the other side of the room and kissed someone's cheek.

"Ignore her?" I repeated.

As if I could. I felt the moment she spotted me. Her confusion mixed with excitement before she rushed toward the booth I sat in. Fuchsia lipstick was stuck to her teeth as she smiled and pulled me into a hug.

"Baby girl! What are you doing here?" The embrace was affectionate, which was my first clue. The second was the way her words ran together.

She was already drunk. Now that she was closer, I could see that her eyeliner had begun to run, and I caught the sour smell of her breath.

"Where's Dad?" I asked as I stood and walked with her over to the bar. Having her sit in our booth felt sacrilegious.

For a moment, she seemed uncertain, as if I had asked about someone she didn't even know. "Your dad? He's at home, I guess."

She guessed. I hadn't seen her for three months. She had missed my birthday. Not that she had been around for many others, but this one stung. She didn't even ask how I was doing. Just rubbed affectionately at my arm while she tried to order a drink from Uncle Rick. I hated her touch.

"Do you have money to pay for your vodka and soda, Anna?" Uncle Rick asked.

"Nope." She popped the *p* when she said it. "But I'll find a way to make it up to you."

He rolled his eyes and mixed her a cocktail while I tried to hold back my disgust. I moved away from her and toward Tenny.

"Where are you going?" Mom asked as she leaned against the bar.

"Over there." I motioned toward Wyatt and Tenny.

A drink was set down in front of her with a thunk.

She turned to Uncle Rick to say thanks and I used the distraction to escape back to my friends.

I felt the lump in my throat as I pulled out my phone on reflex.

"What are you doing?" Tenny's shoulders stiffened because she knew the answer.

I told her anyway. "I'm texting East."

"Seriously?" She couldn't keep the frustration from her voice.

I didn't say anything as I tried to steady my own panic.

"Ellis, this is supposed to be our thing."

"I'm not asking him to hang out."

166

My phone vibrated a second later.

Easton:

OMW.

Tenny's glare was full of venom as my mom sat down in the booth with us. Two shot glasses glittered in her hands. "Here, baby."

I crossed my arms. "What is that?"

"A shot." She smiled wide. "It's your birthday!"

I frowned. "It's not my birthday. It was weeks ago. And I'm only sixteen."

"I know . . ." She didn't. I could see the information come back to her. "It's just one."

Wyatt reached across the table and took the shot in front of me, knocking it back and giving my mom a wink as he set the empty glass on the table.

She gave him a smile that made her look like a panther. "See? Wyatt's not afraid to take a shot!"

Wyatt only shrugged.

Each second I sat with her was an eternity, and I kept my eyes on the door. Waiting.

When Easton walked in, I felt like I could finally take a breath.

His eyes scanned the room, eventually landing on mine.

"Hey." He walked up to us with his keys in one hand,

167

turning them over and over. His other hand was clenched at his side.

"Easton Albrey," Wyatt said with a sly smile. "How's your brother?"

Before he could respond, my mother turned in the booth. *"Easton?"*

He looked like he was considering telling my mother exactly what he thought of her.

"You got tall!" She stood and stepped closer like she was going to measure herself against him.

He took a purposeful step back, but she pulled his bicep toward her. Easton's face transformed into disgust, but my mother didn't seem to notice.

"Mom." I sounded like I was begging. Another thing I added to the list of reasons why I hated her.

Her eyes were wide. "I remember when you were all knees and buckteeth. Not so much anymore."

His brows knit together, though I couldn't help but notice the way his ears turned pink.

"You better get him out of here," Tenny said. Her voice was resigned.

"I'm just going to go tell Aunt Minnie that I'm leaving," I said. "I'll be right back."

I walked into the kitchen and saw Aunt Minnie making sandwiches and putting them into red plastic baskets.

"You leaving?" she asked.

"Yeah. I . . ."

"I saw your mom here." She wiped her hands on the front of her apron and kissed my cheek gently. "I love you. Happy birthday. Call your grandmother."

Tenny's mother was what I expected a mom should be. Not quite Sandry with her easy life, but a mom who had it hard and still showed up for her kid. It made me resent my own so much more.

I nodded and walked back to the booth.

My mother stood uncomfortably close to Easton, her hand on his chest. I was too shocked to move as she whispered in his ear. A blush rose on his cheeks as he took her wrist in his hand and pulled it off him. She laughed, throwing her head back and exposing her neck as she fell into him purposely.

His eyes moved to her lips as she licked them.

"Goddamn it." I moved without thinking, placing myself between my mother and Easton. "We're leaving."

"So soon?" my mom whined. "Let's have a drink first."

She said it to Easton, not to me.

"You don't need another drink," I told her. "And he's sixteen. The same age as me."

I expected her to be embarrassed, but she ran her tongue against her bottom lip and smiled. "He doesn't look sixteen." Her gaze drifted to his pants.

Why had I expected anything different? I looked at Wyatt and Tenny. "Thanks for the help."

Tenny shook her head. "You invited him."

And that was it.

Easton deserved what he got because I asked him there and they thought he didn't belong. The worst part was, they were right. I didn't feel the need to protect *Wyatt* from my mother.

But.

Easton was mine. The one thing I had that was for *me*.

Outside, I took heavy lungfuls of the cool night air and pulled Easton's jeep door open. We sat in silence, the muffled music from the Tavern floating toward us. Under the neon lights. In the darkness without stars. I had always loved neon lights. The bright colors painted onto everything they touched. Blues and yellows and pinks and greens. I tried to remember what my mother's face looked like without them, but I couldn't.

Pink on her cheeks as her head tilted back laughing.

Blue as she lifted a drink to her mouth.

Yellow as the glow of the night faded.

Green on the darkened streets as we walked down them, back to the house.

Black under her eyes.

I could paint my mother with the lights from the Tavern, but I couldn't seem to remember her in the daylight.

"You can cry," Easton said eventually.

I didn't want to cry. I wanted to scream. I spoke softly. "No."

"It's not like your mom meant it."

I turned toward him. "What part? When she forgot my birthday? Or how old I was? Or when she tried to make out with you?"

"I don't care what your mom does, Ellis. She's a terrible person who only embarrassed herself."

And me. She embarrassed me. Because no matter how far I ran or tried to distance myself from her, I would always be her daughter. Nothing would ever change that. It was a humiliating truth. "I just— Can we go?"

Easton started the truck and pressed a foot on the gas and I watched as the lights from the Tavern faded.

And I knew sometimes—sometimes parents tried to take what wasn't theirs.

17

THE SOUND OF RUSTLING wakes me.

Before I open my eyes, I consider what I will do if an animal has made use of my house while I've been gone. It would be fitting to have one live here now.

Then I hear the animal swear.

"Shit." The mattress dips as someone's weight presses against it.

I open my eyes with effort to see Tenny sitting at the end of my bed.

Her hair is wild around her shoulders, like a lion's mane, as she looks at me with her nose scrunched up in disgust. "There isn't even any electricity," she says instead of a greeting.

I push up and rub at my eyes.

The room is worse in the daylight. My dresser is covered in a layer of dirt; there's garbage and broken glass on the ground. Pictures ripped from books and magazines of destinations that have yellowed with time hang from tacks on the wall and all my travel guides are still stacked in neat rows as they accumulate dust.

But I'd still rather be here than at the Albreys'. With Easton. His argument with Tucker. The look on his face when I said I didn't need him to come with me to see my dad. My anger makes it easier to justify being in this house.

Tenny lets out a long breath. "You look terrible. Is there even any hot water here?"

"I don't know. I've been awake for like thirty seconds."

"So?"

I run a hand over my face. "So, I haven't checked the water, Ten."

She looks around the room with a frown. "Why are you here and not at the *Albreys'*." Tenny spits out the name. I know she wants me to feel bad about staying with them. "How long have you been in town?"

"Not long." I don't tell her exactly because I know she's already upset about me not calling her.

"So which Albrey did you fight with? The mom or the boy."

Tenny knows their names but it makes her feel smug to be petty. I let her do it.

"How did you know I was here?" I ask.

She tosses my phone at me. "Were you missing this?"

I pick it up and check my alerts on reflex. "Easton told you," I surmise. Not smug enough not to talk to him.

"He did." She stands and wipes her hands off on her jeans. "Let's go. It's gross in here and you need a shower."

I'm not ready to go back to the Albreys'. The thought of walking back into the house when I pouted like a child makes me feel foolish. "Go where?"

"Grandma's. I've been staying there because my mom's working in the city. You can borrow some of my clothes." Tenny makes a face at the bed as I stand, but I ignore her. "Maybe we should check you for lice, too."

"You're staying at Grandma's?" I look down at my shoes when I say it as I slide my feet into them. The rejection stings. There has never been room for me to stay at Grandma's. Not long-term. She might be worried about her son in jail, but not about his daughter without a parent.

"Yeah, with everyone else." Like it's an inconvenience.

I stand and take a breath, forcing my resentment down past where I can reach it.

The drive to our grandmother's is quiet and I feel the grime of last night settled against my skin. I can't wait to wash it off. Her house is exactly the same as it has been every day of my life. Worn blue with broken white shutters. The grass is patchy and the front planter has an overgrown rosemary bush. Several old cars are in the driveway and my cousin Jesse is sitting on a plastic lawn chair in the middle of the yard, wearing only a pair of swim trunks. A cigarette hangs out of his mouth and a beer can sits against the leg of the chair. I don't have to be close to know it's open. His head is bent over his phone and he types on it furiously. He's almost seven years older than me, but he's never lived anywhere but with our grandmother.

I get out of the car and walk toward him. "Hey, Jess."

He gazes up at me slowly and lets out a drag of smoke from the side of his mouth. "Well, look at you, California. When'd you get back?"

"She's not back," Tenny says on her way inside the house. "Just visiting."

"Probably good," he tells me, reaching down to the beer. "You look like shit."

I point at the can in his hand. "Breakfast?"

He smiles, lopsided. "Gotta stay hydrated. Want some?"

"Not right now."

"Wild night with the rich kids? Crazy game of badminton?"

I lift a brow. "Do you even know what badminton is?"

"Ellis!" My grandmother's voice reaches me in the yard and I see her standing on the porch. Bright silver hair is pulled over her shoulder, her face lined with age and a hard life that never did her a single favor. Her round hips and narrow shoulders are covered in a light pink matching pants and tee set. "I was wondering when you'd turn up. Get your butt inside and get cleaned up so I can see your pretty face."

I smile. This is how she talks to all the grandkids. Somewhere between annoyed and in love. It's where Tenny gets it.

175

My arms wrap around Grandma and I smell the baby powder and lavender that belongs to every recollection I have of her. "Okay. Okay," she says as she pats my back. "Hug me after you shower."

Inside the house, everything is the same. My grandma had five kids. Four boys and my aunt Courtney. Their accomplishments and lives are memorialized in knickknacks that cover the surface of every usable space. Honey-colored oak furniture and bright but worn knitted blankets draped over the back of well-used couches. Everything smells a little like the cast iron on the stove and cigarette smoke. The only rule in the house is *Don't make a mess in the kitchen.*

My cousin Eric comes out from the dining room holding a sandwich. "El Bell? What happened?" He takes in my rumpled clothes. "Must be bad if you're here."

He's joking but it still stings.

"You better have cleaned up after yourself," Grandma tells him.

He waves at her. "What are you doing back?"

"Showering."

He nods because at Grandma's that's a perfectly acceptable explanation. Grandma's is a way station, a safe house. The door is always open. No one knocks here, no one asks to get something out of the fridge, everyone is expected to treat this place like it's their own.

Except for me. When I asked if I could live here for my

senior year of high school, after everything happened, my grandma told me that she didn't have the room. Which really meant she didn't want me here because I had somewhere else to go. I could always go to the Albreys', to San Diego. She had to prioritize beds. And I was not a priority.

I stand here and feel *other*. Not quite one of them, but not quite something else. It's how I feel everywhere.

The hall to the bathroom is covered in framed photographs. Old ones of her and a grandpa who died many years before I was ever born. My uncles in different school photos and celebrations in sepia tones are littered between homecoming and baby pictures of all thirteen of her grandchildren.

In the bathroom I see a dozen drugstore shampoo and conditioner bottles lined up on the windowsill. There is a tattered, dusty-pink towel and a set of clothes that I know Tenny must have put in here when I was talking with Eric. I wash as quickly as I can and dress, then follow Tenny out to the backyard, which is littered with rusted and broken lawn furniture.

Tenny sits in the weathered wicker chair that I've always known was her spot and I sit on the bench next to it. "You hungry? There's food in the kitchen," she tells me.

I hear Grandma's voice raise as she yells at Jesse and shake my head. "I'll get some in a minute."

Tenny takes a cigarette between her lips and flicks her lighter. She's never vaped. Says it doesn't have the same feel. I'm sure it doesn't have anything to do with the fact that she can steal cigarettes from our grandmother. "You going to see your dad?"

I rub at the tension in my neck. Escaping this question seems to be never-ending. "Yeah. I'll go."

She inhales the first drag, lighting the end bright cherry red. "That's about how I feel about mine." Gray smoke curls from her mouth on an exhale. Her dad isn't incarcerated; he's in Alaska working on a fishing boat the last we heard. Her mother was left with a baby and no family.

Grandma takes care of them. She pays for her sons' mistakes.

Because that's what family does.

"Have you talked to him at all?" she asks. Which is weird anyway, because we don't really talk about my dad.

"A little bit. He just asked about school and California." I lick my lips. "He didn't even apologize."

"Apologize?" she asks. "For what?"

Right. Me getting arrested wasn't his fault. Not here. The cops are responsible. How could they arrest a kid? Why were they going through my dad's stuff? If they would have just left him alone . . .

What I did wasn't kind, or stupid, or rash. It was expected. Because family is like that.

You pay for things that aren't your fault.

My head shakes down as I stare at the dirt covered in cigarette butts. "I just don't want to go."

"How much longer till you have to go back to the Albreys'?"

I should be there now. Helping Sandry cross things off her checklist. "I might not go back."

Tenny gives me an annoyed face. "Yes, you will."

She says it a little like it's expected and a little like she's disappointed. I hate that. The expectation that I will just choose the Albreys. Even when they sent me away.

We spend the rest of the day watching my cousins drink and smoke too much while they complain about how no one will pay them a fair salary. They complain about rich people and the government. About college. And college kids. They plan get-rich-quick schemes and dream about what they'll do with all the money they will make. They drink and tease each other and bring up embarrassing stories and my grandmother points out all the ways we are just like our parents.

I think about my dad and what he would look like here. How he'd laugh a little louder than he should, a canned beer in one hand and a cigarette in the other. I can see him in all the faces around me. I think about Aunt Courtney and don't miss the fact that neither my grandmother nor anyone else has asked about her. I notice all the ways she wouldn't fit here now.

I wonder if that will become me. I wonder if I ever fit here to begin with.

When my phone chirps in the afternoon and everyone is tired from drinking all day, I check it. Dixon's text is simple.

Dixon:

Dinner?

Ellis:

At my Grandma's. Come get me?

Dixon:

Meet me outside.

My phone slips back into my pocket and Tenny shakes her head at me before I even tell her what I'm doing. More disappointment.

What I don't expect is for Dixon to show up in his squad car. I don't expect all my cousins to look at me like I've betrayed them. And the resigned acceptance of my grandmother.

"Go," Tenny tells me. "You were going to anyways."

"Ten."

But. But I don't have anything else to add to that. She's right.

She smiles sardonically at me. "I'll see ya next time something goes wrong."

And that's fair.

18

Sixteen years old

EASTON'S PHONE CHIRPED NEXT to me on the night-stand. His arm was slung over my waist, like it typically was when the alarm went off on a Saturday for his morning swim. I nudged him, trying to hold on to the sleep that was already leaving me.

His elbow pressed into the mattress next to my head as he lifted himself up and leaned across me, grabbing for the phone. I felt the brush of his chest against my cheek and tried to hide the way I leaned into him out of habit.

It should have been simple. He'd hit the button and then fall back asleep. But he spent too much time staring at it, which is how I knew something was wrong.

"Shit." He sat up. "Shit, shit, shit."

A second later, he was out of the bed and grabbing his swim trunks. I stared at him as he went into the bathroom, not bothering to shut the door completely.

Easton came out running a hand through his hair and looked out the window. "You need to get up and you need to go to your room."

"What?" I asked. He never told me to go to my room.

"Sara is here."

I sat up. "Here? In the house?"

"On the porch waiting for me to let her in."

I dropped my head back to the pillow. "So?"

He stopped moving around and gave me a leveled stare. "Ellis, you can't be in my *bed* when Sara comes up here."

On my tongue was an argument. Everyone knew how close Easton and I were. But the way he was looking at me. This was different, and it wasn't about me.

Was I supposed to stop him? Was I supposed to tell him not to go to her? My skin felt hot from embarrassment, but I smiled as I sat up. "Fine, but can you make coffee before you go swim?"

He let out a frustrated breath and headed to the door. I went to my room and watched through my window as the two of them held hands to the dock and then as she kissed his cheek before they both dove into the freezing water. I tried not to hate that Sara swam with him. Easton had asked me a hundred times to go swimming with him in the morning and I had refused every time.

Maybe that's what Easton wanted. A girl who went swimming with him.

182

Eventually, the door to my room was pushed open lightly and Tucker came in.

"You're in here?"

I nodded and focused back on what was happening outside.

Tucker followed my gaze and came to stand next to me. "I wondered why no one had made coffee."

His words bothered me more than they should have. It was silly, but Easton had forgotten the one thing I'd asked him for. Tucker let out a deep breath as we watched Easton smile at something Sara said. She hit him gently on the shoulder and they walked right next to each other up to the house. Like a couple. "She's cute."

I let out a little groan.

Tucker should have laughed or made a joke at my expense, but instead he went still. "Don't do that."

"Do what?"

"This. Where you can't allow him to be happy. Let him have this. You know it won't last. Let him have fun."

What if this did last? What if it wasn't just fun? What if he kept forgetting my coffee? Forgetting me?

"Ellis, you always do this. Every time you think East might pay attention to someone that's not you, you pull him back in. Don't do it this time." Tucker walked out of my room.

I waited for Easton, but I could smell Sandry's bacon and could hear Sara's laugh. I lay down and threw my hand over my eyes, feeling all the rejection piling on top of me. If Easton wanted me, he would come find me. If Sandry was worried about me eating she would call for me. *If. If. If.*

But hunger got the best of me and I wandered into the kitchen. Sandry was dishing biscuits onto a plate for Sara, who sat at the kitchen island. Tucker and Dixon were laughing and Easton was arguing with them.

"Don't listen to them, Sara. They're liars," Sandry said, giving her a wink.

I took a deep breath.

"Hey, El!" Sandry greeted me. "I wondered when you were going to get up."

"I didn't smell any coffee," I grumbled as I sat between Dixon and Tucker.

"Hey." Sara gave me a bright, welcoming smile and I almost felt guilty for not returning it. Almost. Sandry put a cup in front of me and I began to spoon sugar into it.

"That's going to be really sweet," Sara said with wide eyes.

I looked up at her and poured another spoonful.

"Sara drinks her coffee black." Easton put his hand on the back of her chair as he leaned back in his.

I added another scoop just to spite them both.

They went up to his room after that and muffled music drifted out from behind the closed door. And I felt sick.

I wanted to leave, go home, go anywhere, but for some disgusting reason I couldn't make myself.

Dixon pulled on my ponytail as the two of us sat in the kitchen together. Alone. "If you could have one superpower what would it be?" he asked.

"Flight," I said.

He made a weird noise. "I'd pick immortality. That should be everyone's answer."

"If I could fly I could travel anywhere."

"If you had immortality you could actually see all the places you want to go."

We went quiet, listening to the sounds around us.

"Sara's nice," he added. For no reason.

"Yep."

Then he added, "I don't trust nice people."

I hoped he couldn't see my smile.

At dinner, Sara and Easton came down holding hands. The secret of whatever had happened in his room clear on their faces.

I was never going into that room again.

"You're not going to stay for dinner?" Sandry asked Sara, clearly disappointed.

I moved into the living room and sat on the floor with my plate. I had no desire to watch their goodbye. Tucker and Dixon were already there staring at the TV for some show Tucker couldn't wait to binge-watch.

He had his legs out on the coffee table and Dixon sat with a plate of dinner on his lap.

The door shut behind Easton.

"Press play," I told Tucker.

"At least wait for him to say goodbye," he responded.

"I wish she could have stayed. She's nice," Sandry said,

sitting down next to Dixon.

Tucker looked at me before he spoke. "I like her."

Before I had to respond, Easton came back, which was better. I didn't think I would be able to get the lie out of my mouth. Tucker hit play, and ten minutes in, Easton fell asleep at the end of the sectional. Between episodes, Sandry asked if I wanted a glass of water while she was up. I shook my head no.

"Did you lose your voice?"

"No." That wasn't what I had lost.

I got up and moved over to Easton, curling my legs underneath me and sitting flush against him. His breathing was steady and I kept replaying Tucker's words in my head. Easton wasn't wearing a shirt and his swim shorts hung low on his hips. My eyes caught on the tanned skin of his torso. We were through our third episode of a Korean period drama with zombies when I felt him stir.

He sat up and stretched his arms over his body. With an exhale, he dropped his hands. Then he looked at me and I felt the way his eyes flickered over my body.

Easton wore a particular expression when he was going to have a hard conversation. Part caution, part unearned confidence. I knew what was coming. He didn't want me around when Sara came over anymore. I watched the words find their way to his lips.

I cut him off. "I forgot I needed to run to the store."

"We're in the middle of the show, El." Tucker groaned.

"Tell me what happened when I get back."

Easton blinked, and then blinked again. "I'll go with."

"You don't have to," I said, standing and moving toward the bathroom. When the door was shut behind me, I leaned against it and took deep breaths. It was fine. I hadn't completely messed everything up. It was going to be fine. If I could just escape.

I opened the door and Easton was standing there, swim trunks gone and a shirt and shorts replacing them. "My mom gave me a list." He held up a piece of paper like proof.

My jaw tightened before I gave him a bright smile. I hadn't wanted to go to the store, I just wanted to . . . "Let's go." I hadn't escaped him. I had trapped myself with him.

The air still carried a chill from spring, not fully chased away by the sun, and the view caught my breath for a moment. Blue and black and green and gold. Sunset on the lake.

Once we had settled in the car, Easton plugged in his phone.

I would know what kind of mood he was in based on what he chose to play. A low, sad song came on, and I braced myself for what would come next. He focused on the road, his forearm flexing as he steered, his jaw tightening, his lips . . .

Did he kiss Sara softly or was it rough?

Guilt grew like a weed inside my belly.

It was none of my business how he kissed Sara.

Silence filled the spaces between the notes of music.

We wandered the aisles of the store together, picking up items and putting them in the small red basket he held. Brown sugar, half-and-half, Dixon's favorite kind of bread.

"What did you need?"

I didn't answer him.

He didn't bring up what he really wanted to say until we got to the candy section. "Are we not going to talk about this?" he asked.

I looked over at him, but his focus was on a candy claiming to be the original chocolate bar.

"Talk about what?"

"Ellis." He still didn't look at me.

The ache in my chest was even worse. "I'm sorry, fine. I'm listening."

"Listening," he repeated like he was trying to understand the meaning of the word. Trying out the cadence on his tongue.

"Actually, I don't really want to talk," I said.

His head shook gently once. "I know you're mad at me."

"What?" I couldn't keep the confusion from my face.

"You've been sulking all day. You barely spoke to Sara when she was over."

I tried to shove down my frustration. "What did you want me to say? Hey, scoot over so I can sit with you guys while you make out?"

"No, but you could have been nice to her, like everyone else was. I know you might be jealous—"

"Jealous?" I cut him off. "You think I'm jealous?" I was. He hadn't even denied that they had spent the day kissing.

His anger fell from him in heavy waves. "If you're not jealous, then talk to me. Tell me what you're thinking."

"It's not a big deal, Easton," I lied to him.

Because I thought it's what he needed.

Because I thought it would make him happy.

Because I thought I would die if I told him the truth.

"Do you like Sara?" he asked.

"Do you?" I threw back. "When I'm around her I don't . . . I don't know what I'm supposed to do. It feels weird to be there."

"You shouldn't feel weird about being at home."

"But that's it, right? That's what's wrong."

Now he looked at me. And I wished he hadn't. His face was annoyed and frustrated and confused. And if it was only those things, I would have been okay. But somewhere in there, I could see the hurt. "What do you want me to do, Ellis? Never date anyone because I have you?"

"No." I swallowed. Surrounded by brightly colored packages and smiling cartoons of candy. "I just wish it didn't feel like you were taking something from me to give something to her."

Easton shook his head. "If you can't see that your place isn't anything like hers, then I don't know how to change that. It's not the same, Ellis."

And that was the problem. I already knew we were different.

But not enough that I wasn't replaceable.

Because I was still the same girl who stood in the candy aisle and thought about stealing.

19

FROM MY BEDROOM WINDOW I watch deliverymen roll round tables out of white trucks. They move like clocks, counting down the seconds till the party.

Such a different scene than the one at my grandmother's the day before.

Four days. Only four and I still cannot remember where I put Sandry's necklace. I rub at my temples and try to think about the last place I had it before I moved to San Diego. But memory can be a slippery thing.

Instead of searching for it, I make my way to the kitchen. I stare out the open doors to the backyard, trying to get rid of the feeling that rubs against me. Everything feels raw. The sun. A bright blue sky. Picturesque white clouds that dance over it. It's beautiful, and for some reason it stings. The green grass, the beautiful people scattered across it, the soft music filling the air that only complements the lulling waves of the water.

I grab a glass and hold it against the fridge to fill it. A long sigh escapes me, and when I turn around Easton is standing at the kitchen island staring at me.

"What?" I throw the accusation at him, but he doesn't even flinch. Like he expects it.

He simply shrugs as an answer.

"What?" I repeat, but this time it's a question.

"I'm not trying to fight with you, Ellis."

A loud screeching sound shoots through our conversation from the speakers set up outside the open doors and we look over to Dixon, who raises a hand with wires in it. "Sorry!"

I drain the glass in three long gulps and set it down on the counter with a loud noise. "Then don't. It'd be easier if we didn't talk anyway."

"Sure, Ellis," he says, sounding tired. "Whatever you want."

I walk through the back door just as Prince comes blaring from the speakers. The opening chords of the song trill and everyone seems to realize at the same time what is happening.

Kiss.

"Ohhhhhhh." Tucker stands from the table he's been sitting at folding napkins. His hips move seemingly without his permission and he gives me a devilish smile and crooks a finger at me. I ignore it, but I don't move. If I try to, he'll come for me.

Tucker sings the opening lines to me, but I keep my frown. *"You don't have to be beautiful to turn me on."* His voice goes high and he makes a face that I think he assumes is sexy.

His head moves side to side with the beat as he dances toward me. *"I just need your body baby . . ."*

Tucker grabs my hips and forces me to sway with him. And because Prince is more contagious than a cold, I'm dancing. Dixon turns up the music and moves toward us. He's picked up a glass vase and is pretending it's a microphone. Sandry sways as she puts together flower arrangements and Ben grabs her hand and drags her over to where we are all dancing.

Still frowning. But dancing. I pretend that this isn't affecting me. I am not having fun.

Until the chorus, and I join everyone in making air-kisses with the song. I'm grinning now. There is no way to dance to Prince without it being all about your hips. I think that's the whole point of his music. I remember a hundred days where Prince was the soundtrack to our lives.

Ben stealing kisses from Sandry. Dixon singing in the highest register possible as he tried to flail around. Tucker with an air guitar. Easton trying to do the splits.

I look at Easton. He's only an arm's length away. Sandry pats him on his cheek.

And I look away.

The music changes to another Prince song, but the spell is broken. Everyone returns to setting up and I watch Easton's broad back as he moves toward Dixon.

Tucker throws an arm around my shoulders and I take a seat next to him at a round table in front of a huge pile of white linens. He folds the napkins as he sits, transforming the flat squares into blinding bright swans in the sunlight.

I take my square and fold it.

"That's not a swan," Tucker says next to me.

"It's mostly a swan," I say, studying what my hands have created. It's *not* mostly a swan. It's mostly a blob.

"That's a duck and you know it." He frowns. "Why are you making that face?" Tucker's hands move deftly over the linen.

"I'm not making a face."

"Did you stay at your grandma's last night?" he asks.

"No. Dixon came to get me for dinner and I slept here. Why?"

From his throat comes a thoughtful sound and he adds his finished swan to the pile of completed ones. "You get moody when you leave your grandma's."

"I do not." Maybe I do, but I don't want him to talk about it. I don't want anyone to talk about it.

"Was Tenny there?"

I make a noise that means yes and watch Dixon move a speaker toward the dance floor.

"What about your grandma?" Tucker continues.

He's fishing and it grates on my nerves. "Was my grandmother at her house?" I repeat so he can hear how ridiculous it sounds. "What are you trying to ask?"

Tucker looks up at me and then back at the napkin. "Did you talk about your dad?"

I bite into the flesh of my cheek so hard I taste blood. "Yes."

He continues, "Are you going to go—"

But Easton interrupts before he can finish his sentence. "Leave her alone, Tuck."

He's collecting tiles from the pile next to the table we sit at. They will latch together and make a dance floor. Sandry has been begging Ben to make it permanent. But Ben won't agree, something about resale value and investment properties.

It bothers me that Easton is trying to fight with Tucker *for* me. I don't need him to. I knot the napkin in my hand instead of folding it into a duck.

"I'm not picking on her," Tucker tries to explain. "She's just been—"

"Just let it go," Easton says, moving the tiles to the other side of the lawn. "If she wants to see her dad, she will." Like his defense of me isn't a big deal.

"Speaking of things you want me to let go, what are your plans after the summer?"

I look at Tucker and then Easton, confused.

Easton glares back to Tucker with a furious stare. "Shut up." His voice sounds tense. "And leave Ellis alone."

I swallow down the words that fill my mouth and only open it when I'm sure my voice will sound steady. "I don't need you to defend me. I have a voice."

"I . . ." Easton stops what he's doing, face transforming to surprise. "I wasn't . . . I just . . ."

The truth is, Easton knows that I don't want to talk about

my dad. Of course he does. He was there, too. He's just as mad as I am. But he's still *my* dad, and the anger that comes with speaking about him belongs to me.

I make my voice sound frustrated and final. "Well, *just* don't. We aren't friends. We don't talk. So *just* stop."

Easton opens his mouth and then closes it. And opens it. And . . .

"Ellis," Ben calls me. He's holding up a tall wooden post. "Can you give me a hand?"

It's then that I see all the eyes watching us. The Albreys' friends who have come to help set up go back to their work quickly and Tucker only shakes his head as he returns to his napkin.

Stupid.

"Hold this upright?" Ben directs and hands me the dark wooden post.

He shimmies it into the hole as I steady it and stands back to view his handiwork. "Nice job," he tells me as he dusts off his palms and inclines his head to the next beam.

I hold it up, and when Ben clears his throat, I know it's going to be more than just a *nice job.* "You've been pretty hard on East."

I don't know what to say to him. I can't tell him about all the things that have piled against my heart and hardened it, forming walls so high I might never see over them. But like most things with Easton's dad, he doesn't waste time pretending he doesn't know what I'm thinking.

"He really hurt you, I know." He pushes the post in. "But you really hurt him, too."

He hurt me worse, I want to say, but even I can hear how petulant it sounds. "A lot of things happened."

"Yep." He picks up another post. "I know all about what happened with the cops. I'm your dad's lawyer." He winks at me, trying to keep the conversation light. "And I know that you didn't want to go to San Diego. But no one didn't want you to go more than Easton."

We move to another post, this one next to the retaining wall, and I want to tell him he's a liar, but I can't find the words. I know Easton wanted me to go.

"When you left, Easton took it pretty hard. I'm not saying that he was right, or that you weren't miserable, too. But I think you should remember that it wasn't only you who was hurt."

"I know that."

"Sure, El, I think you do know that. But I think you only *care* about *your* pain."

I close my eyes as we put the last post in the hole.

And that's when I hear it.

"Hey, East."

I know that voice. I look over and see her. Shiny hair. Big smile.

Sara.

20

Sixteen years old

"HOW LONG IS THIS going to take?" Tucker groaned from outside the open bathroom door and stomped his feet like a kid being told to go to his room.

I swiped glitter eyeshadow onto my lid and stepped back, studying my makeup. "I'm almost done."

He hit his forehead against the wall. "You said that twenty minutes ago."

I ignored him as I fixed my lipstick for the hundredth time. The dark color was bleeding at the corners.

"We have to go. Halloween is all about the treats," Tucker announced with a stupid grin. "Kids get candy and we get . . ." His face turned suggestive as I pushed him back from the bathroom.

"You think you'll find a *treat* tonight?"

Tucker sighed and stood up straight, showing off his broad chest under his Roman toga. "My dear Ellis. *I* am the treat."

Dixon stuck his head around Tucker and frowned at my makeup. "Are those caterpillars?"

"Eyelashes," I said, putting one on.

Dixon's head tilted to the side. "What's wrong with the ones on your face?"

"Dixy," Sandry called from downstairs. "Leave her alone. We're going. Make sure to set the bowl on the porch for all the kids."

"Where the hell is Easton?" Ben shouted.

"He went to get Sara." Dixon's voice came from his room.

A dark feeling swirled in my chest and I didn't miss the way Tucker's eyes watched me.

Three more swipes and I declared my makeup finished, setting my brush down harder than I meant to. Tucker gave me a pointed look.

"What?" I challenged.

He lifted a shoulder at me. "Just waiting for you to stop being stubborn and actually talk about what's making you break stuff."

"I'm not being stubborn." I pushed him out of the way as I walked into my room, grabbing my black high heels from the closet and stepping into them. Tucker watched me wobble for a few moments before he moved over to stand next to me. I put out my hands to hold onto his arm and stomped my foot as the heel caught on the carpet.

Tucker's eyebrows went up in an *exhibit A* way. "Your

victims disagree with your claims of nonviolence."

I groaned. "I just don't know why he's going with Sara and we aren't all going together."

"Sara is his girlfriend."

"Of, like, three months. This is *our* thing."

"El." He spoke my name like he wanted me to understand something that was just outside of my reach. The softness made the word feel like a punch.

"I'm not jealous. I like Sara." It was true. Mostly. Sara was smart and kind. She wasn't arrogant even though her dad was the mayor and her mother was rumored to have money from an early Apple investment. They threw a giant fundraiser every Halloween to support the food bank in town. And Sara spoke to every person with the same amount of respect. She read books with one leg pulled up against her body and hair tucked behind an ear. She played softball and coached a kids' team for free.

Sandry loved her.

That was the whole problem with Sara. She had no faults. I had been looking for them for the past four years.

"I'm not jealous," I repeated. "She's my friend."

When she'd asked me about Easton months before, I *had*, in fact, told her I was okay with her going on a date with him. I *had* told him I thought she was nice and pretty when he asked what I thought.

I *had* . . . completely misjudged how much I would hate seeing Easton with someone else.

"Listen to yourself."

I shoved at him. "I can't because you won't shut up."

He held out a hand to me with a soft expression. "Wanna be my date?"

"Why? So you can ditch me to make out with Kalley Farrow?"

Tucker clutched his chest as if I had wounded him. "I already made out with her, but if Jordan Mitchell is around . . ."

"You ruin every sweet thing."

"It's actually my greatest gift and burden. Imagine how tired *I* am."

I looped my arm in his and smiled when I almost reached his height.

"Those make your legs look amazing."

Dixon coughed from the doorway. "You need a longer dress. Everyone is gonna hit on you."

"You need a muzzle," I told him.

"Oh." Tucker reached back onto the bed and grabbed my hat. "Can't forget this, little witch. Without the hat, you're just hot."

"Have fun at the party," Dixon told us as he opened the door. The front porch was filled with Disney princesses and superheroes and zombies. Dixon was dressed as a doctor and standing in the middle of a swarm of children. "One at a time! I'm going to—"

I couldn't hear the rest of the sentence because he was

overrun by screams and shouts as Tucker and I drove away.

All the kids in our town made the rounds, all the important people went to the fundraiser, and all the people my age went to the north side of the lake.

The cove was only accessible by walking down the beach into a more secluded spot. There was already a bright fire burning. Light reflected off high rock walls, making it feel like our own little kingdom. Sexy nurses and exaggerated politicians mingled with vampires and girls with enormous fairy wings.

A silver keg stood off to the side with a huge pack of red cups next to it. I immediately kicked off my heels and let the sand squish between my toes.

"Those shoes were a bad call." Tucker winked.

A group of boys Tucker's age called us over to the keg, handing us red cups. I took a sip of the flat, warm beer and tried not to make a face. But someone laughed, and when I looked up, Aaron Nam gave me a grin. I had seen him around school, but we never really spoke.

"Here," he said, holding out a cider. "This is better."

I took a sip. It was fizzy and tasted like pears. I liked it immediately. Aaron inclined his head and I sat down next to him on a long log by the fire.

"No shoes?" Aaron asked.

"I forgot about the sand, so I took them off."

"Well, now you can put your feet in the water." When he smiled, it felt like something more than just a smile. It was direct and it didn't have anything to do with Tucker or any of the Albreys.

Aaron asked me about school, and my costume, and the anime I had recently become consumed with. It felt nice to have someone ask about me. It was nice to not be known.

I knew the minute Easton and Sara arrived. Blond hair hung down her back in loose curls and a white dress with wings spread out behind her.

And Easton.

Red horns, black fitted suit, and a smile that seemed only too appropriate.

"Couples' costumes," Tucker said, sitting down next to me with his drink. "It's so gross it's almost cute."

It was goddamn adorable.

"Whatever."

They walked over to a group of Sara's friends. Easton had his hand on her back. The small part that girls always say is so romantic. He smiled at her as she said something.

And my heart hurt.

"Ellis." Aaron smiled back at me with a dimpled grin. "You and Easton fighting?"

I opened my mouth to tell him that we weren't fighting. Instead, I grinned. "He seems busy."

Aaron's eyes moved over to the group toward the end. "Ah. I always thought you two were together."

"What?" I laughed.

"Tenny said you were close."

My face scrunched in surprise. "You're friends with Ten?"

He nodded. "Wyatt was on my Little League team."

I had always assumed that Aaron was like the Albreys. Middle class with bills that were paid on time and two parents who talked about things like vacations and going to dinner at restaurants.

Aaron asked question after question. About what I thought about something random, about why I thought it, about how it could have been different. It was sometime during a conversation about Nutella as a dessert or a breakfast food when Tenny showed up and Tucker took off to find himself a treat.

Aaron handed me another cider and another, until they were gone. He sat close enough that I could feel the heat from him against my leg.

Out of habit, or maybe something more, I looked up for Easton.

His eyes were already on mine, a frown on his face. At that exact moment Aaron leaned over and whispered something to me.

I laughed, even though it wasn't funny. Or maybe it was; I hadn't really heard it. I smiled wider than I should have. And when I met Easton's eyes again, I prayed he felt as punished as I wanted him to.

"Easton's staring at us," Aaron told me. As if I hadn't already figured that out. "He looks mad. He's not gonna come over here and hit me, is he?"

"No." Probably not. I could never tell what was going to set Easton off sometimes.

I asked Aaron to get us another drink. He came back with a cheap beer and a small bottle of Jäger.

"This tastes like licorice," Aaron said.

It tasted like medicine, but I washed down the shot with terrible beer and felt the tightness in me unwind a bit.

As I was pouring my second shot, Tucker appeared over my shoulder, taking the bottle. "Absolutely not."

I narrowed my gaze at him. He had his dad's antique flask in his hand like a hypocrite. "You can drink but I can't?"

"You're more than welcome to drink, but you really shouldn't do it with a guy you barely know." He looked at Aaron. "No offense."

Aaron shrugged. "I mean, her cousin is right here and I'm more scared of Ten than I could ever be of you." He grinned. "No offense."

Tenny smiled with narrowed eyes. "I'm terrifying." She winked at Tucker.

He gave Aaron a long blink before turning back to me. "If you want to get wasted, you do it with a friend."

"I am with a friend," I argued. The words were a little harder for me to find.

"Relax, Albrey," Tenny told Tucker, her contempt clear in her voice. "I think I can handle it from here."

I didn't go with Tucker, but I didn't drink anything else either. Instead, Tenny and I danced with people whose names I couldn't remember. Girls, boys. I closed my eyes and pretended that Easton wasn't on the other side of the crowd with his arms wrapped around Sara and his lips pressed against her neck.

Someone stood behind me and I leaned back into them. I pressed my body against theirs and I didn't even care that I didn't know who it was. I wanted to chase the feelings that made me forget the way my heart hurt.

"Ellis." It sounded like Easton.

Even my mind was pretending now. I kept dancing with my eyes closed.

"Ellis."

The body behind me was suddenly gone and I stumbled without the support. I opened my eyes and Easton stood in front of me.

His jaw was set and his hands opened and closed into fists. "Time to go."

Sara stood a few feet behind him, her eyes wide like she could feel the storm in the air. "No," I said, pulling my dress down. "I'll find Tucker—"

"Get in the jeep," Easton growled.

The idea of sitting in the car with him and Sara made the alcohol in my stomach feel like it was writhing.

"Easton," Sara said. I hated the way her voice sounded. Soft, concerned.

I was backing away from them. "I'll ride home with Ten, and if not, I can find Tucker. You take Sara home."

She put her hand on his. "I can get my own ride, East. It's not a problem. You should take Ellis home."

She was so . . . kind.

"What a great idea," I snapped. "Except I don't want to ride with your *boyfriend*."

As soon as I said it, I watched understanding move over her face. She knew. She knew the real reason I hated her. "Ellis." She said my name slowly and my fear rose. "I'll find another ride. Just go with Easton."

The air around Sara felt thick with my own shame and I couldn't stand to be there another moment. "I'll tell Tenny."

It only took me a few steps to see Tenny. She was passing a joint back and forth in a group of a few people. Tucker was sitting next to Aaron, and I watched him hold the joint up to Tucker's lips.

Of course. He didn't want me. He wanted what was on the other side of me.

I didn't bother to find my heels as I stalked off to the jeep. If I turned around, I might see Easton kiss Sara goodbye, or thank her for being so understanding, or . . .

"Where you going?" A chest came into my view. When I looked up, I recognized a guy from class—Lucas, Louis, Larry? "Are you leaving?"

Before I could answer him, Easton was standing between us

and the boy was sitting in the sand. Because Easton had pushed him.

"What the fuck, Albrey?" he said, shaking off the cheap beer he had spilled.

"I already told you once tonight, Liam. Don't make me hit you." Easton was ready for a fight.

A second later Tucker was standing in front of his brother. "Get out of here, now. Liam is twice your size and if he gets backup both of us are gonna get black eyes."

The night had grown into something that was spiraling out of control, and I was ready to go home. At the car I pulled the handle on the door. Again and again and again. Easton's hands came over mine and pushed them away. "What are you doing?"

"Let me into the car."

As he walked to the other side, Easton hit the button and slid into the driver's seat next to me. I crossed my arms in the passenger seat and turned my whole body away from him.

He played with the keys in his hand. "What the fuck is your problem?"

I refused to answer that question. "Just start the car."

"No."

I turned to him. "Easton."

"Tell me why all of a sudden you're all over Aaron and—"

"Are you jealous?"

It took him a beat too long to answer. "No. I care that you've had too much to drink and you're dancing—"

My cheeks burned. "I don't know why you care."

"Because you're my friend."

"Your *friend*." I repeated it slowly.

"Ellis, just say whatever you're trying to say."

God. I was being so petulant.

"I'm just feeling stupid. Or . . . whatever. I'm not anyone's first choice."

His face showed his confusion. "I don't even know what that means. Are you mad that I went to a stupid party with my girlfriend and not you and Tucker?"

"It's not just that and you know it."

"I wouldn't have a girlfriend if I brought you with me to everything."

"Fine." I threw my hands up. "Don't have a girlfriend."

"I want a girlfriend."

He didn't say "Sara."

My eyes met his. "Get a different one." I leaned back in the quiet of the jeep. The dark leather absorbed all the light and made it feel like we were in a bubble of our own universe.

"Ellis."

I let my words sit as they were. I waited for him. I would always be waiting for him.

"Do you really want me to break up with Sara?"

Yes. But I couldn't say that. Instead, I looked up at Easton and asked him a question I knew he wouldn't answer. "Do you want a different girlfriend?"

I knew what was coming next. He was going to say sweet words to me, assure me. But—

He let out an angry laugh. "You're such a coward. You can't even say it, can you?" A muscle in his jaw ticked and he turned his body toward mine. "You want me to spend all my time with you and not a girlfriend? You can't keep treating me like your boyfriend because you don't want to get one. I *want* a girlfriend, Ellis. I want it."

I wasn't enough. He needed something else. I wasn't enough. He was going to leave. A tear slid down my cheek without my permission. "You don't want me?"

His lips parted softly and a small breath escaped him. I watched him stare at my mouth. The pad of his thumb brushed the tear at my cheek. "Ellis."

His hand came to rest on the side of my neck, like it had a hundred times before, but this time I wondered if he could feel my pulse hammering. "I don't want to have this conversation. Not like this."

"Please," I whispered. "What are you thinking?"

His eyes looked pained. "Tell me the truth and I'll tell you the truth."

Except I couldn't. I couldn't because I was afraid. I was worried. I was a hundred things and none of them were brave.

Because Easton was the most important thing in my whole world. He stood at the center of my universe, holding me still while everything spun around us.

And if something happened to him . . .

I couldn't be brave. That was for people who had nothing to lose, and I couldn't lose Easton.

But when he put the keys in the ignition, I knew I already had lost more than I was willing to admit.

21

SARA. SARA IS HOME.

Her name plays on a loop in my mind, over the music playing from the jukebox in the Tavern.

I'm not running away.

And despite the text from Tucker in my pocket, I'm not a coward. I just don't want to see Sara. Or Easton. I didn't even know she was in town.

The neon sign above my seat at the Tavern is blue. A melancholy color even though it's bright, making me lift the red cup in front of me to my lips again and again. The side of it says *Cola* in white script that has washed out against the warped plastic, but there is no "cola" in this drink.

No one even told me Sara was back. She showed up in the Albreys' backyard. I smiled and let her hug me—

I take a large gulp from the tumbler, feeling the burn of alcohol slide down my throat painfully.

She said it was good to see me and that I looked *beautiful*.

I take another sip.

She asked if I wanted to get coffee. Catch up. She wanted to hear about California.

I hate that Sara is nice. I hate that she's done nothing to truly earn my anger. I hate my hate.

The alcohol burns my throat.

"Slow down or I'll be scraping you off the floor, and trust me, this place is disgusting." Tenny is leaning against the tall table I'm sitting at. She has a rag in her hand and her own drink in the other.

"I'm fine."

She shakes her head at me. "Fine is the last thing you are." There is a pause that is filled with judgment. "Why are you here?"

Sandry is going to be upset that I haven't come back, but . . . I can't. "I'm visiting."

Tenny makes an annoyed sound. "I'm not off for another four hours, so you need to pace yourself if you want to make it to the car." She looks like she wants to say more, but a couple gets up from a table and she moves to clean up the glasses.

I keep going, until the tumbler of vodka and ice is empty. The Tavern is mostly unoccupied, which is how Tenny snuck me the alcohol in the first place. The neon lights move on the fake wood of the dance floor. They swirl and change and shift.

Light is never the same.

Light never stays.

I slide off my chair and lie down on the cool floor, right in the center, with my eyes closed. The brightness moves behind my eyelids and makes me dizzy and disoriented. Or maybe it's the alcohol.

"Ellis, get up." Tenny's grabbing my arm, but I've gone limp. "Goddamn it, get up."

"I'm fine here," I say, keeping my eyes closed.

She tosses my arm back at me and it lies across my stomach. "You're unbelievable. Uncle Rick is going to fire me."

"Who cares?" I mumble.

She does. I know she does, but if I stand up, I'll lose this moment. The one with the lights.

"Ten," Uncle Rick says with a warning riding on his voice. "Get her off my floor."

Tenny curses as she tries to pull me again and then drops my arm. "You're going home."

"I don't want to go home. I don't . . ."

I don't have a home, but I don't tell Ten that. Because I never have to explain who I am to her. She knows.

I lie there on the floor, staring at the ceiling and thinking about Sara. I can't stop seeing her smile at Easton. Or the way she placed a hand on his. She walked into the backyard like she belonged there. Like she was expected.

"Your ride is here," Tenny tells me.

Easton stands above me, swirling in the moving light.

213

"You called Easton?" I throw my question at Tenny, who has the decency to appear marginally ashamed. "Why?"

"Because you need to go home." She's telling me that my home is with the Albreys. She's making it real. It hurts.

What she doesn't realize is that I will never be one of the Albreys. And I can't be like her, either. I exist in the undefinable space between.

"Where is Sara? At the house?" I can hear the pettiness in my own voice.

Easton shakes his head once and puts his hands in his pockets.

"Fine." I push up to sit and feel my head swim. "Fuck you, Ten."

"Ellis." Her voice is sweet but her eyes are sharp. "Actually, fuck you."

My anger overrides the alcohol and I stand up and stumble. With my arms out I push through the door to the sidewalk. Easton follows me and the music and noise disappears behind the walls until it's only the sound of night on an empty street.

"I don't need you to take me home," I tell him, hoping I sound sufficient.

He scoffs. "Clearly."

I pretend like I don't care. My hand waves in the air as the sidewalk waves under me. "You can stay or you can leave. Go back to Sara, or whatever."

"Knock it off, Ellis."

"Why are you even here?" I turn to him and wobble on my feet.

His arms are folded over his chest now and his eyes stare back at me, unflinching.

I think about the last time Easton collected me from the Tavern. I hate the way my heart bends at the memory. "I don't need you to save me."

"Ellis, get in the car."

I make my voice sound mocking. "Easton, fuck off."

"I think you're overusing that word."

He's probably right. "Well, fuck."

His tongue pokes at the inside of his cheek. "I'm not going to ask you again. Get the fuck in the car." Even through my drunken mind, I know he's serious.

"What will you do if I don't?" It's suggestive. I don't mean it to be . . . or maybe I do. I can't tell if it's the alcohol or Easton that muddles my mind.

Something flashes in his eyes and I feel my pulse quicken. I want another hit of Easton's resolve cracking. I open my mouth to speak but he cuts me off. "Let's go get you a coffee. And water."

"I'm not thirsty."

Easton puts his hand on my elbow as I sway. I let him, even though the vodka does nothing to numb the burn of his touch. "You're wasted."

"You have to pay for the coffee." I close one eye when I say it.

"Obviously."

For some reason this upsets me more than I think it should. The assumption that I can't pay for myself. "Forget it. I can pay for myself. I have my own money. I have a *job*."

"I know, Ellis."

He's trying so hard not to fight with me, but it all sounds patronizing. I slam the car door as hard as I can. Easton sighs and turns the engine over.

"I don't need charity."

"That's your problem. Friendship isn't charity."

"I don't have friends. You have friends." I drag it out when I say it, hoping he knows I mean Sara.

He doesn't speak. My words fall into the blackness of the night.

"So you don't care that I don't have any friends in San Diego."

"You had Tucker." He lets out a laugh. "Your new best friend. And *Will*." His voice carries an edge to it.

I love it.

"And you still had your whole life. And Sara."

His hands tighten on the wheel as he turns into the parking lot for the Quickstop and parks the car. The LED lights glow against his face in beautiful curves that I've missed. They steal my breath and my anger. I close my eyes and lean my head against the window, refusing to let my frustration with him diminish.

"Are we going to keep having this conversation? The one

where you blame me for what happened? You had to go. I couldn't have stopped it if I wanted to."

My mind catches on those last four words.

He looks away. Takes a breath. Gets out of the car. I watch him inside filling a Styrofoam cup with bad coffee and dumping a handful of creamers into it. I watch him pay for that and a water bottle with deft fingers that I can remember the feel of and say thank you with lips I remember the taste of. I bite at my own.

He gets back into the car and hands me the coffee. "Drink." And then he places the water on my lap.

"Remember when we first met?" I ask him. "You asked me to break into the school."

"That's not when we met, Ellis. That's just when you stopped pretending I didn't exist."

I swallow a sip of hot coffee and let the silence eat away at the questions that sit between us.

"Did you want to stop it?" I'm not talking about him existing. I'm talking about California.

He lets a breath fill him. "No, Ellis. I didn't want to stop it."

I turn back to the window as each one of those words hits me in the heart. Everything feels raw and exposed. My tears fall, embarrassingly, and I hate that I'm trapped in this car.

A memory of Easton wrapping his hand in mine on the porch finds me. *Me and you.* He whispered it to me, with his lips close to my ear and his breath dancing against my skin.

"You lied to me." I mean for it to sound angry, but I only sound broken. "You chose everyone over me."

"Yeah, well you chose Tucker over me."

I turn to him. "I chose him over you?"

"Stop talking to me like I'm an idiot. I'm not the one that forgot. *Me and you,* remember?"

We pull into the drive and get out of the car. I take my coffee and water, ready to go inside, but Easton puts his hand on my waist and moves me to the side of the house. "You're not going inside until you sober up."

We move around the tables set up on the lawn and sit down at the edge of the dock with our feet scraping at the top of the lake.

"Ellis. Tell me what you're thinking."

"Thoughts aren't free. They cost something, and you don't have anything I want anymore."

"Ellis."

I should have known he wouldn't let it go. I take another sip of the coffee but I don't feel less drunk. I feel even more jumbled. "It hurts. You hurt."

He watches me. His eyes follow the swallow of my throat, the way I wipe at my mouth with the back of my hand. It feels unsettling and yet familiar.

Our eyes meet. His pulse beats at his neck. I want to reach out and touch it. To feel him underneath me, against me. My body wants what it can't have. "Easton."

He looks . . . scared, and something else that has hard edges. "Don't say my name like that."

"Why?" I whisper. "Are you dating Sara again?"

He laughs and stares out at the lake. "You are unbelievable."

"Why? Are you dating someone else? Have you . . ."

Have you moved on? Do you still think about me?

"What does any of that matter?" he asks.

But I can see the cracks. "Because . . . I miss you." I put my hand on his thigh, much too high to be friendly. I just want to see if I can. If he will still let me touch him like this.

His eyes move to the hand and his breath stills.

"I miss . . ." I lean into him.

"Goddamn it." He pushes me off and stands.

I follow him, stepping into his space. He has very few places he can go on the narrow dock. "Easton."

He curses.

I take another step closer until my chest is flush with his. My arms wrap around his shoulders and I press my face into his neck like I've wanted to do since the day I left. "East." I let his name mingle with the smell of his cologne and skin.

His face turns down to me, a mistake for him and an opportunity for me. Softly, I rub my lips against his and let out a small breath. Not a kiss. Only the promise of one.

The next moment my back is against the post of the dock and he's pressing against me. His body's hard curves pushing into all my soft ones. His hands hold on to my waist. "Like

219

this?" he whispers against my neck. "Is this what you want?"

Suddenly, I feel like my game has gotten out of hand. I've lost the control I thought I possessed.

His mouth drags against the skin of my shoulder. "Do you still miss me?" His hips roll into me and I moan. His mouth is on mine, rough and angry as his teeth pull at my lip. I reach up toward his neck and then—

A hand tightens around my wrist and he's stepping away. I feel the cold air replace my chance.

Panic claws at my gut. "You're just leaving?!"

He steps back to me so quickly I flinch. *"Shut up,"* he says. "You're going to wake everyone up."

But I'm too far gone to understand his words. The implications of them. "How can you be so mean?"

"Mean?" His face shows how shocked he is by my words. "First, I don't want to talk about your bullshit right now. And second, if you wake up my parents—"

"This is *your* bullshit!"

"No, it's not. You saw Sara and now—"

A light comes on in the kitchen.

"Fuck," Easton curses again.

A second later he's pulling me into the dark space of the boathouse with a hand over my mouth and an arm wrapped around my body. He's quiet as he listens for the back door to open or for someone to call for us or . . .

But seconds go by and all I can think about is that his body is still touching mine. The way he smells like home and smiles and every tear that has ever been wiped away. I remember how it felt to be kissed by him and the way his face transformed when I touched him. What his voice sounds like when he's whispering against me.

I take a hand and slowly move it under the soft fabric of his shirt. The skin of his stomach is smooth under the tips of my fingers, and his breath stutters.

The rush finds me.

I move across his waist as slowly as I can, watching the agony of pleasure play out on his features.

And then he takes his hand from my mouth and I see the hunger in his eyes.

It's the last thing I see before the memories of gold fade to black.

22

Seventeen years old

SOMEONE WAS MAKING DINNER. The scent of garlic and something buttery found me before the front door to my house was even fully open. My throat tightened as music, upbeat and sensual, poured from the living room and flooded the house with an excited chaos.

Food and music meant only one thing.

My mother was home.

She stood in the center of our small kitchen, dancing and humming along to the song. I watched her lips move as she popped a piece of the fruit she'd cut into her mouth. I didn't have to hear her to know what she'd said. *"One for the bowl and one for the chef."*

I wanted to ask how she knew where the knife was. I wanted to ask what she was doing there. How she had gotten money for food. I wanted to ask . . . but I was only relieved.

The part of myself I hated was glad to see her and it let her stand in our kitchen like she belonged there.

I bit the inside of my cheek to keep from running and wrapping my arms around her waist or greeting her with happy words. I was afraid it would scare her. And if she was scared . . . she would leave. Despite how often she was gone, my mother was always Dad's true north. All roads pointed to her.

And nothing was worse than picking up the pieces of my father when she left.

Now he stood with his back bent in front of the open refrigerator, humming to himself as he rooted through the shelves for something, which was strange. What could he even search through? He straightened eventually and handed her a tub of Cool Whip I didn't know we had.

"Thank you, baby," I heard her say as she leaned up on her tiptoes to kiss his cheek. My eyes couldn't help but notice the way the light caught on the dark circles under her eyes, and the reason my mother was home suddenly became clear. She had run out of money, which meant she'd run out of whatever her latest vice was. And it was payday for my dad.

He finally noticed me standing in the doorway, and for a second surprise flittered across his face.

At me, standing in my own home.

As if he'd forgotten I ever lived there.

I swallowed down the bitter taste that was bubbling from my throat. We'd been spending more time together. I'd even been coming home for dinner most nights. I never told him that I was avoiding the Albreys, but he seemed to sense it, as if he could tell my heart was broken from watching Sara and Easton. But all it took was my mother returning to erase all that. I dropped my school bag on the floor during the change of songs.

Mom turned around and looked down at the noise and then up at me. "Ellis! What took you so long?"

What took *me* so long? She hadn't been home in months. "I was studying," I told her and leaned in to kiss her cheek. The skin was papery and smelled like cheap cover-up and waxy lipstick.

"Studying? At school?"

My dad's eyes pleaded with me not to correct her. He knew where I'd been.

Sandry's.

But he didn't want me to ruin this moment. The one where my mother was content. He didn't want the restlessness that lived under her skin to steal her away from this.

And what did it matter if I told her a lie? She had told me so many.

"Yep."

He nodded gratefully at me and then wrapped his arms around my mother's waist, swaying with the music. He didn't care what my lie had cost me.

"Set the table?" she asked.

We had only sat at the table a handful of times in my whole

life, on holidays and special occasions, but I did as I was told, placing mismatching dishes on the table and cheap plastic forks next to them.

My phone vibrated in my pocket.

Easton:
I need to talk to you.

I read it three times, trying to understand what could be so urgent. He was with Sara tonight, which was one of the reasons I was here. With my mother. She set the food at the center of the table and my father turned down the music. I snapped a picture and quickly sent it to Easton.

His reply was almost instant.

Easton:
Where are you?

Ellis:
Home. My mom is here.

And then.

Easton:
Are you okay?

"Nope." My mother held out her hand. "No phones."

225

I gripped it tighter. How dare she come here and act like she was my mother, like she could tell me what to do. She'd be gone by next week.

"No phones, El," Dad echoed, and my mother looked smug. He had chosen her over me.

If it wasn't for my father's face, the one that seemed like all the pain he felt had finally left him, I would have stormed off. Instead, I handed her my phone.

During dinner she told stories about different places she had visited and people who had odd nicknames. My father laughed with her the whole time, never telling her that those stories were all at the expense of her family.

He seemed happy as the two of them sipped cheap wine and barely touched the food on the table. They looked like happy people should. They sang songs to each other as music played softly.

My mother was the most powerful drug my father was addicted to.

Three bottles of wine later, I finally slipped into my room. They didn't want me there anyway. And when the music was quiet and the house had stilled and the silence crept over everything, I could feel the wrongness in the air.

Slowly, I pushed open my door and walked past the table with plates piled on it and a kitchen full of dirty dishes to find my mother standing at the hall table, where my father kept his keys. She had a duffel bag on the ground next to her and in her hands was my father's wallet.

My mom pulled out a stack of cash. The first of every month my father got a check. That was all the money he would have for the whole month, sitting in her hands. Dinners and breakfasts and electricity and medicine.

I should have stopped her, but all I could think was maybe this time she would stay gone forever. Maybe this would be the time that she wouldn't be able to come back. Maybe the cash in her hands was all it would cost to never see her again. If I just let her take it. If I lied one more time.

She glanced up at me without an ounce of shame, gave me a wink, and slipped into the humid night.

By the time my shock wore off, she was gone.

I had let her leave because I hated her. Because of my selfishness. And when my dad woke up, he would have that look. The one that was hurt and confused but mostly just broken.

I couldn't be there to see it. I didn't want him to see my guilt and my relief. I couldn't . . .

The path to Easton's house was ingrained in me from habit. I didn't think as I walked up their drive, my feet crunching on the gravel and the smell of gardenias blooming in the planters. The locks on their house were automated, so I punched in the code and tiptoed up the stairs.

Easton barely moved as I slid into bed next to him. "Mmmm." That was the noise he made as I folded myself against him. My front against his back as my face pressed into the place between his shoulders. I wrapped an arm around his waist. Here, I could cry if I wanted to. I could talk about my mother, or not say anything at all, and he would understand.

But I was sick of thinking about them. My mom and my dad. They were in charge of all the ways I was allowed to feel. I wanted to be in control of something.

"So, it was bad?" he asked, between sleep and awake.

I bit the inside of my cheek so hard I tasted blood. "She already left."

Easton didn't say anything else, but when I moved my leg over his hip, he put a hand on my bare thigh.

I pressed my chest farther against him and felt his body stiffen.

My heart pounded as I chased a feeling that consumed all the other ones snaking around my emotions. With light fingers, I traced the strip of skin between his shirt and shorts. My arm wrapped around his waist and I set my palm at his belly button.

"Ellis," he whispered. It was supposed to be a warning, but I pretended it was a challenge.

I moved my hand lower, slowly . . . and his fingers wrapped around my wrist. Holding it in place. He turned toward me, his face next to mine, and I didn't want to spend another moment thinking. I pressed my lips to his. Slowly at first as I let the taste of him chase away all the feelings that had been building from before. I moved closer to him, my fingers running over his body, under his shirt with touches I had only thought about before.

I could feel that Easton wanted me. His want pressed against my hip, and each time I moved he let out a groan that made me feel drunk with my new power.

Hands moved over my body, lifting my shirt, pulling at my shorts. His mouth was against my skin, fevered and desperate. And suddenly I wasn't in control anymore. Suddenly, it was Easton making *me* feel.

"Easton." I breathed his name into the darkness.

"Tell me what you want," he said. In the moonlight, I could see the muscles in his shoulders shifting, the side of his face and the way his jaw worked as his lips found the sensitive parts of me.

I let out a soft cry.

And then he was pushing me away.

His forehead was against mine, and his face turned down toward the space he had put between our bodies. Space I desperately wanted to close.

After three steadying breaths, his eyes met mine. "Damn it, Ellis."

I was so angry I couldn't form words. I needed this. I needed him.

But like everything, I wasn't allowed to have what I wanted. I— "Please," I whispered. "I need you."

His thumb brushed against my cheekbone.

I hadn't realized I was crying. "Ellis."

I didn't want his sympathy. I didn't want to talk about my

family. My mouth opened to demand he kiss me again . . . "She took all the money."

My tears multiplied and he pulled my face to his chest. The smell of Easton and the Albreys' detergent filled my nose, and instead of stopping my tears it only made them worse. But it was safe to cry here. In the dark, on Easton's twin bed, our little island.

He pressed his lips to the top of my head and left them there.

Connecting us in a way I needed more than the way I wanted.

Somehow Easton knew. He always knew.

"She didn't even clean up the kitchen. She does this. Explodes all over our life and then doesn't even care that she's made everything a mess."

He rubbed circles over my back with a flat palm. Comforting.

The words I chose next were filled with the most truth I had ever spoken. "I wish she was dead."

His hand never paused when I said it. He was never shocked by my anger. He just let me be.

And I'd tried to use him. . . . I was no better than my mother.

"I'm sorry, Easton." My voice broke and cracked over the apology. "I'm so sorry."

"You have nothing to be sorry for, Ellis," he said against my hair. "I'm here."

"What if you move away and I'm left all alone?"

"You can call me and I'll listen to you cry from wherever I am."

I swallowed and tried to believe that Easton wasn't going to leave me. That he would always let me cry in his bed. That he would always forgive me for not knowing how to love him in the right ways.

"I hate being like this," I told him.

"Honest?"

I started to deny it . . . but "honest" was the best description for what I never felt like I could be.

"You can be a hundred different things in the same second. I'll still be here." He said it the same way he said everything about me. As if there was no way I could change its truth.

I pressed a kiss to the soft skin where his neck and collarbones met, but this one wasn't like the ones before. This one was filled with gratitude.

Because I could always trust Easton Albrey.

23

MY EYES OPEN SLOWLY, one after the other, and the movement is painful. I press a hand to the center of my forehead and take a deep breath. I'm in the room.

My room.

My room . . . at the Albreys'.

Fuzzy memories at the Tavern, on the dock, of Easton. They feel like *almost* truths.

Everything in here is white and bright. The sun filters in through the gauzy curtains and I groan and swallow. My tongue feels like lead. Something chirps and from the corner of my mind and I recognize it as my cell phone.

With a fumbling hand, I reach for it.

Tucker:
Take the pills.

I read the text with one eye open before setting the phone

back down on the nightstand. It clatters next to my jewelry. My necklace, a bracelet, my earrings.

Hands brushing against my neck to the clasp at my throat.

My vision is blurry.

"Shit."

The nightstand has a glass of water and two red ibuprofen tablets. I swallow them and then look back at my phone.

Five calls to Easton. In a row.

I go to my texts.

Ellis:

Come back.

Easton.

I'm sorry.

I pull a pillow over my head and wonder if I can smother myself. It might be less painful than dying of the embarrassment I feel right now.

In the bathroom, I brush my teeth and wash my face and attempt to piece together what happened last night, but it doesn't matter how many times I try to remember past the boathouse— *my hands on his body*—I can't seem to get past—*hungry eyes*—that moment.

I debate living in the bathroom forever. Maybe if I stay here, at least until everyone leaves for the day, I can avoid Easton.

Coward.

I am such a coward. I pull open the door and pad down the stairs and into the quiet kitchen. Coffee is brewing and Tucker leans against the counter, scrolling through his phone. When he looks up, I see the frown on his face.

"She lives."

I cross my arms and lean my head on his shoulder as we wait for the coffee to finish. "What the hell happened?" I ask. But I also don't really want to know.

"You did your best impersonation of 'teen returning to her no-good town and trying to drown her sorrows with underage drinking' cliché."

A groan escapes me.

"Don't worry, I don't think Dixon is mad."

"Dixon?"

Tucker's face is patient, if not patronizing. "What is the last thing you remember?"

The screen door pops open and Dixon walks in wearing his sheriff's uniform. "Elvis, you're alive."

"Alive?" I ask. "Oh my god . . ."

Dixon takes a coffee mug and pours the still-brewing coffee into the cup.

"Hey!" Tucker yells. "You're messing with the potency."

Dixon lifts a shoulder. "It's all the same."

"That's not how science works, asshole." Tucker gives an angry glare to the mug. "Aren't you on duty?"

"It's coffee, not heroin. I think I'll be able to keep my job if they find out."

But I can't take another moment of this. "Stop talking about coffee, right now, and tell me what happened."

Tucker's eyebrows go up. "Why don't *you* tell us what you remember."

I can feel the blush crawl up my face.

"Oh." Tucker's eyes widen. "Please start with what you just thought of."

"Oh god." Dixon looks disgusted. "Please don't. That's my brother."

"I think I made a mistake."

"Some," Tucker corrects. "Some mistakes. Definitely not one."

A scoff sounds behind me and I watch as Easton runs a hand over his stomach under his shirt. He takes a cup from the cupboard and pours coffee and then walks out of the kitchen without speaking to any of us.

"Holy fuck," Tucker mutters with wide eyes. "You are in so much shit."

He's loving this.

I take my coffee and pour too much cream into it. My hand tightens around the mug and I hate that I draw a comparison from my cup with too much cream to my life right now. I've poured too much in and ruined everything. Tears prick at my eyes and —

"Here." Dixon takes it from my hands and pours it into a bigger cup and then adds more coffee until the milky color turns to a caramel one. "Fixed. No need to thank me."

I look up at him, my eyes still wet.

"Jesus, Elvis. It's just coffee."

I wrap my arms around his middle, careful of his belt. It takes him a second but he wraps his arms around me and presses his cheek to the top of my head.

We stay like that longer than Dixon normally allows, and thankfully Tucker doesn't make a stupid comment. Until Dixon whispers gently, "You smell like the floor of a bar."

I push at him.

"Assaulting an officer is a felony."

I take my mug and find Easton sitting on the porch with one hand on his coffee and the other scrolling through his phone. When he hears the door open, the phone in his hand goes dark.

He's texting his friends to save him. He's texting Sara about what a mess I am. He's texting . . .

"Hey," I say.

Instead of an answer, he only glances at me. I take the seat next to him and cross my legs, staring out at the mess that is all over the lawn. In two days, this will be beautiful, but right now it looks like the carnage of a hurricane.

"I'm sorry about last night."

The only way I know he's heard me is because his hands tighten on the coffee mug before he brings it to his lips.

I let out a short laugh. "I don't even remember everything that happened."

He unlocks his phone and goes back to scrolling through an app. Probably Instagram, maybe Reddit.

"You don't want to yell at me?" I ask.

"What would that change? You don't remember what you did."

"And you don't want to help me out?"

"What part don't you remember? Shouting at me in the house? Calling Dixon? Tucker and I trying to shut you up so you wouldn't wake up my mom?"

I try so hard to see a glimpse of the things he's talking about, but those memories are empty.

"Or do you not remember the boathouse?"

My face heats at the mention of it and I can't hide the blush.

"No," he says with his eyes on my face. "You remember that." He watches the way I respond to his words, hearing all the things I'm not saying.

"Easton . . ."

"What? Continue. Please." His hands make wide exaggerated gestures. Like this conversation.

His anger, my contrition. Exaggerated.

My words are all lost inside my embarrassment. Easton stands. The movement is so fast I look back at the Adirondack chair that scrapes behind him. His hands move up to his hair and then back down to brush against the sides of his pants. He reminds me of a tiger in a cage. Pacing. I watch his broad back as he walks down to the water and wonder when he got so long and lean. Where did the youth that was in his face go?

I follow him to the dock. He's standing on the soft patch of worn dirt where grass has never been able to grow, right before the wood planks start.

"Easton, I don't know what to say."

When he speaks, it's with his face turned toward the water. "Start with 'I'm sorry.'"

"I am. I'm embarrassed and I feel stupid and—" I take a deep breath. "I didn't mean to . . . the boathouse was . . ."

His mouth opens in shock but it only takes him a second to recover. "You think this is about you and me?"

I hate that I can't seem to stop being confused.

"Ellis, I don't give a shit about you trying to fuck me. That's just a regular day in the whiplash of being your friend. I got over that shit a long time ago. I'm pissed about my mom."

I don't have time to feel the vicious sting of his words. "Your mom?"

"Oh my *god*." He groans. "Yes, my mom. The person whose birthday you're here for. If you get wasted like that again and ruin the week—"

"What?" I tilt my head. "What will you do, Easton?"

When his face goes still and his breath becomes shallow, I know he means his next words. "I've spent the last year without you."

I feel fire burn in my veins and I know the moment it turns to angry words in my mouth. "So what? Are you going to stop speaking to me? Make me move to California if I don't behave?"

"Ellis—"

"There isn't anything to threaten me with because I don't actually give a shit anymore. I'm here because I choose to be, but don't expect me to act the way you tell me to."

"As if I could ever fathom that. You always do exactly what you want."

"Yes. I do. Because when it comes down to it, you don't. You pretend to be sad about me and act like a kicked puppy. *You* sent me away. *You* were the coward. You did this and your mom and I are this way because of *you*. However I treat your mom, that's all on you."

His face turns furious. "So, what? You're going to be a bitch to my mom to make me suffer?"

I smile. "Not everything is about you. You write all those poems and pretend like they mean something, but they don't. They're full of lies so that you can feel important when really you just sound pretentious. It's all fake. So why don't you go write a shitty poem and pretend to be heartbroken about it."

"*Shitty.*"

"Shitty. You write bullshit words about pain and love that you're incapable of feeling. Your words are *bad*."

He isn't angry anymore.

Only I am.

Only I am breathing hard.

Only I am throwing insults.

Easton looks . . .

His dark eyes don't blink as he stares back at me. The disappointment there isn't something he even tries to hide. His hands hang limply at his sides and his shoulders fall. He steps back, but his eyes stay on mine, making sure I know what I've done.

Making sure I understand what I've said.

"Hey!" Sandry calls from the porch. "What are you two doing?"

Easton studies my face and I hope he can see in my eyes how sorry I am. How much I regret my anger.

"Just stay away from me, Ellis. Don't call me if you get drunk. Don't text me if . . ." He shuts his eyes tight and then opens them again. "Just don't."

He walks toward his mother and kisses her cheek as I trail behind.

"Are you two fighting?" she asks.

"No." He gives her his liar's smile and I wait for Sandry to call him on it, but instead she looks at me.

I tell myself to smile. To laugh. To pretend.

But I can't.

"We aren't fighting," Easton says, putting an arm around my shoulders.

It feels stiff and awkward.

"Okay. Fine. You have your list?" she asks Easton.

He sighs and nods. "Yes."

"Well, then you should probably get going."

I nod and she turns into the house. Easton's arm falls from my shoulder and the absence feels painful.

"Easton," I whisper, reaching for him.

But he pulls away and I'm left with only shitty words echoing in my mind.

24

EASTON HAS BEEN GONE all morning. His absence aches like my head.

All the tasks that don't require being at the house have purple *E*s next to them. Which leaves Tucker and me to do the rest.

The boxes in front of us are all filled with pictures. Memories pressed onto pieces of paper like dried flowers in a book.

There are so many photos of the boys. So many photos of Ben and Sandry holding one of their babies up to the camera. And there are so many pictures at the lake. Easton's poetry along with Tucker's drawings, a phase from his junior year of high school, is scattered throughout.

Everything here captures a feeling, or a promise, more than an event. All glossy paper and flashes that turn backgrounds black. Faded edges and overexposed people.

I take a deep breath and press the heels of my hands into my eyes as I let out a groan.

"Are you sure these are all the boxes?" I grumble behind closed eyes. "Because if there is another hiding somewhere—"

Tucker laughs and whispers to me, "It wouldn't be the end of the world if you weren't so hungover."

Behind us, Sandry is making something in the blender. When she turns it on, she smiles at me. "Something wrong?"

I give her a tight smile.

The next picture I find is of me sitting on the dock. My arms are wrapped around my legs and my cheek is pressed against my knees as I look at Easton next to me. His smile is full of too many teeth and freckles take up most of the space on his face.

I remember this moment.

Tucker leans over to me and smiles. "I love that one. Add it to the pile."

Sandry looks over to the picture. "Me too. I love all your summer freckles." She pats my shoulder.

"You don't have to—" I begin, and Tucker cuts me off with a face. One that tells me he will not allow me to continue my thought. I let the end of my sentence fall away.

"And don't forget the one from Ellis's graduation," she continues. "The one Easton sent me."

My brows come together. "Easton?"

Sandry's hands still as she wipes down the counter. Tucker looks at her. Something is off.

"You mean the one Tucker sent?" I clarify.

Her hands move again. "I don't know who sent it, all the boys are the same to me."

"Thanks, Mother. I'll put it in. I have it on my phone." Tucker holds up a picture of a young version of Sandry and my dad with their arms around each other at night. They are smiling down at the ground. "I like this one, too."

I squint at it before Sandry comes sweeping in and snatches the picture from his hands. Her smile is fond. "God, I look amazing here. Add it."

Tucker cocks his head to the side and tucks a fist under his chin. "You do look great, but you also kind of look like a couple."

She rolls her eyes at him. "For the millionth time. I never dated Tru. I met your dad freshman year of college and Tru met . . . Ellis's mom at our twenty-third birthday party. This picture was at our party . . . sophomore year of college, I think?"

This feeling in my gut is always there when we talk about my dad. A little curious and a lot nervous. He's a fine line, and it seems inevitable that someone will cross it. But I can't escape the odd sense of genetic loyalty I know I don't owe him. "You had birthdays together?" I ask.

Sandry's face has a faraway expression, the one she wears when she's thinking of things that are outside of the life she has here. "When we could. Sometimes Tru was gone. Sometimes he was in prison. Sometimes he wasn't."

244

She says it so matter-of-factly it almost feels more painful that way, and I realize Sandry's been dealing with my dad in jail longer than I have.

"Did he miss a lot of them?" Tucker asks.

"More than he didn't." She sighs. "But the ones he was there for . . . Tru always made me feel like he was stealing all the light in the room and shining it back at me."

Sandry flips through a stack of photos that I recognize are of her and my father. Her face grows nostalgic and I wish I could read her thoughts. "The woman who lived on the big piece of property by the rail line, she would have Tru out there every day digging in the dirt looking for gold she said her father had buried. She sat in a dining chair and directed him as she told stories. He knew there was no gold out there, but . . . he also knew she was lonely."

I'd never heard that story and I wondered how many more were hidden in the cracks and crevices of their pasts.

Tucker gives her a look of disbelief. "You sure that you *never* dated?"

Sandry rolls her eyes but her voice stays soft. "Tru and I were something different. He was my first love, but you get to a point where you realize that love isn't always enough. It doesn't go away, but it shifts. Addiction changes things."

I don't flinch, even though I want to. This is one of the few times Sandry has talked about my dad's drug problem directly. Normally it's something that she only alludes to. She'll refer to his moods or call it a vice. But now Sandry seems to be done talking around these things.

With a deep breath she holds a photo out to me with a smile. It's my dad standing on the dock just outside the house we are sitting in. His arms are wide and he looks like he's trying to hug the whole lake.

"He had a way about him. Before." She clicks her tongue.

I can't quite process how she can remember this version of him after what he did. I hate that this is the version of my father she has decided to keep.

After everything.

I stand. The barstool underneath me scrapes on the floor. "I'm going to get some air."

Tucker holds up a stack of pictures. "Sure. I'll do this by myself." It's snarky.

I don't have the energy to come back with a comment of my own.

The hot air outside doesn't change the heat in my face. I can hear the water lapping against the wood slats on the quiet dock and the sounds of birds in trees as they hide from the sun. Suddenly I wish everything out here was louder. I wish it was loud enough that it drowned out every thought.

"Ellis."

Sandry stands behind me. In her hand is a small three-by-five photo. It's turned toward her, not toward me. Like it's private.

I look back to the water and wish I had remembered to grab my sunglasses.

"You doing okay?" Her tone is soft and I hate it.

I narrow my voice to a point sharp enough to stab. "I'm fine."

But Sandry isn't deterred. She comes to stand next to me and sighs as she stares out at the lake. "Birthdays are strange. You spend a lot of time thinking about the past."

The waves continue to lap quietly. The birds still chatter.

"We don't talk much about your dad."

I close my eyes. "I don't want to talk about him."

"I know." She clears her throat and looks down at the photo. "But I wonder if I did you a disservice by not talking to you about him."

"He's my dad."

"Yes, and being a dad is different than being a friend. It's different than everything else." Sandry smiles. "Caleb Truman was the most earnest person I've ever met. If he said something, he meant it. He had a kindness to him that felt sincere. I also watched him stab a guy in the leg." She laughs. "People have layers. Your dad was always peculiar like that. And then it changed."

I wish I could read her thoughts. She holds up a photo of my father with an older woman I've never seen before.

I can't seem to stop myself. "How did it change?" I ask.

I know what she's going to say. My mother. She's generally considered my father's downfall. My grandma says so, my uncles, everyone. And I've never seen anything that would tell me different.

"The same way most things change. So slowly you don't know it's happening." She smiles wide and passes me the picture. "Tru met the wrong people. It wasn't a big deal at first." She lets out a breath and sets down another picture. "Life is just a series of small choices, and you can only see the one in front of you, but it leads you to the next and the next. Eventually you've ended up somewhere you don't even recognize."

I press my teeth against each other and try not to show emotion.

"You're a lot like him."

I scoff.

"It's true," she tells me. "You and him. You both are the same kind of strong. Survivors."

I want to scream. Or cry. But I can also feel something like pride swell inside me. I don't want to be a survivor, but I also feel it deeply. I add it to the list of words I hate.

"Easton is a lot like me."

And there it is. The reason we're talking. My feet shift underneath me and I think about walking away.

She keeps her head toward the lake, like looking at me is hard and the glare from the water is softer. "I watched him follow you out of the house the day you were arrested. And when I saw the two of you . . ."

"I didn't ask him to follow me."

"I know, I do, but I also was reminded of every time I

followed your dad. He never asked either. You just *do* for the people you love."

Anger bubbles inside me. This is the same argument my grandmother uses when she justifies all the exceptions she makes for her family. "It's so unfair to punish me for something that I didn't even do. I'm not my dad."

"You're right, and I'm sorry, Ellis," Sandry begins. "I realize it doesn't mean much now that it's done, but I was selfish. I was scared. Easton . . ."

"It's all right." The conversation causes the break in my heart to widen and I don't want to even acknowledge what's happening, so I try to stop her.

"It's not. I was scared for him. As a mother. And I looked at the two of you and . . . two kids shouldn't be that close. You and Easton have your whole lives. I was so worried that you would burn too bright and too fast."

I've heard versions of this so many times I just decide to finish her words for her. "Well, now Easton and I don't even talk. We don't burn at all."

Sandry got her way and proved everyone right. We are apart even when we stand in the same space.

"Yeah, I don't know about that. Your dad and I—" She clears her throat. "Your father is always going to make the wrong choice, Ellis. I have watched him do it his whole life, and I can't let you and Easton fall into those same choices. Easton would have followed you into anything."

Would.

Past tense.

"I sent you to California because I thought it was the best thing for you. Your aunt escaped all this and I thought it would be good for you to escape, too. To put space between your life here and the choices that you were making."

"So I wouldn't drag Easton into those choices," I add for her.

"You lied to the police, Ellis. You were going to take the blame for your dad. Do you understand how that could have affected your whole life?"

The anger building in my throat makes my hands shake. These are all the things she told me before I left. "You just said you were sorry."

"Yes, but I never said I was wrong." Sandry stares at her hands. "I know you and Easton aren't your dad and me, but . . ." She trails off. "But Easton has loved you for a long time now. You don't want to live like this. So wrapped up in another person that you're only trying to survive." Her voice is filled with a resilience I don't fully understand. "I *am* sorry, but I don't regret it."

25

Seventeen years old

I HADN'T BEEN BACK to the Albreys' house in five days and I hadn't been to school in just as many.

But I could still count the minutes that didn't have Easton in them.

It was a game I had begun to play with myself since I had kissed him. I would try to hold my breath for a full sixty seconds and will myself not to think about him. Eventually I might be able to go an hour, and then a day.

But even in the dark of the room at my parents' house, Easton still found a way to sneak into every second of my life.

I hid in my house avoiding him. Avoiding the memory of what had happened when I snuck into his room. The pain of my mother leaving with my dad's money. My lips on Easton's.

Sandry had called to make sure I was okay. Tucker had sent messages during school, demanding proof of life.

Easton sent texts. Never asking me where I was or why I

hadn't responded. They were normal texts, like nothing had happened, like I hadn't kissed him.

Like I hadn't asked him to hold the broken parts of me while I cried.

Easton:
Tucker ate eleven pancakes for breakfast. He's going to get cancer from all the sugar.
I walked to school today. The sunrise was pretty.
[photo attached]
I'm going to fail Econ. Tell me I won't need it when we grow up.
Everyone is asking where you are.
I haven't been writing.
I miss you.

It felt like he was trying to ignore what had happened and I couldn't tell if I loved him more for it, or if it made me hate him. Either way, I wasn't ready to face him or Sara.

After school, I was alone in my house. My father would pop in between shifts at work and whatever was consuming his evenings. He was so preoccupied that he didn't even ask why I was home or notice my mood. I had nothing to do but think about the whens.

When had things changed with Easton and me?

When was there no other choice for me but to love him?

When would I be able to make things go back to normal?

Whens were the worst kind of question because they asked time to be kind, and time never was.

On the sixth day, Dixon showed up with a meal his mom had made. My favorite stir-fry. Dixon ate a dumpling and gave me a smile that was more food than teeth.

"When are you coming home?"

"I am home," I lied. He didn't challenge me on it.

He took a bite. Chewed. Swallowed. "Did you and Easton break up?"

"Break up? We aren't together." My laugh pulled at the lies it tried to cover up. "He's dating Sara."

He made a noise. "Did you fight?"

"No." We hadn't really.

"What happened then?"

Honesty was a bandage I needed to rip off. "I kissed him and he's dating someone else."

"Ahhhh." Dixon leaned back. "Well. That was stupid."

"Helpful, thanks." I ate another dumpling and wondered why I had even told Dixon what had happened. Now that he knew, I wouldn't be able to pretend it hadn't.

Maybe that was why.

He finished eating and picked up all the plates, setting them in the sink.

"Just so you know, he's not dating Sara."

It didn't make me feel better like I thought it would.

I lay in my bed at midnight staring at the moon outside my window, doing what I had done for the past six days. Thinking. The ache in my chest felt all-consuming in the quiet house. A gentle tap outside my window caught my attention, and when I sat up Easton was standing in the place a flower bed should have been.

I pushed open the window. "You could have come in the front door."

"I didn't know if you would answer," he said, climbing in.

Easton settled on the bed next to me, his elbows resting on his thighs and his shoulders slumped. A deep breath expanded his chest. "I'm tired."

"Tired?"

"I haven't been sleeping." It almost sounded accusatory, but that wasn't his way. He was simply telling me.

"Me either."

"Where's your dad?" Easton asked.

"Gone." I wanted to leave it at that, but Easton seemed to always be able to pull my words from me. "He's been gone a lot at night. Busy. A side job, I guess."

We both knew that *side job* was just code for doing something that neither of us wanted to ask about. If I didn't ask how he was going to replace the money my mother had stolen, I could pretend it wasn't happening. I could pretend that I wasn't worried he was going to get caught again. So I let Easton hear the things I wouldn't say between my words.

I lay back and Easton fell down beside me. His body next to mine made me feel relief so intense I had to swallow the emotions rising in my throat. I didn't deserve this.

His eyes closed and his breathing grew steady as I stared at his face.

"Why are you avoiding me?" he asked into the darkness.

"I'm not." It was easy to pretend it was true.

"Yes, you are." He didn't even open his eyes when he called me on it.

"I just . . ." My words were whispers. Saying them with anything more felt like too much. Too full. "I don't know what you want me to say."

He opened his eyes. "I want you to tell me what I did."

I couldn't believe what he was saying. "What you did?"

"Just tell me, El." He propped himself up on his elbows and looked at me without any pretense. "I'll make it right. I just can't— I don't want to do this anymore. It's exhausting."

"You didn't do anything. It's me . . . I don't know how to be around you."

Hurt flashed against his confusion. "Be around me?"

"I didn't mean for you to break up with . . ." I couldn't even say her name. "I'm sorry."

"I'm not." He lay back down with his hands laced over his chest, the two of us staring at the ceiling, moonlight and unspoken words lighting our faces. "I'm not sad that we broke up. Sara broke up with me before. . . . It's just . . . When you came

255

over that night, we had already ended it, so if that's what this is about—" He cleared his throat. "You have to tell me what this is. I can't guess."

"I have to tell you?"

"Yes."

My hands played with the hem of his shirt. "Thoughts aren't free."

He turned toward me so our bodies were facing each other. "I don't want to get this wrong. If you don't want . . . maybe you don't want . . . what I do. Just please talk to me."

Easton seemed so sincere, like he wanted the truth, but the thing about the truth was that it meant more than all the other words spoken. Once I said it, I wouldn't be able to take it back. "Close your eyes."

He frowned at me, but his eyes eventually shut.

"I'm afraid."

"Afraid of—" He was opening them, so I put my hand over them gently.

Easton sighed.

"I'm afraid because I don't want things to change. But . . . I want things to change. I don't really know. I'm afraid because what if I tell you what I want—how I feel . . . and you don't feel that way?"

He opened his eyes. "Fine. I'll tell you first." He wasn't fearful about the cost of these moments. "I love you, Ellis. More than anything. And that isn't going to change things between us, because I've always felt this way. It doesn't matter if you love me or not. I'll wait until you figure out that you love me, too. Or until you're brave enough to do something about it."

"You shouldn't wait for me."

"Don't tell me what to do. I don't want to be anywhere you're not. Me and you."

I reached over and put my hand on the side of his face. His perfect face. No matter how many times I touched him it never felt like *enough*. I could never be close *enough* to him. I ran my thumb against his bottom lip and he let out a sigh, closing his eyes.

"Ellis." He was warning me that I was starting down a different path than the one we had been on.

But I kept my hand there. "Me and you." I pulled at his lip gently and a second later he was over me. My wrists pinned at my sides.

"You can't do that to me," he whispered. "It's not fair. If you don't want me, don't pretend."

But all I had been doing was pretending. I was sick of it.

My mouth met Easton's and he let out a small noise. It was a question more than anything. When he deepened our kiss, I took it as permission to feel the way his lips moved against me, the way his hands let go of my wrist and found other parts of my skin to touch. His lips found my neck. His hands slid under my shirt, against my stomach.

"Easton." I said his name like a plea, a prayer.

He grabbed my hips with both of his hands as he settled on top of me, every part of him pressed against my body.

"You're going to kill me," he said as he kissed me again.

I pushed him up until he was sitting back on his haunches and pulled off my own top and waited for him to say something. To make a joke or tease me as I sat there naked from the waist up.

Instead he met my eyes and only said one word. *"Beautiful."*

Easton pulled off his own shirt, and when we met again I could feel the sensation of his bare skin against mine. Emotion welled in my throat and made me hungry. Our hands became frantic against each other and I lifted my hips to his. A groan fluttered from him as I pressed and rolled my body. But I needed him. To be as close to him as I could get. To feel all of him.

"Ellis, I won't do anything you don't want to."

I reached my hand between us and felt him thick in my palm just to make sure he understood exactly what I was asking for. "I want all of you."

He went still above me as his eyes searched mine. "Have you . . ."

"No," I told him. "Have you?"

He paused and I waited for my heart to break. "No." Easton reached down and touched my face, gently taking his thumb to the top of my cheekbones.

When we kissed again it was different. Slower, but with the same fever that had been there before. He pulled my pants off and pressed his lips to my hipbone with reverent and gentle kisses.

258

And then it was just us. Nothing separating him from me. He pulled a condom from his wallet and I didn't make a comment or laugh. Because this was different.

Easton pressed a kiss to my temple and whispered words that crashed together like waves. His face twisted like he was in pain as he slowly moved into me, and once fully inside, he took a deep breath and leaned his forehead against mine.

"Does it hurt?" I asked.

Easton let out a little laugh. "I'm supposed to ask you that." He swallowed audibly. "It feels . . . incredible. You are incredible."

I had thought about this moment before. A hundred different times and a hundred different ways, but when our bodies came together, over and over again, all I could think was how I could have never dreamed of this moment fully.

And when it was over and Easton kissed my cheeks and shoulders and neck, I realized that I could never have imagined this because I had never understood love like this.

"I love you." When I said it, I waited for . . . something to happen. The world to stop. My heart to stop. Him to realize he had gotten what he wanted and leave. None of those things happened.

The words were as simple as they were intricate. They just were. *I love you.*

26

Seventeen years old

I WOKE TO THE rustle of fabric.

Easton stood, pulling his pants up and buttoning them with shaking fingers.

"Shit, shit, shit." He kept repeating the same word over and over as he frantically looked for his shirt. "Shit." I had heard him say those words before. When Sara had come over.

My stomach sank as he searched my floor. Somewhere down there was my self-respect because I knew without a doubt Easton regretted last night.

I must have made a noise because his eyes finally found mine and his face changed from worried to something different. A look I had never seen before. "You're up."

My stomach soured as I tried to pretend like I was fine with him leaving before I woke. I was. I was fine.

It was fine.

"Get dressed. My mom has been texting me all morning. And last night. And calling."

"What?" I sat up.

"She's pissed," he said, sounding embarrassed as he continued. "I guess I forgot to tell her I was staying the night . . . here."

The words weren't making sense to me. "What?"

"My mom wants us to come home. She wants to . . ." He plucked his shirt from the floor and pulled it over his head. "Talk. But I'm sure that just means yell at both of us."

"Your mom wants *both* of us."

"Yeah," he said, throwing a pair of my own pants at me. "Like, now. So get up."

I fell backward onto the bed and put my arm over my eyes. The relief I felt was so intense that it was embarrassing. Easton leaned over me and picked up my arm, peering underneath it. "Hey."

I pulled it back over my eyes and rolled to my side.

"Oh," he said quietly. "You thought I was leaving."

"Shut up."

He laughed softly and wrapped his arms around my waist as he settled down behind me. "Ellis Truman, you have got to be the dumbest person I've ever met."

"I said shut up." But I didn't take my face from my hands.

His breath hit my neck and his lips touched the skin gently. "I love you."

I always thought those words would feel heavy, like a stone tied around your neck that pulls you under the surface. Unescapable.

But *I love you* was light. Like a feather. Like a breeze. Like being set free.

I love you coming from Easton Albrey was nothing like the *I love you*s I had heard before.

"Anything you want to say to me?" he asked, pushing his hip against mine.

I had already said it last night. "Your breath smells."

He dug his fingers into my side, tickling me.

Easton's finger found a lock of my hair and ran over it again and again. "Do you only love me because I loved you first?"

As if Easton could have possibly loved me first. I thought back to the moment I knew I was in love with him. Sitting in the back of the cop car in front of his house at eleven years old. He was so determined. So sure. I hadn't ever met anyone my age who was so confident. He had never taken a step that didn't feel like the right one. And even in this moment, he was so sure of his feelings. Confident that I could only love him back. Knowing that we would work out. It was contagious.

"I loved you first," I told him.

He fell onto his back, his arms out wide as he stared at the ceiling. "It's not a competition. But if it was, I would win."

"I doubt it."

"Five. That's when I knew I loved you."

I narrowed my eyes. "You can't love a person at five. We didn't even know each other."

"Oh, I knew you. And you can't tell me how I feel."

I groaned. "You're just trying to win."

His eyes skimmed over my face slowly. "You had an army-green jacket and white shoes. You would blow your breath into the air while you waited for the crosswalk light to change. I thought it looked like smoke."

"Smoke?"

The corner of his mouth lifted slowly. "I wanted to walk to school because you did. I wanted to do everything you did, and you didn't even know who I was."

We stared at each other as we lay on the remains of a fevered dream from last night. And I believed in the hope he had for both of us.

I believed when he took my hand on the porch of his house and when he whispered, *"Me and you."* When we walked into the kitchen, I believed that whatever came next it would be *us*.

Sandry stood at the kitchen island. Her face was pinched and the coffee cup in front of her had left a ring on the marble underneath it. I wondered how long she had been standing there.

Easton's hand gently squeezed mine under the counter as Sandry waited for one of us to speak. Her green robe was pulled tight and the white mug in front of her said "LAWYERS GOTTA LAW" in black block letters. Her hair was escaping from her bun and I could tell that she had been up longer than we had.

"So good of you to come home." Her voice was even. Not a good sign. "Where were you two?"

"Sorry," I began. "We fell asleep at my house."

Her eyebrows rose and I watched her expression grow suspicious. "All night? You were there all night?"

"Yes," I answered.

"Was Tru home?" she asked. "If I call him will he say you were there?"

My guilt felt colossal and I struggled to understand why. Easton and I shared a room all the time, but it seemed like Sandry could sense the change in us. I swallowed.

"Mom," Easton said. "Why would we lie?"

She leaned back on her heels and her eyes moved to where East held my hand. He shifted closer to me so that there was no space between us. Sandry tracked the movement.

Her next question felt like a bullet. "Are you two sleeping together?"

I was stunned by her words. "We, I— No, we—"

"Yes." Easton looked his mother directly in her eyes when he said it. Not an ounce of shame or embarrassment.

Sandry stared at her son before running a hand over her forehead. "Perfect. Just . . . *perfect*. How long?"

"Mom." That was as close as Easton would get to chastising his mother, but still.

She shook her head and pointed a finger at me. "You need to get on birth control, right now." And then she moved to point at Easton. "And you need to have a talk with your dad about how to use a condom."

"I know how to use a condom," he told her simply.

How could he be so calm?

She smiled tightly. "Let's make *sure*. I cannot allow the two of you to—"

The phone rang and Sandry held up a single finger. A single aggressive finger.

"Hello. Yes, this is her. Caleb Truman? Yes. Yes." Her eyes landed on me. "When was he arrested? For what? Yes, I'm aware of his parole."

As she spoke, her words went from sharp to fuzzy, but it only took a second for me to realize what had happened.

My father had broken his parole.

Sandry paced in the kitchen. Back and forth. Nausea flooded me as I listened to her conversation. I prayed I was misunderstanding.

Maybe I had heard her wrong. Maybe—

"When was he arrested?" she asked.

And in a matter of seconds, all my hope dissolved.

They had called Sandry because she always bailed him out. Literally and figuratively. How he had broken his parole didn't really matter. If they searched our house . . . I was sure my father had things he wasn't supposed to have. And if they found them, this time he would be tried as a habitual offender. I thought about all his late nights since my mom had taken all his money and I knew what was going to happen next. He wouldn't get a lighter sentence; this would get him real time.

"Damn it," I cursed, and was already walking toward the door.

"Ellis." Easton's hand on my arm stopped me. "El."

"I have to go. I have to make sure they don't— I have to go back to the house. Tell your mom she can finish yelling at me then."

"The house? What's at the house?" he asked, walking alongside me.

"Probably about a hundred things my dad isn't supposed to have." There was no point in telling him everything. I was wasting time.

"Stop," he said, and I did on reflex. "Tell me what you're doing so I can help."

"Drugs, maybe," I answer, thinking about all the places I knew he kept them. "He might have other things in his room. I never really check. There might be nothing, or there might be something."

I could see the frustration in Easton.

"You don't have to come," I told him. And I meant it, even if I wanted the opposite.

"Yes, I do," he told me as he started walking toward the door. He pulled his keys from the hook and turned the knob, waiting. "Me and you."

I tapped my hands on the door handle of Easton's jeep as he drove the few streets to my house. His eyes took in my shaking leg, my fidgeting fingers, the way I kept rolling my shoulders. The car pulled into my driveway, and before it completely stopped I had the door open. As soon as I was in the house, I went straight to the garage. If there was anything

266

in the house, it would be there.

An old tackle box he had used on our fishing trips was filled with pretty yellow pills. The same color as the bedspread he had bought me when I was seven. I pulled out the sandwich bags full of opioids and went back into the house and set them on the counter.

"What are you going to do with these?" Easton asked.

It was a good question. What was I going to do? I couldn't take them to the Albreys'. I couldn't take them to my grandma's. Flushing them made my stomach uneasy. It was so much money in a little bag. If I took them to Uncle Rick's, he would never give them back. "Tenny's?"

I pulled another tackle box from under the couch. This one only had half a sandwich bag full of blue pills. A pretty sky blue.

Easton held it up. "More?"

I ignored him and moved back to my dad's room. I searched through his dresser, his nightstand, his closet. And then I found a revolver. It was old and rusted, but it was still a gun in an ex-con's house.

I added it to the pile and wrapped it all in a pillowcase, picking it up like a trick-or-treater. Easton held open the door and unlocked the back of my dad's car. He didn't offer his jeep and I didn't suggest it. Something about putting these things in something that belonged to Easton felt like a line I wasn't willing to cross.

"Now what?" Easton asked.

I didn't really know. This wasn't something I did a lot,

moving drugs for someone. But I knew if they found these . . . Intent to sell at the least, trafficking at the worst. And the gun? Altogether this would put my father away for years. He would miss my whole life. This felt like the loss of all the hope I had. There wouldn't be a next time for him to do better, because he would be gone.

It was so unfair.

I slid into the driver's seat and Easton slid into the passenger's, pushing aside papers and a pair of shoes and an outfit I had changed out of last time I was in the car. "What are you doing?"

"I'm going with you."

"*Easton.*"

"Just drive the fucking car."

I gave myself a second—a full second—to feel like shit for dragging him into this with me. And then I turned over the engine and made Easton an accomplice.

When the red and blue lights flashed . . . and I pulled the car over on the side of the road . . . I knew that I should have made him get out of the car.

When the officer opened the trunk. When they asked us to put our hands on the hood. When they put us in the back of the cop car with our wrists cuffed behind us.

When Easton wouldn't look at me.

I knew the *me and you* Easton had talked about was over.

27

IT'S ALMOST DINNERTIME.

All the pictures and memories have been sorted and scanned and arranged for the party in two days. Everyone's gone to see to their own to-do lists, and I've been left on the porch to fix Dixon.

Or his speech, at least.

He has one arm over his eyes and the other limp at his side as he lets out an annoyed groan. We've been sitting at the table on the porch for more than an hour now, trying to start his speech for his mother's birthday. I'm considering drowning him in the water when he says, "What about 'Dearly beloved, we are gathered here—'"

I take a deep breath and tell myself not to shout. "It's not a wedding."

Dixon sits up. "I was going more for a Prince thing. Mom loves Prince."

"You're not Prince. You're her son and this is your gift to her."

"Yeah, but this is under duress. It's not a gift if you're told what to give. What are you gonna do for her?"

I run a hand through my hair and look down at the paper that has only two lines. My mind goes to the necklace. I still have no idea where it could be. I'm beginning to worry that I won't be able to find it, but I don't examine the feeling. I'm not ready to acknowledge that my anger might be fading. "Just worry about your gift and write something."

He picks up his pen to mark his paper but is rewarded with only an indent. "Stupid," Dixon grumbles as he tries to flick the ink into the bottom.

"Here." I take it and try to draw circle after circle in the corner, until finally giving up. "Wait here. Don't move," I order.

He rolls his eyes, already picking up his phone as I move inside. Sandry keeps a stationery caddy by the breakfast nook, and I open it, rifling through the pens and paper and . . .

My hand stops on the parchment I know by heart. Slowly, I pull out the cream-colored paper that has a touch of gloss on the corners and run a finger over it.

"She sat there every Tuesday with her coffee and wrote you a letter."

I turn around and press the paper to my body as if I could hide it, but it's already too late. Easton has seen that I'm holding his mother's stationery. My heart skips a beat at the sight of him. I remind my traitorous heart that he hates us. And we hate him.

"She gave up thinking that you would write back sometime around January."

An apology is on my lips before I remember I don't owe him one for that. His mouth tilts up, reading my thoughts.

Easton's phone rings and he looks at the name and then back at me. With a tight jaw, I watch him step outside to take the call. It's clear he doesn't want me to hear his conversation.

There was a time when Easton and I didn't have secrets.

On the kitchen island are a notebook and a pen. Probably a speech Easton has written for Dixon because he doesn't trust me. I move over to it and see the black ink on white paper.

It's quiet in all the places she's supposed to be.
It shouts at me from the canyon I've gone deaf waiting in.

Easton's poetry. He's always written it privately. Something he rarely shared. I feel guilty as I flip to another page.

I can taste her.
The whole sky at my fingertips when I touched her.
Tracing silver stars on her skin.
Night and secrets.

"Those aren't done." Easton stands casually in the doorway. I would think he didn't care, except for the white of his knuckles around his phone.

These poems feel like something that speaks in the spaces

271

Easton and I don't. They feel like they belong to me as well, which is why I foolishly do the next thing and turn the page to read out loud. *"'She sleeps next to me. Her head on the pillow. A shock of light hair that is in such contrast to the dark hollow of my chest when I look at her . . .'"* I want to read more, but . . .

He sees the moment I realize that head isn't mine. Whoever this poem is about, it's not me. My hair is dark. Easton wrote a poem about sleeping with another girl.

I can't decide what hurts worse. That he slept with someone else, or that he wrote about it.

"Keep reading." He motions to his private words. Ones that I now realize aren't for me. "They're just my shitty poems."

I swallow down a response. It's bitter and burns.

I take the pen Easton was using and go outside to Dixon. "Here."

His brow pinches together at my tone. Behind the reflection of darkened glass Easton moves around the kitchen.

"What happened now?"

I focus on the table. "Everything is fine."

Dixon seems like he wants to argue, but instead he puts his pen to paper. Scrawling letters dash across the page in aggressive black scratches. When he's written the last word of his speech, he looks at me. "You don't have to keep doing something that makes you feel bad."

I wonder if he tells Easton the same thing, or if he's just overprotective with me.

"I'm not." But I can't meet his eyes when I tell the lie.

"I know you think—"

"Dinner's here," Ben says as he pushes out the back door with three large boxes of pizza.

Like moths to flame, the boys circle around the table and begin to eat. The sun starts to sink and Sandry pulls out two bottles of wine. She passes us glasses of dark liquid and winks. "Just a little bit because it's a special occasion."

I like the way the glass makes me feel grown-up while I eat something with my hands. The wine is red. Served out of beautiful wide glasses that catch on the light while the pizza is dished up on paper plates. I take a tentative sip, remembering the way the alcohol from the Tavern made me feel when I woke up.

The fading sun shines down on my bare shoulders and my face, heating me from the outside to the bone. Van Morrison plays from the house and Sandry kicks off her shoes. She crosses her heels on Ben's knee and wiggles her bright pink toes to the music.

It's perfect.

Eager stars poke through a sky where the sun still refuses to leave and we stay and watch until it blackens and shines.

I still feel the heat when everyone goes inside. Maybe it's the wine. Maybe it's the remnants of the sun. Maybe it's this place.

Easton sits in the chair next to me with silence thicker than the air and he reaches for my glass, taking a sip from the wine before setting it back on the table.

He doesn't speak. Only lets out a heavy breath.

"Is Sara coming to the party?" I ask.

The silence that Easton allows between us feels excruciating and it takes everything in my power not to fill it.

"Yeah." That's all he says. One word.

"Are you two—" My words fall off the cliff of my curiosity. It's a stupid question anyway.

"You don't get to ask me questions like that." He takes a sip of wine and makes a face.

It reminds me that we are still pretending to be grown. Not kids who've just graduated from high school. I try not to let the anger that flares inside of me get the last word. "I'm trying, Easton."

His body turns to me, broad shoulders angled in my direction, sharp jaw softened by the bistro lights above us, and fingers still stained with ink. "Trying to what?"

"Apologize."

"Apologize for what?"

I lick my lips and his eyes follow the movement. "For what I said to you. About your writing."

He leans back in his chair and his eyes grow dark. I've said the wrong thing.

"What?" He looks surprised before shaking his head gently. "Not everything is about you."

274

No. Some things are about blond hair spread out on pillows.

He takes another drink. The long, tanned column of his throat working. I press my mouth together as if I can feel his lips on my own through the cup. "You weren't even supposed to be here. You were supposed to be in Mexico until the party."

"Yeah, well. We all do stupid shit."

"Coming home early was stupid?" I ask. When he doesn't answer I decide to say what I need to. "I'm sorry about last night." The memory of my hands on his skin and his mouth on my shoulder flash in my mind. I have to remind myself I *am* sorry.

He sighs. "I forgot how much work it is to be around you."

Easton's words crack my vulnerable armor. *I'm too much.* "You don't have to be around me."

"You're sleeping across the hall from me, Ellis."

"Yeah, but you don't have to be out here with me right now . . . I mean."

"Really?" He lifts a brow. "Weren't you apologizing?"

"I really am sorry about . . ."

"About trying to use me?" His words are sharp and pointed. All the vowels hard and the consonants piercing. They are meant to embarrass me.

I turn and look at him. His cheeks are flushed and I focus on the wine in his hand. The empty glass. I can't remember how many he's had. "I . . ."

He licks his lips. "I know what you were trying to do. It's what you always do when you feel like shit. You use the people around you. You use *me*."

"Easton."

"You don't get it." A scoff. Again. "I'm done, Ellis."

Done. The word is thin and when it wraps around my heart it cuts into it like wire. "Done with what?"

He motions between us. "Whatever the hell this is."

"Maybe I'm the one who's done."

He laughs. "I could never be that lucky."

Easton gets up and I wait until I know I won't run into him upstairs before I follow. I don't wash my face or brush my teeth, simply slip under my covers and pull them up to my chin, ignoring the way my body aches all over from heartbreak.

It makes me feel all the things I hate as I lie in my bed staring at the void above me. I grab my phone and can't stop myself from clicking on Sara's social media profile. And then I scan through Easton's friends' photos, searching for proof that he's dating her. That he loves her.

Or that he doesn't.

I pull my blanket tighter around my shoulders even though my room is warm.

His last photo is a picture of him from tonight. He's scratching the back of his head with one hand and his face is turned down with a slight smile. He looks like he has a secret. The background is dark from the lake at night and there is pizza and wine on the table in front of him.

I wonder what made him smile.

A text comes through and I click on it to read.

Tucker:

I'm starting a new series on my IG.

Ellis:

Cool.

Tucker:

Wanna see my first pic?

I don't respond because he's going to send it anyway.

Tucker:

It's called USE YOUR WORDS

The picture he sends is of Easton. It looks like the one from Easton's Instagram. But it's zoomed out so Easton isn't the center. I sit not far from him. And.

There is no mistaking the way I'm staring at him.

With longing. With anguish. With . . . love.

Ellis:

Do not post that.

He sends me a string of laughing/crying emojis and a picture. It's a screenshot of a conversation with Easton where he sent him the same text, but with a different picture.

Easton responded with the same words. I try to zoom in on the picture. It's from later in the evening; I can tell because I'm holding the wineglass and Easton is sitting next to me. But it's small and grainy and I feel like I could kill Tucker for sending it.

I get another text.

Tucker:

What will you do for me if I don't post it?

Ellis:

You're such an ass.

Tucker:

Gross. Stop talking about my ass.

Ellis:

You're gross.

Tucker:

So, what will you do for me?

Ellis:

I will attempt to not murder you, but I can't

promise anything.

Tucker:

I'll settle for you and Easton to just talk. And because I know you're trying to enlarge like crazy.

He sends another picture and I don't hesitate to pull it up. I'm greeted with Easton staring at me as I look down at the wineglass in my hand. He is clearly frowning, but . . . there is more there. A deep abyss that has me staring at the photo longer than I should.

The glass around my heart breaks and shatters.

Tucker:

I have more if you want them.

Ellis:

Stop taking stalker pictures.

He sends me another screenshot of Easton saying the same thing.

Tucker:

You two are so annoying.

I can't help the smile that finds me. In the dark of a room where I'm alone. Only a few steps and a few inches of wooden door separate us, but still I feel safe here.

My fingers move on their own and I pull up Easton's number. Not for the first time, I regret deleting the thread months before. *Just come* is the only text from him. And then the series of messages I sent to him after I got drunk at the Tavern.

That's all that's left of us.

What can I even say to him? I shouldn't say anything. I should let it die. But the gnawing feeling in my chest only becomes more painful as I imagine what he's thinking.

Ellis:

hi.

My stomach falls and regret instantly fills me. Why did I send—

Read. The word appears directly under my bubble and I wait. And wait. But Easton doesn't respond. My thumbs hover over the keyboard, waiting for those three dots, waiting for something to happen, waiting for me to figure out what words will take back my *hi*.

Ellis:

Tucker text you, too?

I wait again for a response, but all I see is the *Read* underneath the bubble.

Ellis:

I told him not to post it.

And because I can't seem to stop myself, I keep texting him.

Ellis:

Not that it would matter if he posted them or not.

I don't even know if you're with Sara since you won't

answer me about it.

And I know you said that I use you, but

I type out four different things and delete them. But none of the words are the right ones. They either tell him too much or they make it sound like I don't care. I'm typing my fifth response when his text comes through.

Easton:

Just say whatever it is you're trying to say.

I stare at my phone and feel something dangerous. Hope. It slithers around me like a snake and I'm waiting for it to squeeze me until I stop breathing.

Ellis:

I hate that you think that. It's unfair.

Easton:

You only hate it because it makes you feel bad.

Ellis:

No. I hate it because it makes it sound like
you don't use me too.

He doesn't respond and I close my eyes, wondering if I've pushed him too far.

Easton:

I don't use you.

Yes, you do. You need to save me.

When I say it, I know it's true, but that doesn't make my guilt any lighter.

Ellis:

I don't need to be saved.

Easton:

I didn't say you did.

Ellis:

That's how you treat me.

Easton:

Bullshit.

You spend so much time reminding me that we aren't the same and how different your "real" life is and how I couldn't possibly understand.

Ellis:

That doesn't mean you don't try to save me.

You followed me to my house that day we got arrested.

You wanted to save me.

You want me to need you.

Easton:

That's what you think I was doing? Saving you?

You can say whatever you want about me, but I know that you don't need me.

I think this past year proved it.

I want to respond with something witty or clever or biting or angry. But not the truth. I do need him. And then he says—

Easton:
But that's the problem, isn't it? You don't need anyone.

Somehow I've managed to convince Easton of my lie. The fact that he can't see through it makes me direct my blame at him. But how can I be mad at him for believing me?

And I realize Sandry was right. Sometimes love isn't enough.

28

Seventeen years old

HE WOULDN'T LOOK AT me.

The blue plastic chairs at the police station were side by side and I shifted uncomfortably on the hard seat. Bright fluorescent lights shined down from a foam tiled ceiling and caught on all the angles of Easton's fallen face. White walls with posters hung in cheap metal frames gave information about rights, and processing, and the creed of the police department. The metal desk in front of us was empty except for two pieces of paper. One with my name.

And one with Easton's.

His eyes were on his wrists and I watched his fingers rub at the spot where the handcuffs had been. Like he could still feel them against his skin.

I bit my lip and studied my own hands.

This wasn't okay.

I shut off the voice that repeated those words. Over and over. This wasn't the place. If I felt those words . . . if I allowed myself to acknowledge the things that weren't normal—

I cleared my throat.

An officer sat on the corner of his desk closest to Easton and crossed his arms. His name tag read "Kelly." "We're waiting for your dad to get here."

When I looked up, I realized he was talking to Easton. Not me. And the fissure in my chest widened.

"Your dad is already here," he told me. "So once we get Easton sorted, we'll start processing."

Easton's brows came together. "This isn't processing?"

"No. This is waiting." Officer Kelly smiled. Smiling officers were my least favorite. "You're minors and your dad is a friend. So we wait."

"Of course." Easton's head tilted back to the ceiling, exhausted. "I can't even get arrested right."

Officer Kelly clicked his tongue and put a sympathetic hand on Easton's shoulder. "You're not arrested. But you will need to answer some questions."

We both tensed, but it was Easton who found his voice first. "What questions?"

His words were gentle. "Whose pills were those, son?"

For a long moment, Easton did nothing. He stared forward and shook his head.

The officer continued, "I know they belong to Caleb Truman, but he's saying he's never seen them."

This time Easton lifted his shoulders. The officer still wasn't asking me.

"If you don't tell us, you'll be charged with possession."

"I thought you were waiting for his dad?" I remind him with a bit of edge to my voice, an edge I knew I shouldn't use with a police officer.

Officer Kelly's eyes scrunched at the sides and his face turned disapproving.

"We're just talking. I'm reminding both of you that this is serious," he continued. "A charge like that could change your whole life."

Easton shifted.

This was my fault. Easton was here because of me. Dread and panic laced themselves inside my stomach, churning and mixing together like acid.

"They're mine," I said.

The officer looked at me, not surprised, but clearly disappointed. "Yours?" He didn't even bother to hide his disbelief.

"Yes. Mine."

"Ellis, if you lie it will be even more of a mess." Officer Kelly said my name like he knew me. He only assumed he did because he knew my father.

Something I had learned early in life was to dig into a lie. People either began to believe you or got tired of fighting and gave up. "I'm not."

He sighed. "I think we should wait for—"

There was yelling on the other side of the metal double doors. The officer swore and stood as if he expected a physical altercation. Another shout broke through the steel and wood. A shout we recognized.

I watched the set of Easton's shoulders relax as we both realized it was Sandry.

He was relieved. Except.

A tear fell from his eyes and I knew it wasn't relief he felt. Not *only* relief. Shame.

Fuck. Fuck. Fuck. Fuck. Fuck.

I said the word so many times in my mind it became an incantation. I prayed it would erase everything that was happening.

Sandry burst through the double doors into the large room and I watched as her eyes scanned the desks until they landed on us.

Another officer walked over to her and she completely ignored them. "Kelly," she breathed. "What the hell? Drugs? And a *gun*?"

"Tru is saying they aren't his."

Her whole body grew still as we watched her process the information. "What?"

"Sandry, you know if he doesn't say they're his, both these kids will end up charged with possession of drugs and an illegal firearm."

"What the fuck were you thinking?" Sandry looked between the two of us with an even voice. It almost made it worse that she didn't shout.

Easton's lip trembled.

"I want to talk to Tru," Sandry told Officer Kelly.

"You know that I can't—"

"Let's pretend I'm his legal counsel and take me to him right now." Her mouth was in a flat line as she waited for Officer Kelly to answer her.

The war on his face was clear as I watched him trying to decide if Sandry's wrath was worth it.

It wasn't.

"Ellis, get up," Sandry ordered.

Officer Kelly shook his head gently as he motioned for me to follow him down a long corridor lined with gray doors. The fluorescent lights dimmed as we walked into a small room with only a table and a few chairs grouped around it. My dad was sitting with another officer. His hands weren't cuffed and he was holding a white paper cup of coffee. He wore the clothes he always wore, dirty T-shirt and grease-stained jeans with work boots. It was odd to see something so familiar in a place so unfamiliar. His smile faded when he saw us.

He had been *smiling*.

"Ellis." His head tilted to the side and he glanced from Sandry to me and then to the officer. How could he be confused?

"Goddamn it, Tru," Sandry said in way of greeting.

My father's brows pinched together. "What's happening, Sandy?"

The nickname didn't have the desired effect. "What's happening?" She sounded almost hysterical. "Ellis was arrested.

She just told Officer Kelly that thousands of dollars in prescription opioids were *hers*."

Dad didn't speak. He didn't deny it or tell me he was disappointed or act confused. He didn't even look proud of me, which hurt more than I expected.

No, my father was relieved.

"Easton was with her, too." Sandry spoke through her rage.

Dad leaned back in his chair and brought the paper cup in his hands to his lips. He nodded twice, a habit he had when he was thinking. "Arrested."

Sandry's head tilted to the ceiling and she let out a groan. "You better fix this shit right now and tell the truth."

My dad looked at me, his blue eyes going soft around the edges. "It's your first offense, so the court will go easy on you. They always go easy on pretty girls."

In the second before Sandry started yelling, I heard it.

The sound of my father falling from the last pedestal I had put him on. When he hit the ground, the broken pieces of him lay next to the ones of my mother.

"You owe her more than this, Caleb." Sandry's voice was like a string ready to snap, but it didn't matter.

It was my first offense. I stood there numb as I watched Sandry yell. I couldn't hear her over the ringing in my ears. Or my father as he eventually relented and admitted they were his drugs. Only after Sandry threatened him with everything she could think of.

I barely understood when they sent me back to sit with

Easton. Each of us as broken as my love for my father.

After the processing. After the fingerprinting. After the hours of waiting in silence when Easton wouldn't speak to me, I was released into Sandry's custody.

We went back to the house in an oppressive silence. I immediately went upstairs and locked the door to the bathroom.

Only here, alone, would I let myself cry. I pressed the back of my hand against my mouth to muffle the noise and started the shower.

The water was scalding. I was trying to wash off the police station. Trying to wash off the look in the police officers' eyes. Trying to wash off Easton's disgust.

Trying to wash off my dad.

All I wanted to do was the right thing. The weight of it pressed down on my chest. If I made my dad proud, I disappointed Sandry. If I made Sandry proud, Tenny said I was forgetting my family. If I made Tenny proud . . . Was I always going to be this way? Caught in between not knowing what to do and not knowing what I wanted?

I pressed the heels of my hands into my eyes and tried to erase the recollection of Officer Kelly telling me that my dad said the drugs weren't his. My stomach sank every time my mind replayed it and I scrubbed at my skin as if the vision sat there.

In the end, I had done everything wrong. Sacrificed my word for someone who was going to throw me away. Ben had

290

been furious and threated to never represent him again. Had called my father "that man." As if he wasn't even worth a name, and maybe he wasn't after what he had done.

But in the end, my dad had told the truth. And I hated the way I felt relieved by it because it meant I wasn't strong enough to be loyal.

When my clothes were on and my hair was brushed and my skin was as pink and raw as my eyes, I went downstairs to find Easton. I needed to see him. I needed to feel the weight of his arms around my shoulders. I needed to look at him and know it was okay. After everything, I just wanted Easton.

The voices found me first.

"—you had a gun, Easton."

It was Sandry. I took another step, ready to defend him. But then I heard my name.

"Ellis is—" I could hear the breath that Sandry released. "This will only get worse. Trust me, son."

I was frozen on the staircase, my hand on the railing and each foot on a different step.

Easton's voice was clipped when he responded. "I know."

"Do you?" Sandry asked him in a sure voice. "I have seen this time and time again."

"She's not her dad," Easton said, but he didn't sound like he meant it.

"No, but she is Tru's daughter. Her first thought was to go to the house and hide those drugs for her dad. And a gun."

I heard Easton clear his throat and then say, "She was trying to protect him."

"And you were trying to protect her. You just did it the wrong way." Sandry didn't sound mad. She sounded disappointed.

"Mom."

"Easton, you know she can't stay."

The room spun around me and I fell to sit on the step. I had finally crossed the line. I had broken their trust. I had gotten Easton involved.

"I know." His words were rushed and heavy. I felt each one inside of me.

"You almost got arrested. You probably should have been, but . . . by the world's stupidest luck you didn't. Honestly, if you hadn't been there, Ellis probably wouldn't be here now. They would have charged her. But this is the one time Tru being a piece of shit actually worked in our favor. You were given the benefit of the doubt, son. Something not always given to people in handcuffs. Ellis has to get away from all this."

I wiped at my tears. Away from my dad? Living with the Albreys *was* away from him. If I went back home, I would only be closer. I was confused.

"Mom, I know. Are you finished?"

"Your words say you know, but your face says you don't."

"What do you want me to say?" He was almost shouting. "You were right. I fucked up. I didn't listen."

It was odd that the thing that my mind snagged on was him

cursing at his mother. The way Sandry didn't react told me it was worse than I could imagine.

But Easton had said, *"You were right."* What had she been right about?

"I know this is hard—"

"I don't want to keep talking about it."

"Well, what you want doesn't really matter anymore. She's going to have to go to California."

The ringing in my ears was back. *California.* The other side of the world.

"California?" He sounded as confused as I felt.

"With her aunt. We talked about this."

They had talked about this.

"She doesn't even know her aunt."

They had *talked* about this.

"It's better than her staying here."

I waited for Easton to realize what he was agreeing to. He was going to tell her that he was mistaken. He would.

Silence shouted to me as I wrapped my arms around my legs and buried my face in my knees. They were sending me away. I had finally done something they couldn't forgive. I wasn't good enough. They had thought it for some time.

"Ellis needs a chance at life more than she needs a boyfriend. She needs to be with her aunt and at least be given a fair shot."

Everything was so messed up. I was sinking and I couldn't

stop it. I wished I could see his face. I wished I'd never see it again. I wished—

"Tucker already got accepted to UCSD and will be there in the same city as her. It's like the universe knew. We'll still talk to her all the time."

"Please stop," Easton asked.

"East."

"I don't want to talk about this anymore. I don't—"

"I need you to say it. Tell me that you won't fight this."

This was the moment. I knew that Easton would never agree to this. He was the only person who would never send me away.

But.

My heart, she whispered to me in the quiet. She told me the truth. She already knew what he was going to say. I pressed my lips together as I held my breath, hoping.

Easton Albrey would never reject me.

"I know that Ellis has to go to California."

His words sounded forced, but he had said them. He'd agreed. He had decided to let me go. Of course, I should have known what he was going to say, because my heart had always been Easton's.

And he had just shattered it.

29

I STAY BUSY.

My goal of avoiding Easton is mostly successful. I focus on completing all the small tasks Sandry has listed, one by one. Marking each item off and ignoring his presence in a room.

But when I close my eyes, I see Easton's texts. They float in between the photos that Tucker took of us from last night and confuse me even more.

And by the end of a tedious day, I'm tired. There is a small headache just behind my eyes from staying up too late, and my worry that I won't find the necklace Sandry gave me is growing.

For what feels like the hundredth time, I search through the boxes underneath my bed. Again. I've opened every envelope and every box and flipped through every book in the hopes that the necklace has slipped between pages or has snagged on fabric and is hidden . . . somewhere. Because the alternative is . . .

The alternative is that I have lost it.

"Goddamn it." I punch the box as I mutter the curse, hoping it will make me feel better, but it doesn't.

The more time passes, the more I realize I'm going to have to ask Sandry. And if I have to ask her, she'll know I've lost it. And admitting I've lost her family heirloom feels like disappointing her. I don't want to disappoint her again.

"You don't need anyone."

Why is it always *Easton's* words that are stuck in my head on a loop?

There's only one place left to look. I glance out my open door to the closed one across the hall. It feels menacing, which is ridiculous. Easton's door is cracked. Swallowing my nerves and fear, I knock, hoping he doesn't answer.

The house is silent, so I push it open with my foot. I call his name again, but no one answers.

It feels odd to be in this space knowing I'm not welcome here anymore.

My steps are light on the soft tan carpet and I take a deep breath of his familiar smell. My eyes go automatically to the map hanging on the wall, and the ache in my throat is back. The pins are still there. I had placed every single one as he lay on the bed, arms folded behind his head, and watched me talk about all the reasons I couldn't wait to see whatever place I had just become fascinated with.

I ignore the jealousy and rejection that I feel inside myself. Easton has already been traveling. The spiteful part of me wants to rip out all the pins in Mexico.

Instead, I get on my knees and look under his bed. There are boxes and shoes and a pair of sweats. I check the corners and the places the bed touches the wall, thinking maybe the necklace had fallen down, but I can't see it. I search the back of his closet. I look on his desk.

And I open the drawer to his nightstand and see—

"Are you looking for something in particular, or . . ." Easton stands in the doorway with his arms crossed and his brows lifted.

I stand up so fast that I hit the top of my thigh on the open drawer and wince. How long has he been standing there? "I was— Why do you have this picture in here?" I pull out the picture of me and him sitting in our swimsuits on the dock. He always said it was his favorite.

"Where did you want me to put it?"

I want to ask if he couldn't throw it away but didn't want to look at it. I want to ask what it means that he still has it. And I realize that every question feels like the phantom presence of a limb I used to have.

I can feel the pain of it, but it's not there anymore.

"I'm looking for my necklace." The minute the words are out, they're real and I can feel my panic rise. "The one your mom gave me."

He takes a deep breath and puts his hands in his pockets. "The opal one?"

I nod. "I can't remember the last time I had it, or where—"

Tears prick my eyes and I hate that I'm crying because I'm so frustrated. Helpless.

Because of the necklace. Because of my family. Because of Easton.

His eyes look like he's deciding on something before he finally settles. "I know where it is." The words carry on a sigh.

"You do?"

He nods. "Yeah. I saw it in the car the day we got arrested."

"In the car?"

"It was on the seat with some clothes and shoes."

My dad's car. The one that was impounded and probably sold or worse.

This was the one thing I wanted to do for her. Wear this necklace and show her I still cared. That I still remembered. Despite everything.

My dad took everything. Even this.

Tears fall down my face and I can't even seem to care that I'm crying in front of Easton. Does it even matter? Do I even have any pride left?

"Come on." He motions for me to get up.

"I don't want to go anywhere."

"Just—" His jaw tightens. "Just come with me."

It's already dark outside when we start walking away from the lake and into the dry fields around his house. Walking with Easton feels normal. Our feet on the ground, him breathing next to me. Warm summer air on our skin. This is how we started. Walking. Eventually, he turns down a dirt road that doesn't have a single light on it.

"Where are we going?" I ask.

But Easton stops in front of a chain-link fence with a worn metal sign and red peeling letters. *Pick and Pull Junkyard.*

"The junkyard?"

He pushes the chained gate open just wide enough that we can slip in.

"Easton, are you going to chop up my body and hide me in one of those trunks?" I ask, only sort of kidding as we pass rows of cars and dishwashers and refrigerators.

He holds up his phone and shines the flashlight down long alleys, clearly searching for something, so when he answers, he seems more distracted than serious. "I would have drowned you in the lake and made it look like an accident."

"No one would believe that. I'm an excellent swimmer," I joke.

"Sure you are— There." Easton points to something in the distance and starts walking with purpose. As we get closer, I see what it is.

My dad's car.

I start running and Easton follows behind, shining the light on the path. Pulling at the passenger door, I pray it's not locked. When it opens with a sticking sound, I let out a cry. Frantically I search the seat. My hands rifle through the remains of a life from a year ago. Forgotten things that still sit here like a time capsule.

And my fingers touch a chain.

I clasp it and lift it up. The necklace hangs from my fist and I collapse onto the seat, clutching it to my chest. I'm sobbing. The ugly kind that no one else should see. But when Easton slides into the driver's seat next to me, he only waits, somehow knowing that my tears aren't only about this piece of jewelry.

When I finally go silent, I wipe at my face with my sleeve.

"You could have just asked me."

My laugh is breathy. "I can't *just* anything with you. And . . . I didn't want your mom to think I don't— I don't know. I feel like even if I'm mad—and I am—I still feel like I want to do this for her." I clear my throat. "It's stupid."

"It's not stupid."

"I feel stupid." *Weak.*

"Because you care about her?"

I lick my lips and press them into a firm line. "Because all the people who *love* me don't want to keep me, but I can't stop feeling like I need to please them."

"My mom isn't the same . . ." He shakes his head.

"Your mom is only different until she's not. Everyone chooses something over me." I'm not saying his name, but I know he realizes that I'm talking about him, too. I put the pendant into my palm and hold it on my lap. My eyes focus on it instead of him.

"I don't—I don't even know what that means."

"It means she convinced you to break up with me after we got arrested." I let the implication sit between us. "She wanted me to go because I had pulled you into my bullshit and she was worried for you."

He frowns and turns toward me. "Break up? My mom didn't do that. You did. And she sent you to California because she was worried for *you*, not for me. She—" He curses. "She thought that you were going to . . . she thought that your dad and your family— It wasn't a *punishment*, Ellis."

"Yes, it was. Even if she thought she was doing me a favor. I was being punished for . . . for choosing my dad."

"It's hilarious that you think my mother would punish anyone for choosing Tru." He lets out a barking laugh. "My mom is always choosing your dad."

We haven't said the thing I know we need to. I feel it between us. Festering. "*You* agreed with her. You didn't . . ." *Trust me? Believe in me? Need me?* I don't know which one of those things I want to say, so I say none of them.

He's silent as he stares forward before he finally says, "I didn't agree with her."

"You did. I *heard* you."

Moonlight cuts into the creases of his brow and I can see his thoughts leave his mind and fill the silence. When he speaks, it's a whisper. "What was I supposed to do?"

"You were supposed to say no. You were supposed to choose me."

He scoffs and looks up at the roof. "I thought that's what I was doing."

I don't speak, because his thoughts are costing me more than they cost him.

"You left and you wouldn't talk to me, and then you chose Tucker and not me . . . even then I thought, if she's happy. If this is what she wants, I can . . ." He runs a hand down his face. "God, I'm pathetic."

"I wasn't choosing Tucker."

"You shut me out, but not him." He puts his hands on the wheel of the car and flexes them. It's a habit I used to find so endearing. Now I just know it means he's nervous. "I was a mess, too, Ellis."

I'm supposed to cherish those words. I'm supposed to feel lighter.

Instead, I feel like I'm falling. We move closer to each other like magnets.

"I don't want to forgive you," I lie.

"I don't want to forgive you," he whispers back and lets out a breath.

He swallows and his jaw tightens. I want to lean in, I want to reach out and touch him, and despite everything . . .

A loud noise breaks us apart.

Red and blue lights flash onto his face like a kaleidoscope.

I've seen it before.

It takes me a minute to realize what's happening. A siren lets out a small chirp, and Easton's eyes squint against the brightness that shines toward us.

"What the hell are you two doing?" It's Dixon's voice, scratching through the loudspeakers.

Easton curses again, but he threads his fingers into mine when we get out of the car. Suddenly I can't hear the siren, or the tires I know are crunching on the gravel of the junk-yard, or the words coming out of Easton's mouth as he shouts at his brother. The world has gone silent, and all I can hear is the thrumming of my own pulse. His hand feels perfect inside mine and I take a deep breath. He doesn't let go as he leads me away from my dad's car, or when we slide into the back of Dixon's squad car.

In one hand is Easton's, and in the other is the necklace.

Easton and Dixon are arguing and I can't help my smile. Until I hear something I know is wrong.

"Breaking into private property is still a crime even if you're getting something in Tru's car," Dixon says. "If you think you can pull shit like this when you're at NYU, you're mistaken. Your dad won't know the whole police force and your brother won't be a cop."

Easton stiffens beside me as Dixon continues.

"In a few months you're going to be on your own and there won't be anyone to—"

"NYU?" I ask as I look up at Easton. NYU. I can see the letters on Sara's Instagram and I remember when I thought I should feel happy for her instead of jealous. Now I feel sick.

He keeps his eyes forward.

"Yeah, he didn't tell you?" Dixon answers. "He got into their writing program."

But I can't hear Dixon really. I can only hear three letters shouting at me in my mind. "You're going to NYU?"

Easton doesn't answer as Dixon continues to talk.

"NYU? You're going . . ." I can't even finish my sentence. Easton and Sara are going to NYU. *Together.*

Easton Albrey said he missed me, but while I was gone, he changed his whole life without even telling me. Easton changed and made decisions and I wasn't here to see any of them. He didn't wait.

And he's going to college with Sara.

I pull my hand from his.

"Ellis." He reaches for it, but I pull it back and ball it into a fist.

"Don't," I say through clenched teeth. "Don't."

NYU. NYU. NYU.

It repeats on a loop in my mind. I can't hear Dixon speaking. With *Sara.*

Easton has been going to NYU this whole time. He got in and he never told me. Never brought it up. Tucker never said anything. *Sandry. Ben.* It feels like a secret everyone kept from me.

Dixon lifts the handle of the back door and I am out of the

car before the door is completely open.

"What the hell?" Easton growls at his brother. He shoves his shoulder.

"What?" Dixon looks lost and I understand why.

But I'm already walking away from them. My mind spins, trying to put the pieces of my betrayal together. A betrayal that, even through this anger, I know I'm not entitled to.

"Ellis." Easton's voice sounds pleading as he walks behind me.

I turn around and he almost slams into me. "When?" My voice is a whine when I want it to be full of my rage.

He's quiet. His eyes hollow out my heart as he stares. I watch his T-shirt pull against his chest as he takes breaths.

One. Two. Three. Four.

"December. Right after I applied."

Months. I let out a breath that is more of a groan and start back down the road.

"Ellis."

"Stop saying my name," I yell over my shoulder. I hate the way he says it.

"Ellis." I hear the frustration in his voice, but it does nothing to stop the anger burning in me. "Just listen to me."

"You're going to NYU with Sara." I can't even find words to express how broken that makes me. I'm unreasonable. I know it. But this is the heart of it.

It's not NYU. It's Sara. It's him moving on. It's being left. Again. It's the finality of him and I spending four years on opposite sides of the world.

The ridiculous part of myself, the part I pretend isn't there, had hoped. And I hate that after all this, I can still make the mistake of hope.

He moves to stand in front of me and it stops me in my tracks. I look down at his feet, at the ground, at the things buried beneath us.

"I know you got into UC San Diego."

I swallow. Anyone could have told him. Sandry. Tucker. Even Tenny. But I should have. I should have told him.

"Yeah," he says, reading my thoughts. "You should have told me, and I should have told you."

"That's not the same."

I'm too angry to care that I'm being a hypocrite. I can't look at his face. Dark eyes that can read my own. It's always like this with Easton. Emotion that is all-consuming, larger than reason, larger than I have control over.

"You . . . you said we would travel." My voice is pathetic.

His whole body goes tense. "Ellis, you haven't spoken to me in a year."

He's right. I haven't, but I had hoped that there was a part of him that hadn't given up. Like I hadn't given up. "When were you going to tell me?"

He clears his throat. "I was . . . I was waiting to see if you were going to . . ."

It takes me a moment to realize what he's talking about,

but when I do, I can't believe it. "You were waiting to see if I stayed?"

"When were you going to tell *me*?" he counters.

When did we get here? At this place of tallied wrongs and rights. This place where we speak the same language but cannot understand each other's words.

"You don't even get it."

"*I don't get it?* I don't get that the only way you want me is when I'm chasing after you? No, I get it, Ellis. I get that *you* are the one that's always been selfish. And like a fool, I let you take and take and take from me." His teeth are clenched and he pulls at his tee when he says the word *take*. Like I could take his shirt, too.

I hate this Easton. The angry version of the boy I knew. It hurts more than the words, or him and Sara. Or NYU. His anger is worse than anything, because I know he's entitled to it.

I move around him and start walking back down the road.

"What are you doing?" Easton says, watching me but not following.

"I'm leaving."

His face falls and then I watch him recover. I can hear the snide comment before he makes it. "Are you running away from home?"

He is trying to make me feel childish, but I decide on a truth that we both hate. "I'm going home."

I stop. With distance between us I feel like I can think. "I don't think we're good for each other. I'm not going to stay here and keep pretending." My heart feels broken in a way that makes it hard to breathe. "Nothing good comes from this kind of pain." I pull all my courage toward me. "I think we just need to let this thing between us be over."

He looks up to the sky and back to me with resigned sadness etched onto his face. "It's been over for a long time."

30

I'VE LOST.

On the front porch of my grandmother's house, I watch the bluish light from the television glowing into the living room and know I've failed. There's noise coming from out back—probably Jesse's friends over to drink cheap beer until they get bored and head to the Tavern.

"Must be bad if you're here." My cousin Eric's words feel like the manifesto of my defeat.

It's only been three days since I left this house with Dixon and watched the disappointed looks on my family's faces as I drove off. They won't say anything, though. Which somehow makes the stone tied around my neck feel heavier. The looks of smug vindication and judgment clear on their faces.

This is what happens when you try to depend on someone else.

My lungs fill with the smell of my grandmother's rosemary bush and I push open the door.

Grandma looks up at me from the TV and then down to the bag in my hand. "There she is," she says in way of greeting. "You need a place to stay for the night?"

For the night. Of course. "Yeah."

She nods. Not asking more, because the *why* doesn't matter anyway. "Tenny's back in her room."

I head to the end of the hall where Tenny always stays. We named it the blue room when we were little because of the bright blue walls. The paint is chipped and peeling in some places and others are just dirty. Grandma never comes in this room. It's for the kids so it's their job to clean it. Tenny lies on the bottom of an ancient white metal bunkbed that has all the sheets stripped off it. I can't tell if the large T-shirt and sweats she's wearing are pajamas or clothes she's too lazy to change out of.

She looks up from her phone. "What happened?" It falls to her chest as my bag falls to the floor.

"Must be bad."

"Nothing." I flop down on the bed next to her and the springs creak under our weight. Our sides are pressed against each other as we stare up at the slats from the bed above us. My swallow is loud in the silence as she waits for me.

Instead, tears run down the sides of my face and past my temples into my hairline. I hate the feeling, but I don't want to draw attention to my crying.

"Ellis, tell me what happened or I'm going to go burn down

the Albreys' house." Her face is serious even though I know her words aren't.

"He got into NYU."

She makes a noise. "Holy shit. That is . . . amazing."

"Yeah. It is." And I mean it. In between all the places of myself that hate him for it. "It shouldn't matter. It doesn't really."

"Why would it matter? Are you mad at him?" Tenny is clearly confused.

"It's the other side of the country." How do I explain that I wanted him to choose me and our dream, not NYU? Not *Sara*. But even *I* wouldn't choose me over that college. I recognize what an amazing opportunity this is for him. It shouldn't matter that it's with her.

And then suddenly, her face changes to understanding. "It's about your trip. You thought he would tell you that he still wanted to go."

"It's not just the trip. It's everything."

She leans back and flips her phone in her hand. "To be fair, you didn't tell him about UCSD."

But *I* was punishing him. He wasn't allowed to punish *me*. Which is completely unfair.

"Well, it's done now. It . . ." I trail off. The finality of my words sinks in.

Tenny pushes up from the bed and groans. "Get up," she tells me. "We need Grandma's tea."

"Ten," I whine.

Her long limbs climb over mine as she moves toward the door. My phone feels bulky as I pull it from my back pocket. I'm prepared to type out a text to Tucker and tell him I'm not going to Sandry's party tomorrow. To say sorry, but I failed and I'm a coward who can't go.

Instead, I see a missed call from the prison.

He knows I'm in Indiana. My aunt told him, or maybe Sandry or maybe even my grandmother. Seeing him feels like another thing I don't have the courage to do. I can't go to the party and I can't face my dad.

The door opens again and Ten carries a mug that says "No bad days." It has a dolphin and a palm tree under the words.

She hands it to me and I'm instantly taken back to being a little girl. My grandma made all of us her famous tea. Cinnamon, honey, vanilla, and more milk than water.

I take a sip and make a face. "Too much vanilla."

"Yeah, well, Grandma is already asleep and I didn't want to wake her for your"—she waves her hands in the air around me—"breakdown."

"Must be bad."

I take another sip and Ten reaches for my phone. "Your dad called?"

"Yeah."

She nods.

"You're not going to ask me if I'm planning to see him?"

"You don't owe him anything, El. You'll go when you want."

Pressing the mug to my mouth, I take a sip and swallow down the tears that try to spill from my eyes.

"And you're not going to Sandry's party tomorrow?"

I pull the phone from her hands. "What's the point?"

She's silent. I can see the disapproval pooling around her like a shadow.

"What?"

"I'm just surprised is all," she says with a shrug. "I guess I didn't realize you were that scared."

I try to be angry, but the word feels true. "Scared?"

"It's okay, El. There is no shame in not wanting to go back to the Albreys' or not wanting to see your dad." She takes my mug from me and takes a sip. "God, this is awful."

"I don't see the point."

Tenny stretches her legs out parallel to mine so that we are sitting against each other but face-to-face. "The point would be that you did it." She takes a deep breath. "People like the Albreys think people like us are always giving up."

"That's not true."

"Sure. Maybe not."

"I don't want to go. I don't want to see Easton or all the people Sandry knows. Or people from school."

"And you don't have to, but you're better than *all* of them. I know you think they pity you or they look at you like charity, but you're tougher than all of them put together."

I chew at my lip.

"You should be fucking proud that you got into UCSD.

313

You did that. You should be proud that you have a savings account. Do you know how much money I have in the bank? Thirteen dollars. I can't even get money from an ATM." She laughs.

I forgot about this. People who can laugh at shitty things. People who don't think the sky is falling when something small goes wrong.

They call it perspective. Or being jaded. Or worse, a grateful attitude.

Really, it's just survival. A word I hate as much as I own.

"I don't want to go just to prove something to anyone."

"It's not about them. It's about you. Your dad, the party, UCSD. What do you want to prove to yourself?"

I stare at the missed call on my phone. And I know what I'm going to do. Not because I have to or because I should.

But because I'm not going to live my life just surviving, no matter how bad it is.

31

Seventeen years old

ALL MY THINGS WERE packed.

My entire life's possessions inside a suitcase. Pictures and trinkets that would help me remember where I was from. Even if I didn't want to.

Tenny put a hand on mine. "It's just a year."

I drew her words against my mind like a promise.

"A year isn't that bad." She sat down on the bed in a room that hadn't really belonged to me in a long time.

Only a week ago, Easton and I had been tangled up in those same sheets. The pain of remembering was immense.

Tenny chewed at her lip. "I hate the Albreys."

I shake my head at her. "It's not their fault." The need to defend them was a reflex even now.

"Sure." She leaned back on the bed. "I guess I could come out and see you and Aunt Courtney. Maybe we could Rollerblade on the beach?"

"It's not a teen drama." I refolded the sweater in my hand.

Sandry had told me to bring one because planes could get cold.

She sat back up. "I can't Rollerblade anyway." Her eyes were on the ground and I could see the way her feelings sat in a pile at her feet. She was deciding which one to pick up and show me. "I'm not sure what I'm gonna do without you. Who am I gonna call when everything gets bad or when Grandma does something stupid?"

My eyes stung. I didn't want to cry here. "Call Wyatt or Jesse."

Her lips pressed down on each other. "I don't want to. I don't want you to move."

Tenny wasn't the kind of person who said what she did or didn't want often, and I understood what it meant that she had. Her sincerity hurt my heart.

I sat down next to her on the bed and wrapped my arms around her shoulders. Tenny and I survived. Sometimes together, sometimes separate, but always like parallel lines. Close but not touching.

"Will you miss me?" I asked against her hair.

When she spoke, it sounded wet from tears and emotion. "I think the answer is obvious. No."

We laughed but it was tinged with our grief.

And when she left me standing on the porch, waiting for my ride, she squeezed my hand and made me promise to never love California.

"I hate sunshine. It's the worst." I tried to smile when I said it.

Her face turned threatening. "You better."

I watched her till she disappeared down the road. A fuzzy dot on the landscape.

Tucker didn't start school for another month, but he'd decided to go to San Diego early. He said he needed to check out the town before school started, but everyone knew it was so I didn't have to fly on a plane for the first time alone. He promised me Dixon would drive us to the airport. Not Sandry or Ben or . . .

Only Dixon.

I couldn't handle anyone else.

Easton had called and texted and come over, knocking on the door loudly. I had ignored everything.

He had broken his promise. *"Me and you."* Anything he had to say didn't matter. It wouldn't change the fact that I had to go. Or that he got to stay.

So when the car door opened and Easton got out of the passenger side I felt anger burn through me.

"Ellis." He held his hands out in front of him like I was a scared animal that he didn't want to spook. "Please just let me say one thing."

"No." It was all I said, afraid my voice would give away something precious if I spoke more.

I waited for Dixon and Tucker to get out of the car, but they both sat there. Immovable traitors. Fine. I walked to the car and tried the handle, but Easton leaned against the door.

"Please just listen to me."

So many *please*s. *"No."*

"There wasn't another choice." All his words were rushed and pushed together.

My eyes shut and I counted to ten as I folded my arms over each other. "Okay."

"Will you look at me?"

I wouldn't. I couldn't. I didn't want to see that Easton regretted what had happened. Or that he didn't. And I couldn't let him see how broken I was. My pride was all I had left. But I finally lifted my eyes to him and took in the dark circles that matched my own and the sallow skin.

When he spoke it was barely a whisper over the sound of the car. "I don't want you to go like this."

I felt my facade crumble and I didn't even have time to put it back up before honest words escaped me on a pathetic cry. "I don't want to *go*."

His hand reached out to my arm, but I moved out of the way. "Ellis."

"Tell them to let me stay." I was begging.

"I'm sorry."

His apology only reignited my anger. "If you didn't want this then why did you agree to it?"

"There—" he began, but I couldn't listen to it again.

"If you say there wasn't another choice I swear to god—"

"You swear to god what, Ellis?" His eyes flashed with anger. "You won't speak to me? How is that different than right now? You don't seem to even care that this is killing me."

I stepped closer to him, my teeth clenched. "Your

metaphorical death is nothing compared to my *very* real one-way plane ticket."

"I don't want you to go."

I hated those words because they did the one thing that hurt the most: caused me to hope.

"Why can't I . . . why can't I just stay?" I don't know why I asked it. I knew the answer. I had just heard Sandry explain it. And she was right. I had done the one thing that meant I could no longer call this place home. I had finally crossed the line. "Why can't you take it back?"

The struggle on his face was painful. "I'll come out and visit you. I'll call every day—"

I stepped back until I hit the car. "I don't want that. You don't get to visit me after you did this."

"I didn't do anything."

"You told her I should go!"

"What the fuck else was I going to do? We got arrested for your dad and he was going to let us go to jail because you can't seem to let him handle his own shit!"

He was right, and it made me feel stupid and small.

And alone.

Even Easton didn't understand why I couldn't just let my dad go. "He's my dad."

"He's a coward who wanted to let his daughter take the blame for him. That's not love."

Tears stung behind my eyes, because if that wasn't love, then I wasn't sure I knew what it was like to have a parent love you.

He shook his head. "I could have lost everything."

I *had* lost everything. I *was* losing. "And I guess losing me isn't a big deal."

"Hey," he said, stepping into my space and pulling me against his chest. "Hey. I can't— We'll figure it out. It's only a year. And then we can travel and do whatever we want and college—"

I pushed out of his arms. Everyone kept saying that. It was only a year, but I was the one who would have to survive that year. My heart broke and cracked and split. The shards too infinitesimal to pick up.

"I don't want to travel with you, or go to college. I don't want to talk to you. Don't call me or text." The breaks showed on his face. "We aren't friends anymore." His pain was fierce and manic. "There is *no* 'me and you.'"

This time he didn't stop me when I pulled open the door and got in the car. The hum of the air-conditioning and the silence of Dixon and Tucker filled my ears. I didn't cry. Not as we drove to the airport, not as we went through security, and not as our plane took off.

But when Tucker fell asleep, I pulled out my phone and read through every single text Easton and I had sent with tears in my eyes. Every single one of them was a cut that bled.

So I pressed *Delete all.*

And pretended like I could delete Easton.

32

THE PARKING LOT FOR family visitors is already filling with people. Visiting day at the prison is always worse and better than I remember it. Women change in front of open car doors from fuzzy boots into heels and skirts. They apply lipstick and brush their hair. I watch them in the rearview as kids get out in brand-new clothes. A little boy pulls at the collar of his shirt with a frown.

I consider this a mistake for what feels like the millionth time in the past minute, but we're already here.

With a deep breath, I watch people begin to file toward the visitors' gate.

"You going to get in line?" Tenny asks from the driver's seat.

I nod, and as I get out I let myself be angry that I have to do this at all. That he is in prison. That his choices have forced me to do something I *so badly* don't want to.

My pants are a black rayon that feels stiff against my legs. I hate them. They belong to Tenny and she calls them her prison pants. No jeans allowed behind bars.

The line for the pat-down and the metal detector is long and the woman in front of me pulls out a few of the pictures from the clear ziplock bag she's allowed to bring into the facility.

"Pictures of my granddaughter," she tells me. "She couldn't make it today. But my son should still . . ." She tsks as she trails off. "Who are you seeing?"

"Dad," I answer simply.

Her smile is bright. "I'm sure he'll be glad you're visiting."

My flip-flops fit perfectly into a plastic tub, and the guard rummages through it, making sure they're just flip-flops. Then finally I walk down the long hall to the waiting room. Several chairs and round tables fill the large white room. Men in orange jumpsuits sit waiting for family.

But I don't see my dad.

I run my palms over the tops of my prison pants and find a table to wait at.

The conversations around me poke at my mind uncomfortably and I have to stop myself from standing and leaving. He's not even here yet, so maybe he wouldn't even know if I left.

And then I see him.

His light eyes brighten up as they find mine in the room. He waits at the glass door to be let through with an optimistic expression that makes the seconds I just spent trying to escape fill me with guilt.

He looks happy to see me.

"Hey," he says, a little breathless. His grin is hopeful, and I recognize it.

It's the one he gave my mother every time she came back. Now he gives me that look.

"Hey." I take his hand on top of the table and squeeze it.

"Your aunt told me you were home. Sandry's party?"

I nod. "She flew me out."

He laughs, but it's like lead. "She does always get what she wants."

The silence between us is filled with the noises in the room and I focus on my dad's hands. Tanned and flecked with small white scars. He rubs at the long scar on his ring finger with his thumb. A nervous habit he developed after a drug dealer almost cut it off.

"You look good," he tells me. "Your hair is lighter."

My hair. Apparently it's the only thing people can comment on when they run out of things to say to me.

"How's it been? Being home."

I lift a shoulder and let it drop on a breath. "It's been the same as it was when I left."

"You see your grandma yet?"

"Yep. And the cousins." The hand in my lap fists. I'm making *small talk*. With my *dad*.

323

"And your job let you come? The one at the coffee shop?"

It's odd. My dad knows pieces of my life. Information and facts that he strings together to make himself feel like he's still involved, active, in my life. But my dad hasn't been a participant in my life in a while.

"Yeah, they gave me a week off." I run my hand over the orange table. "It's just a coffee shop. Not saving the world or anything."

"Yeah," he agrees. "You'll be going to college next year, anyway."

My jaw tightens before I force myself to relax. My father has never cared about me going to college and ignored all the pamphlets and flyers I got in the mail as he moved from selfish thing to selfish thing. And now, probably in some conversation with my aunt, he's decided to care about this part of my future.

"Are you and Tucker still planning on going to Mexico?"

My face pinches together. Tucker and I had talked about it one day on the beach, but . . . "What?"

"Easton said you were—"

"Easton?"

I watch my father choose his next words carefully. "He visits and . . . I ask about you."

I should feel grateful that Easton visits my dad. Visiting an inmate isn't just showing up. It's applying, planning, filling out forms, requesting a visit. Wearing fucking *prison pants*. He went through all that to visit a man he's said maybe a handful of words to his whole life.

Instead, I'm angry. "I don't talk to Easton."

He laughs. "I know. He didn't come every week . . . but enough. If it makes you feel better, I think he came because Sandry told him to."

Easton doesn't do anything he doesn't want to. "I'm surprised Sandry didn't come herself."

My dad shakes his head ruefully. "I don't think Sandry will want to see me anytime soon. Maybe ever."

I ignore the reflex to deny it and try to make him feel better. "I would have visited, but I was in *California*." I hope he can hear the blame in my voice.

"Ellis." His voice is patronizing, like I'm the one who made all the wrong choices.

And the rope holding my patience finally snaps and I feel my frustration bubble up. "You never even said sorry."

"Sorry?"

"I was arrested because of you—"

"I never asked you to get involved. I didn't ask you to drive to the house. I didn't tell you to lie—"

"You told me they go *easier* on pretty girls. If it wasn't for Sandry, you would be visiting *me* in here."

He scoffs. "That wasn't going to happen."

I deserve an apology. He should admit that he was wrong, but instead he is trying to make me feel guilty. I know what's next.

"And where was your mother, huh?"

There it is. The abdication of responsibility. A hallmark of all the addicts I know. Selfish justification. "I don't care about Mom. She hasn't been around for a long time, but you were there."

"*Am.* I *am* here."

I cross my arms over my body so I don't try to hit something. "You're in *prison,* Dad. I'm going back to California."

"I'm . . . sober. I'm in the program. I'm going to church."

He wants me to tell him how proud I am. Forgiveness isn't something he cares about; it's the forgetting that matters. If you forget, then when they do it again, the sins don't pile up on top of each other. This is what he does. He gets you excited about tiny victories.

I will not be excited about something that doesn't matter, because he will always be a disappointment. He will always hurt those who he loves. He will always put himself first.

"I'm sorry," he says in a small voice.

Somehow, the words that were so important to me now only feel hollow. Apparently sorry wasn't what I really wanted. And now my dad has taken that away from me, too. Now I don't even know what I want. What would make all this better?

I stand.

He gives me the same big eyes he gave my mother every time he sensed she was going to leave. "Thanks for coming, El. You didn't have to, but I appreciate it." His throat works nervously. "Have you—" He runs a hand over the top of his head. "Is your mother at the house?" My dad clears his throat. "Have you seen her?"

I shake my head and stare at the ceiling. *She's probably dead. It's been too long since the last time she came around. And if she isn't dead, she wants you to think she is because she has never loved you.*

I only say those things in my mind, though. My dad is not a bad man. Not always, at least. He's just the kind of broken that stabs and cuts anything that tries to hold it.

"I haven't."

His face falls even though he tries to hide it. I kiss the top of his head.

"Love you," I tell him. And I mean it. I wish I didn't, but I can't seem to not.

"I'm proud of you, Ellis. You're a fighter."

And who made me have to fight? He says that he's proud of me, but it's just another way he can tell himself that he doesn't have to be responsible for me.

I walk down the hallway to the processing area.

"All done?" the guard asks me.

I nod, not trusting myself not to cry.

I'm not sad; I'm not really angry. I'm just so sick of life being so unfair.

Tenny is asleep in her car, so instead of waking her, I sit on the curb and pull out my phone. I don't even think about what I'm doing when I pull up Easton's contact. There are so many things I want to tell him. So many things I want to be able to say without having to explain myself. So many frustrated statements that I don't want to apologize for later or feel guilty about.

I don't want to feel ashamed that I hate my parents.

My finger hovers on the call button, because I'm just the same as my dad. His vice is different than mine, but neither of us can break our patterns, and we let it destroy everything else in our lives.

I hit the button.

The one on the side that turns off my phone screen, because Easton and I are over.

I press my forehead to my knees and cry. In between two cars. With the smell of hot rubber and brake dust and dirty asphalt as my only comfort.

I cry.

Just like my dad, I've been in prison for the past year, hoping that my rehab was working.

But in the end, I can't escape who I am and I will only disappoint myself.

33

I STAND IN THE driveway of the Albreys' house.

James Taylor and the sounds of melodic laughter drift over the night air. My palms feel sweaty and my mouth is dry as I think about walking around the back to where the party is. I know that all I have to do is take a few steps.

One. After. The. Other.

I'm not even sure how I got here.

Guests stroll past me with smiles in the summer twilight, and Ben walks out from the side of the house to greet them.

His smile never wavers when his eyes finally fall on mine. I watch his sure steps as he weaves in between cars till he reaches me.

"You look lovely," Ben says to me.

No *Where have you been?* or explanation required.

I straighten my dress and put my shoulders back with a small smile.

"Are you hiding from Sandry?" he asks, and I give him a

look that makes it clear I don't understand. "I'm assuming she's going to parade you around and make you tell everyone your plans for the fall."

My plans for the fall. Those five words settle like rocks in my stomach because those words mean the other plans for fall are gone.

And now I have to be honest with myself. Traveling was always a dream, nothing more. And I have to let the dream die.

"Ready?" Ben asks me, holding out his arm.

I loop mine through his and allow him to escort me into the lion's den.

The entire backyard has been transformed. Twinkling lights are hung across the fading sky like stars so close we can touch them. Sunset has almost been chased away.

A beginning or an end?

The smell of the water and fresh cut flowers mix with tables full of all Sandry's favorite foods. Spices and blooms and summer.

Guests mill about the yard holding drinks and tiny plates of food. Several tables are covered in white cloths and arrangements filled with Sandry's favorite peonies sit in the center in delicate colors. The dance floor meets the edge of the grass right where the bank of the lake starts.

Dixon is already dancing with his grandmother, a woman I've met a handful of times on special occasions. He laughs as he spins her in a wide circle. The white jacket he wears should be tacky, but on him, it looks exactly like Dixon. Tucker stands near the food table in a fashionable suit like a model and it makes me smile that even here, he is one of the most stunning humans I've ever seen.

People I've known my whole life fill the yard. Teachers I've had, people from Sandry's church, family friends. Dixon's friends, Tucker's, even Easton's are here. Sandry stands at the center in a gold dress that is classic and makes her glow. She shines even brighter than her dress as she moves from person to person. I can imagine the jokes and questions that Sandry is so good at. This backyard is full and warm because of her. Because of how she makes people feel important and valued and seen without even trying.

My hand goes to the necklace at my throat, and I straighten the opal pendant.

Standing by the dock is Easton. He wears a dark suit and a tie that he's already loosened at the neck. He has an elbow propped on one of the posts. I give myself ten seconds to stare and pretend.

One. Two. Three . . .

His face against the black lake and illuminated by the lights in the yard.

Four. Five. Six. Seven.

He takes a deep breath and rakes a hand in his hair.

Eight.

He swallows.

Nine.

His eyes shut.

Ten.

I turn away.

"El." Sandry stands behind me with a drink in her hands and a beautiful flush to her cheeks that makes her look younger than fifty. The worried Sandry, the one who danced around me all week, is gone. Here, she's all confidence. "You look . . ."

Her eyes catch on the necklace at my throat and her brows pull together. For a moment, I wonder if I've done the right thing. Her head tilts to the side and her lips begin to fall. My hand wants to go to my throat. To cover what I've done. But instead.

Instead.

I put my shoulders back.

Her lips press together in a line, but her eyes are soft. "The necklace goes perfectly with the dress," she says, finally meeting my gaze.

I nod once, because I can't think of anything else to say. I've already said it all with the necklace. This time, my hand does go to it, but not to hide it.

Sandry clears her throat. "I'm really glad you wore it."

What she really means is, *I was worried you wouldn't come.*

What she really means is, *I'm glad you're here.*

What she really means is, *I've missed you.*

"Me too," I say.

And I really mean it.

The smile she gives me is as bright as the sun on the lake

in the afternoon and I remember all the reasons I love her. Because despite the hurt that I feel, despite all the things that have broken between us, her love for me has always been there. It's like the sun. Sometimes I can't see it, but it's always lighting the sky.

She did the wrong thing in sending me away, but I did the right thing by coming.

Sandry threads an arm through mine and pulls me toward the boys' pediatrician. He was the one who treated my broken arm when I was twelve. She tells him I got into UCSD and he gives me a generous smile.

"I'm so proud of you." And he looks like he means it.

My math teacher from sophomore year encourages me to take more math in college and also tells me she's proud. Same with the man who owns the grocery store in town and let me spend a summer bagging groceries when I was fifteen. And Dixon's best friend's parents tell me how impressed they are. The call me a "smart girl." They are all *proud*.

And I can't help but feel like they didn't actually expect me to do well. Sandry squeezes my hand as if she can read my thoughts. "Go get yourself something to drink and make sure Dixon isn't putting all the beer in champagne flutes." She gives me a wink as she releases my hand and I make my way over to the bar.

The amber liquid in Dixon's glass doesn't look like champagne despite the flute it's in. "What is that?" I ask.

"Beer." He takes a long sip from the glass.

"Why are you drinking your beer like that?"

333

"Because I'm fancy." He takes another glass and tips a wide green bottle into the flute and hands it to me. "Drink it slow."

"What is it?" I say, giving the bubbly drink a sniff.

He tilts his head at me. "Do you think it's weird that you know the difference between Advil and oxy but don't know that's champagne?"

I don't actually know the difference, so I roll my eyes. "People are going to be weird if they see me drinking."

He sips his beer again. "Pretend we're in Europe."

I swallow the dig that Dixon doesn't realize he's said. I don't want to pretend I'm in Europe.

Tucker comes up beside me and plucks the glass from my hand, smelling it. "That's not very responsible for an officer of the law, Dixy."

Dixon laughs and hands me back my drink, and I take a small sip. It's sweet and fizzy.

"Tucker, Dixon!" Sandry waves her sons over.

Next to her is Easton. Our eyes lock and I watch his surprise at seeing me turn to something unreadable.

And then suddenly Sara is standing next to him. She's handing him a glass of something pink and smiling as she touches his arm.

I remind myself that it doesn't matter anyway.

Dixon takes a long sip from his flute and sets it down before he and Tucker walk over to the crowd. My eyes stay on Easton even after he turns to speak to someone his mother's introducing him to.

"Go slow on the booze," Ben says, coming to stand next to me with a wink.

"The apple cider is really strong."

He gives me a courtesy laugh. "Sandry already make the rounds with you?"

"Yep," I say, and Ben smiles. "Everyone was *very* proud of me." I can't keep the sarcasm from my voice.

He turns and studies my profile. "And you don't like that," he says, coming to that conclusion without a question.

I play with the necklace. "It feels weird. Like they're saying they had something to do with it."

He smiles and gives me a small laugh. "We don't do things in a vacuum, Ellis."

I look up at him and my brow knots. "I worked hard to get into UCSD, and they say they're proud like . . . like they took the SATs for me."

"No, they didn't mean it like that. All those people have been watching you most of your life. Rooting for you, doing their best to give you a hand when you needed it. They are proud of you because they were hoping that you would succeed."

And there it is. "Succeed my parents."

"Of course. We all want our kids to do better than us. But it's not about your parents." He shifts on his feet so that he's turned toward me. "Everyone needs help. My boys have a lot of help—so many opportunities. The difference between the boys and you is that they were born into opportunity and you weren't. When you do well, Ellis, it feels earned, not given. So yeah, everyone here who was rooting for you, or tried to help, they all feel a little bit victorious that you've done well. Despite the lack of opportunity. They get to be proud of you."

I run my fingers against the side of the glass in my hand.

"I'm proud of you, Ellis. We are all proud of you."

I want to say thank you, but mixed into my pride is the anger that things aren't just easy for me.

Instead, the fireworks begin.

The first explosion breaks across the sky and I feel the boom in my chest. I search the yard for the boys on reflex. Years and years of tradition is ingrained in me and I kick off my shoes and head to the dock. Dixon and Tucker stare up at the sky at the end of the dock and I walk out to join them. Dixon stands at the very edge with his drink and leans against a post. Tucker has his hands in his pockets and his head tilted to the sky, and I force myself to watch the bright red explosions in the sky instead of finding Easton. He's probably with Sara.

It's only a few minutes into the fireworks when Easton comes to stand next to me. I don't look at him. I don't grab for him when my favorite fireworks cross the sky. He's close enough that I can feel the heat from his body and see the way his chest moves up and down.

I just stand on the dock with Dixon, Tucker, and Easton. Staring at the night and pretending for a perfect moment that it could stretch out forever.

And I don't know why, but these fireworks feel like a goodbye.

When the gold ones erupt and shimmer down onto the lake, I feel the tears in my eyes fall. It's only the press of the back of his hand against mine.

Only that.

Easton knows these are my favorite. The urge to ask him what he's thinking grows in me and I let myself imagine what it would be like if I actually said those words. The way he would smile down at me. The wink he would give me. Telling me that thoughts aren't free.

I don't pull my hand away because I'm a coward. This small thing means more than I want it to, but still not enough. And as the last firework erupts, he walks off the dock, leaving me to wonder if I imagined his hand at all.

We are called to sit at the tables for desserts and speeches. I find myself seated with the boys. Two of their cousins, Kara and Kaia, sit with us staring at their phones more than talking to the people around them.

Easton mostly moves forkfuls of chocolate cake around his plate. He won't look at me even though I know he can feel my eyes. I don't ask where Sara is. Tucker makes an inappropriate joke to Dixon, who is barely touching his food.

"Why do you get to give a speech?" Tucker complains. "We should all get to speak. I'm a better speaker. Dixon mumbles his words."

"Shut up." Dixon pushes Tucker's shoulder, and then he's standing and walking to the microphone.

"God, this is going to be terrible," Tucker jokes, and takes

337

a long drink from his glass. "Have you read his speech?" he asks me.

I lift a shoulder and look at Dixon, who clears his throat. The nerves are clear on his face as he holds his flute of beer, shifting it from hand to hand.

"Thank you so much for coming tonight to celebrate my mom, Sandry Albrey. I was told that I couldn't use song lyrics in this speech, and I'm not the poet in the family, so you'll just have to live with the choices you've made, Mom."

The crowd laughs and the set of Dixon's shoulders relaxes.

He stumbles over a few stories about his mom, and the audience laughs at all his jokes and his dad turns slightly red from the attention when he's mentioned. But eventually, Dixon finds a groove when he talks about his mother teaching him to slow dance to Joni Mitchell.

"She told us that it was important to know how to dance. That being close to people was a skill we needed to have. It would teach us how to speak another language. For years, it was us taking turns dancing with her, until Ellis came along. Then we forced her to be our partner."

People laugh and I feel a smile on my face.

"But it wasn't about dancing. I didn't realize that till later. It was about understanding all the ways people speak without using words. The other language wasn't music or dancing even. It was the things that people say between the words. We do this thing in our family where we tell each other three things on our birthdays. Past, present, future. Who you were, who you are, and who we hope you will be. Mom, before, you loved the people around you. Quietly and without apology. Tonight, you're seeing how much the rest of us love you in return. And in the future, I hope we can all take the love we have learned from you and share it with others in those ways that aren't spoken." He raises his glass. "So, Mom, 'I love you' feels small, but I hope that you can hear all the things that I'm not saying. Happy birthday. Let's all raise a glass to my mother, the best woman I've ever met, Sandry."

"To Sandry." We all take a sip of our drinks as we repeat him.

Sandry looks up at her oldest with love in her eyes, and as he walks past, she reaches over and takes his face in both her hands and gives him a kiss on the cheek. Now I know why she picked Dixon.

And then Tucker is at the microphone. To anyone else, he seems fine. But I can hear the way his o's sound a little too drawn out when he says "Hello."

"I wanted to take a minute to talk about my mom, too."

"Tucker." Sandry smiles but it's wooden.

"It's fine, Mom. Listen." He clears his throat and something in my stomach churns. Ominous. "I'm Tucker. The adorable blond kid from the slideshow we've all been watching on repeat tonight." He pounds on his chest once like he's trying to clear a burp bubble.

Dixon leans over to Easton. "Stop him," he whispers.

But Easton is frozen. We all are.

"So, something that people don't really know about my mom is that she always encouraged us to do the things we were passionate about. Dixon. He's a cop. One of the youngest ever on the force."

Tucker claps and the audience follows, but it's awkward.

"Me, I'm not artsy or officer-y. I don't like school, or whatever. But Easton, my baby brother, is actually a poet. My mom read every single one of his poems because she is his"—he makes an explosion sound—"biggest fan, and she deserves credit for helping him get published."

Easton looks torn between rushing the stage and jumping in the lake. *"Tucker,"* he says.

Sandry's face pinches together, but her gaze is trained on Tucker.

"In truth, she deserves at least half the credit for all of our accomplishments. I don't really have a thing yet, but when I do, I know my mom will support me like she's supported Dixon and Easton. His poetry was bad. Like, so bad, but she just kept encouraging him. Because she's a saint." There are tears in Tucker's eyes and my embarrassment for him is overwhelming. Dixon's getting ready to stand when Tucker's face changes. He reaches into his pocket. "You know what? I'm gonna read East's poem that was published in a magazine, 'cause it's good."

"Tucker." This time it's Dixon.

Tucker clears his throat . . .

And the world falls out from under me.

34

"'SHE SAID SHE LOVED words.

Collected them like pieces of memories, tucking them away into the parts of her heart that she could keep for herself.

They were the only things that stayed.

After she left.

And she took all the breath from my lungs.

After all the people who promised to stay left.

And said they understood didn't.

After all the laughter was gone.

After the sun faded from the sky,

I still had the words.

They are all I have left.

Written on scraps of paper that I tuck away into notebooks and boxes and pockets of pants to find later like buried treasure.

I let paper and ink speak since she doesn't anymore.

Bold.

Even when she couldn't be.

Those words are the parts of us I hide.

They keep our secret.

I breathe in and out with wordless breaths.

I smile without language.

I speak words that aren't true.

Only the words she spoke are.

Only her.

Words I feel deep down in parts of myself I can't find without her.

Words that whispered to parts of me that change a person.

They trail behind me like morning fog clinging to the surface of the lake.

They shift on the air and cast a spell.

And they are all I have left of golden smiles, soft breaths, and summer skin stretched over a heart that beats in poetry.

All I have left of mornings filled with honeyed light and whispers that slide across me like velvet.

All I have left of initials carved into wood and the sharp points of dreams pushed into brightly colored paper with faraway names written in latitude and longitude.

I run my fingers against the inky flicks of the words and imagine her lips speaking them.

She said she loved words

and

they are all I have left.'"

35

EASTON STANDS.

His eyes on the table. On the floor. On his mother. On his brother. On the exit.

Anywhere but on me.

And then he's gone, his feet taking him past the tables, past the house, past everything.

Ben is standing at the microphone. Dixon is giving Tucker a furious look. And I can't breathe.

They are all I have left.

I'm watching Easton's back as he disappears into the darkness of the house.

They are all I have left.

The ache in my chest is painful and I try to understand what just happened.

What just happened?

"We are obviously very proud of Easton. And all of our kids," Ben is saying. "Tucker has always been good at encouraging his brothers. He got that from his mom. He's the most like her, always says what he's thinking." He laughs and takes deep breath. "Who's ready to dance?"

A hand covers mine. It's Dixon's, and his face is filled with pity.

I hate pity. It's unhelpful, but worse . . . it means that I've already lost. It means there is nothing I can do about what has happened. I'm going to be sick.

How dare he write those words about me. How dare he put them on paper and give them to someone else. To be read by anyone who picked up the magazine. Words that were supposed to be mine.

How could he?

I stand without realizing what I'm doing and follow Easton. The house is dark but I make my way without turning on a single light. The door to his room is closed and there isn't a light shining under it, but I know he's there.

"Easton?" I knock, but no noise comes. "East," I call again, and then an odd feeling finds me. He's going to lock his door. He's going to keep me out— I turn the handle as fast as I can and push it open.

Easton isn't locking the door; he's pacing.

"What are you doing?"

He rolls his shoulders under his suit jacket. "What do you want, Ellis?"

My mouth opens, but I don't know what I want.

"Are you here to make fun of me?"

344

"Make fun of you?"

He yanks the jacket off and throws it on the ground. He pulls at his tie until it's loose enough to tug overhead, and his fingers undo the top buttons of his shirt. "What do you want?" he asks quietly.

"Easton."

"No, I'm not doing this with you right now. Goddamn Tucker."

But he doesn't move. He stands in front of me and I stand there. Bare feet and bare soul.

His voice breaks when he speaks. "Yesterday, you said it was done. We were done. And then Tucker reads a fucking poem I wrote . . . forever ago, and now you're *standing* here?"

"You wrote it a long time ago?"

"I wrote it when . . . you first left. Almost a year ago."

He's not telling me something. "When did you submit it to the magazine?"

Easton takes a step back. "It was for a competition."

"When?"

"Three months ago."

It all seems so unfair. He can tell the world that I broke his heart, but on the other side of that poem is a person who had their heart broken, too.

"Easton, look at me."

"Why? So you can see how embarrassed I am? So you can make yourself feel better knowing I feel like shit, too?"

"That's not fair."

"None of this is fair, Ellis! You fucking broke me." He runs a hand through his hair roughly. "I have about a hundred poems just like the one Tucker read." He turns around and pulls a worn notebook from his desk. The brown Moleskine cover is tattered and stained. He tosses it on the floor between us. "Here. Have it."

I can't keep my tears to myself. "Why are you doing this?"

"You ruined me when you left and you acted like you were the only one who was hurt."

"I was the only one who was alone."

He steps toward me with fury in his eyes. "*I* was alone. *I* had no one."

"Your mom. Your dad. Your brother and friends—"

"I wanted *you*!" His eyes fill with tears that slide down his face and I want to reach up and brush them away . . . but that's not my job anymore. "I didn't want anyone else. I didn't know that when you left—" He chokes on his next words, but it's me who can't seem to breathe. "Why did you go?" he whispers.

"I never had a choice."

We keep having the same argument with words that circle the same hurt over and over again.

He swallows with an audible click of his throat. "It's supposed to get easier. It's not supposed to always feel like this."

"How do we stop?"

He presses his lips into a line and shakes his head. "I don't know that I can. I don't know that I want to." He runs his tongue against his bottom lip. "This pain is better than nothing."

The truth forces its way up inside of me. It presses against my chest and demands me to speak my next words. "Easton, I don't know how to be without you. You're the only person who has ever really seen me. You're . . . I can't live without you. *Please.*"

It's a shattered plea. One that cost me so much more than one word should.

His arms are around me a second later, pulling me against his chest. "El." My name is a whisper on his lips. His hand is in my hair. "Ellis."

A sob breaks the night. It carries the words that hurt.

They are all I have left.

I don't want this to be all we have left. Easton's shirt is wet with my tears, which I can't seem to control.

"Please don't leave me." All my emotions are strangled and sincere. I tug at the necklace around my throat. It feels too heavy and I unclasp it.

I'm pathetic.

My heart is messy and cracked, but for the first time since I can remember, it's the truth. His hand runs down at my back and he lets out a small laugh. "There isn't anywhere I can go that you aren't."

I wrap my arms around his middle, my hands beneath his shirt, and I feel the muscles tense there. My head tilts up and I run my nose against the soft column of his neck.

"Ellis."

Without thinking, I press a kiss to the hollow underneath his ear. His pulse beats wildly, and a second later he's stepped back, his chest moving up and down as he stares at me. Thinking. I've seen this look so many times I could tell him his own thoughts.

He's thinking about this. Deciding if he should let me kiss him. Deciding a way to let me down.

"You're wrong," he tells me, interrupting.

"What?"

"Whatever it is you're thinking, it's wrong."

"Then what are you thinking?"

He lets out a small laugh that's more frustrated than humorous. His eyes are dark. "I'm thinking it's not ideal to make out with you while there is a party going on downstairs. I'm thinking I don't really care if there is or isn't. I'm thinking of all the things I want to do to you now that we are finally alone. I'm thinking it's been a long time since the last time we were together and I'm not sure I can wait to take you somewhere that you deserve. I'm thinking—"

He doesn't have the chance to finish because my mouth is on his, hungry. "I don't care," I say in between breaths. My hands run over him and I love the way his groan sounds against my skin.

Easton pushes me against the door, his hips against mine, and I wrap my legs around his waist.

His mouth moves to my neck, to my shoulders. "I'm thinking about how good you taste."

My teeth scrape against his jaw and he lets out a moan as he presses harder against me.

"I'm thinking about how many times I've thought about this."

I push back on his shoulders and he steps back. Easton looks wrecked. His shirt has begun to come untucked; his hair is mussed and his lips are pink and swollen.

From me.

I've done this to him, and it makes me feel greedy. My palms push Easton onto the bed and I climb on him. With fumbling fingers, I work at the buttons of his shirt, pulling it from his pants fully until I can run my hands over his chest. It inflates underneath my touch.

"I'm thinking about all the places my hands can go," I tell him, and his hips lift toward me. I press back against him and watch the way his face transforms into a painful pleasure.

I look at him. Messy and beautiful and completely mine in this moment. It takes only a second for me to reach down and pull the hem of my dress up and over my head. I settle back down over Easton. His gaze could be a hundred different places—my thighs, my chest, the swell of my backside. But Easton is looking into my eyes. Waiting. I'm the one in my underwear, but Easton is the one who is vulnerable. Exposed.

Raw.

"I love you," I whisper to him.

A slow smile changes his face and he tries to hide it by biting his lip.

He lifts up and unclasps my bra and takes me into my palms. My hands move slow as I unbutton his pants and unzip them. His whole body tenses, and when I slide down him he puts a hand on my wrist.

"You don't have to . . . you don't have to do that," he says.

"I know," I tell him. "I want to."

And when I take him into my mouth, his head falls back with a dark groan. I love the way it makes me feel. I love the noises coming from him and knowing I'm the reason.

"Stop," he says, and I pull away from him, sitting up.

A second later, he has me underneath him. Dark eyes filled with intense desire stare back into mine.

"I'm thinking about how I don't want the night to end like that."

He kisses me as he works his pants the rest of the way off and then the remainder of my clothes. His mouth is on every part of me, and suddenly I know what he felt like only moments ago. Completely at the mercy of someone else as my body tries to chase a feeling I can't hold onto. Like holding sunlight.

I hear the crinkle of the condom as he opens it, and he looks up at me. "Are you sure?"

"I'm thinking about how much I've wanted this," I tell him as I move my hips toward his.

And then we come together, our bodies moving back and forth. He's careful and soft and I can see the concern for me in his eyes.

We move faster and faster.

He groans into my shoulder as his head drops against it. "Ellis," he whispers. I turn my head to kiss him and our noises mingle together as he sets his forehead on mine.

And when we are finished and our breathing grows slower, he pushes the hair back from my face and gives me a small smile. It's filled with honesty.

"I'm thinking about you," he tells me. "I'm always thinking about you."

36

Easton

HER GRADUATION HAT WAS blank.

For some reason, that hurt the most.

I found her in the crowd immediately. Sitting there, staring at the program in her hand. No one was talking to her or laughing with her. I could imagine how it was supposed to be. Me, leaning over and whispering something funny in her ear. She'd hide behind her dark hair and I would brush it out of her face. That was how it was supposed to be.

But a ghost sat in her chair. And I'd help create it.

I thought back to my graduation the week before. It had been full of teasing and jokes and cheers. And family. Not Ellis. But enough that her absence didn't feel like the abyss it normally did.

Things she didn't have.

"Fuck," I whispered under my breath. A gray-haired woman sitting next to me on the stadium bench gave me a judgmental glare and I mumbled half-heartedly, "Sorry."

But it was all so . . . sad.

My phone vibrated with a text from Noah, sending me a series of pictures.

Noah:

Albrey! Get here. Now! Mexico is lit!

Lit. Jesus fucking Christ. Noah was an idiot, even if he was fun.

The first picture was of the ocean from a balcony. The next three were of the suite that Sara had booked for us to stay in with her parents' time-share points. I typed back a quick response.

Easton:

I'll be there soon.

Noah:

You're already missing two days. Hurry up or we'll leave without you!

I waited to feel the urgency that Noah's text was meant to inspire. We were going to backpack down the coast and it was supposed to be "the trip we would never forget." But I couldn't stop thinking about another trip I was supposed to take. Another girl I was supposed to see the world with. The announcer began calling *T* names, so I kept my phone out and waited for them to get to the end. When they said Ellis's name, there was barely a clap for her. Somewhere in the distance I could hear her aunt and Tucker yell. I shouted as loud as I could. Ellis climbed the stairs to the stage with her back to me. The hat was blocking most of her face.

And then she turned.

Ellis Truman stood with the corners of her mouth barely lifted as a man she didn't know handed her a piece of paper and told her congratulations.

Even from this distance, she was still stunning. I took a picture as she put a hand on her hat and looked briefly up to the sky. Ellis was always beautiful, and I couldn't breathe. Now more so than ever. I rubbed at the spot over my heart.

She took her seat again and I stared down at the picture I had taken. I felt like I hadn't seen her in more than a lifetime. My eyes were on the picture through the rest of the alphabet, until—

"Well, well, *well*." It was Tucker's voice. My head snapped up to him and my eyes went wide. "Aren't you supposed to be in Mexico, baby brother?"

I searched for a sarcastic comment, something to hide that I had been caught. Tucker had replaced me in Ellis's life, and every feeling I had toward him was complex and involved some form of harm to his person. I was never going to forgive him. But what I felt the most, more than unforgiving, was the right to be at *my* best friend's graduation. Even if she wouldn't talk to me. "I wanted to come."

My brother put a hand on my knee and squeezed it. "I'm glad you did."

His kindness felt wrong. I sat there, relieved that he understood why I was there and also angry that he could be so generous.

"She'll be happy to see you," he said. "Even if she acts like she's not."

"No." I said it fast. Like a shot from a gun. "I don't— I'm not— She doesn't need to know I'm here."

Tucker's brows came together. "What?"

I had flown across the country just to avoid her. It sounded ridiculous. I knew that. "I just wanted to watch Ellis graduate. I wanted to— I don't need to see her . . ." *Without me.* I didn't want the reality of all the ways Tucker had replaced me to be real. I didn't want to search for the ways that he hadn't, wondering if there were still spaces waiting for me to fill them.

Tucker shut his eyes and let out a heavy breath from his nose as if I was being absurd. It made me want to punch him. "You should talk to her, East."

That was never going to happen. "Don't tell her I'm here," I said, and then added, "Please."

I hated that I had to beg my own brother for something about Ellis.

He clicked his tongue like he was disappointed. "It'll mean a lot that you came."

The fear that I would see her and it wouldn't mean "a lot" kept me in the bleachers. I still couldn't acknowledge the truth: Ellis and I were the kind of people who *didn't* mean a lot to each other anymore.

I sat in the stands and watched her as she stood off to the

355

side and Tucker made his way toward her. She was like a flower tilting to the sun as he approached her. They took selfies and she smiled, but it wasn't her real one.

Tucker didn't make her happy. I couldn't tell if I was glad, or if it made me feel more miserable.

Her aunt appeared and kissed her. Ellis made a face because she hated it.

My phone buzzed. Tucker.

Tucker:
Are you really not coming down here?

Easton:
No.

My answer was simple, but I'd hoped he'd get the point. Instead, I saw the typing bubbles.

Tucker:
That is an expensive flight just to watch Ellis like a stalker.
You must have gotten more money for graduation than
I did.

He was baiting me. I ignored his shit. It wasn't worth engaging.

Tucker:
Actually, you're being a child. You both deserve more than

this and you know it. We will be at the beach if you decide to stop acting like a baby and want to tell Ellis congratulations yourself. Fucking coward.

I would have rather stabbed myself in the face with a butter knife than watch the two of them at the beach. The third wheel in a friendship that didn't have room for me.

Biting down on my cheek to stop my thoughts, I opened the Lyft app for a ride to the airport. If I was there, then I couldn't be tempted to try to see Ellis.

I scrolled through Instagram in the back of the car as it sped down the freeway. Ellis and Tucker's picture came up in my feed and I clicked on his profile. Most of the pictures were of the two of them or of just her. And they were all beautiful. Tucker had always been a talented photographer. I was spending too much time on a picture of burritos and a beach when I got a text from Sara.

Sara:
Everything all right?

Easton:
Just leaving.

Sara:
Did you see her?

Sara knew why I had come to San Diego. She was the only person, other than my mother, who I had told.

Easton:

From a distance.

Sara:

You didn't talk to her?

Easton:

Not this time.

There was a pause that encompassed all her disappointment, and then another text.

Sara:

I'm sorry. I know how much you wanted to see her.

I hated seeing my own feelings reflected back at me in text. I waded through the TSA security line at the airport to get into the terminal. I took off my shoes and took my cell phone and wallet out of my pocket. The plastic tub that I put them in was blue and reminded me of the bins they used at the prison.

If Tru had made a different choice, would Ellis and I be in Europe right now? Would we be together instead of me hiding in an airport and staring at her picture like a stalker?

I gathered my things on the other side of security and found a chair next to a window, putting my AirPods in. The tarmac outside grew dark as the sun disappeared, and I couldn't help my own disappointment.

She had graduated and Tucker was the only Albrey there.

Was he enough for her? Had she even thought of us? Of me? Maybe she really had moved on. Maybe—

The phone vibrated in my hand.

Blocked Caller.

My pulse beat erratically because I knew who this was. Ellis.

"Hello?"

She didn't speak; the only sounds were her breathing and the occasional inhale, which sounded like it had tears in it.

Ellis hadn't wanted me at her graduation but she called.

And it made me feel just as victorious as the first time she had done it when she left for San Diego.

I had spent so many nights listening to Ellis breathe on the other end of the phone. It hurt every time because she had never once answered one of my calls. But this was something I could have. The two of us, not speaking, but being.

I waited for her to say something. Yell. Argue. Anything. The announcement at the airport said my flight was boarding in a few minutes, and for a moment I thought I'd have to choose between getting on a plane to Mexico and staying on the phone with her. But she hung up first, her muffled cries finally ending. Which was better.

Because I would always choose Ellis. Every time.

37

THE MAP ON EASTON'S wall has all the same pins as the last time I stood in front of it. I pull on my dress and I look at them now, feeling sad. Each one is the loss of an adventure I had dreamed of. Red and blue and green plans all just enamel tacks now.

Easton hands me a glass of water as he slips back onto the bed next to me. I tap on the side of it, staring at the blue pin in Morocco. He places a kiss on my bare shoulder, quick and gentle.

"I never took it down." He states the obvious.

"Why?"

I don't say, *You went without me.* I don't say, *You're going to NYU.* I don't say, *This hurts still.*

"I just . . . . It's better than . . ."

I understand that on some odd level. "Do you still have the journal?" I ask.

Easton nods his head yes and takes out the composition notebook from his desk. Somehow, I missed it when I was looking in his room for the necklace. My sloppy handwriting in purple ink covers the *Subject* section. Papers and pictures printed from the internet stick out from inside. They come up from pages where they were taped or pressed with a glue stick.

I open it, listening to the creak of the spine. *Itinerary* is the first thing I see.

June 1st: leave for England.

My fingers run over the words.

"We're late," Easton says over my shoulder.

My throat tightens and I push back an angry response. "We aren't going."

"Why not?"

"What?" I frown, ready for a fight. "You went without me. Mexico is on the list." I don't say *our list.*

"I went to Cancún." He flips to the page with Mexico. "You wanted to go to Mexico City. And there was a whole rant about tourist traps and ruining Chichén Itzá. Why can't we still go?"

I make a noise.

"Te amo." He runs his fingers against the soft part of my stomach. "It's better than hello and thank you." He takes the water from my hands and swallows a long drink. "We could go."

I laugh, but I can feel the hope beginning to bubble up. "Sure."

"I'm serious," he says, sitting up in his bed. It still smells like us in here. "We can still go."

"Easton. Stop." And *I'm* serious. How dare he tease me like this.

"Ellis." He says it against my throat, and I fight down another shiver. "I would go tonight if you wanted to. We could just follow the itinerary."

My eyes roll without my permission and I hit him in the stomach gently. "Shut up. I really wanted to go. You're not funny."

He looks back at the map and lets out a breath that I can feel. "Before you lived in Indiana and dreamed of the ocean. Now you live in San Diego and have stood in the Pacific. I hope in the future you can put your feet in every ocean on the earth."

Three things. Even though it wasn't my birthday. My nails dig into my palms. "You're going to NYU and I'm going to UCSD."

He makes a sound affirming me and rubs small circles into my shoulder. "I have the paperwork to defer."

"You . . . you have what?"

His face tells me that he's trying to be patient. "I honestly don't know how to keep saying this to you. I applied to NYU because when I won the contest for the magazine, they waived

362

the application fee, but the first thing I did was look up deferring."

"You looked into it." I repeat his words in flat tones.

"This is what I've been trying to tell you. That was always the plan. We would defer. I thought . . ." He lifts a shoulder and glances back at the map. "I've looked at that map for the past two years. Obviously I want to go."

I let out a small laugh. "When would we even . . ."

"We could go now. Right now. Throw things in a bag and . . . go."

My mind whirls. I'm trying to find a way to make this possible. "But your mom—your whole family is downstairs."

He gives me a devilish smile. "We're eighteen. This is our summer. Our *last* real summer before we're in college. And we've been talking about this for years."

I'm starting to think about the steps that I would take to leave with Easton right now. Pack a bag, grab my passport, buy a ticket, go to the airport. They are surprisingly few.

"All of the money we saved, I still have it. Plus the money from graduation."

I read the itinerary. "We're way behind."

He shrugs. "I didn't want to go where they speak English anyway. It's boring if they don't think my incompetence is adorable."

My hands are shaking, so I put them under the blanket. "Easton."

"If we go now, no one can tell us not to. No one can stop us or say we're being stupid or that we should wait. If we go right now . . . we actually will."

I want this so bad my heart physically hurts with hope. "Are you sure you want to?" I ask him.

"Do *you* want to?" he throws back at me.

What a ridiculous question. "Yes," I say.

He shrugs. "Then go get your shit."

The smile that blooms across my face is one that I can't stop. It's . . . happiness.

I cross the hall to my bedroom. The sounds of the party float into the room quietly. Downstairs is Tucker. Dixon. Ben. Sandry.

I want to say goodbye. I don't want it to be like the last time when I went to San Diego, because this time is different. I'm leaving, but I'm choosing to leave. I'm making the decision.

Under the bed is the box I brought with me all the way from San Diego. The real present I have for Sandry. Every letter she's ever written me. They are all placed in chronological order, and tucked in between the stamped ivory envelopes are pieces of paper.

Each one is an answer to her.

Some I wrote in classes. Some I wrote on breaks. In the middle of the night, with tears in my eyes, wondering what I had done to deserve my exile. Wondering if I could ever earn my way back to the Albreys'.

Now I know they were looking for ways to earn *me* back.

I take out a piece of paper and write one more note. This one I fold in half and write her name on it, then place it at the top of the box.

After shoving everything I have into my bag, I change from my dress into pants and a baggy T-shirt. When Easton comes in, he gives me a smile. "What's that?" he asks, pointing to the box.

"It's for your mom."

Easton looks at the box and I can tell when he recognizes the letters. He smiles but doesn't ask any of the questions I can see on his face. Instead, he asks a different one. "You ready?"

I swallow. I'm not, but I won't ever be ready for Easton. I could never fully be ready for something that feels like taking in the sky with every breath.

"What about your dad? Your aunt?"

I lift a shoulder. "It's me and you."

He takes my hand and laces his fingers through mine. "I don't ever want to let you go again."

"All right," I tell him, and let him lead me out of the room.

And as Easton and I drive away from the yellow house with white trim and lights that shine on the love that lives inside the walls, he holds my hand. I finally realize something so obvious it almost makes me laugh. I never belonged to the Albreys. They have always belonged to me.

"What are you thinking?" I ask him one final time.

"I'm thinking that this is what always should have been."
He presses his lips against the back of my hand. "What are you
thinking?"

"I'm thinking better late than never."

He laughs. I laugh.

And for the first time in a long time, I tell myself it's okay
to be happy.

Because I am.

Happy.

38

DEAR SANDRY,

In this box is every letter you ever wrote to me. I'm sorry I didn't send my responses. You'll see why when you read the first one. I was angry. I still am sometimes. And then sometimes I'm just sad. But mostly, I was confused. I knew why you sent me away. My mind knew, but my heart didn't.

Being back here at the house, I see all the things I forgot. I remember what it's like to live in a place where love is so heavy that you feel like it's inescapable.

Tucker took that love with him to San Diego. He never once doubted that you loved him or me. But I didn't. I left all of it here. Coming back, slowly I remembered. And I'm not mad anymore.

Not all the time, anyway.

I hope when you read these letters you will pay attention to the ones that talk about my day, my life. Not the ones that said things in anger and frustration.

367

I want to tell you something that I've never really told you before, but I should have.

Thank you for loving me. I know when I first came around, you were only looking after Tru's daughter. But I still remember the day I realized you loved me. Just me.

We were sitting out on the dock. You had a glass of wine and I had a strawberry freeze. That was the year Ben made them all the time. "The Boxer" by Simon and Garfunkel came on the radio and you told me it was your dad's favorite song. You told me your dad had a hard life, but he made sure everyone in his home knew how much they were loved. We sat looking at the water together listening to the song, and you turned to me and said, "One day you will understand that home isn't walls and a roof, it's a feeling that you get. And you get to pick who lives there."

I never felt like I had a home. I still don't feel like I have the kind with walls, but it was that day I knew you had picked me.

I love you, Sandry. Thank you for loving me the best way you knew how to, and I'm sorry that I didn't always recognize it for what it was.

Love,

Ellis

EPILOGUE

Easton

Mom:
You need to at least tell me you've read this. Dixon wants to
file a missing person report.

My mother's text is typical.

Half worried, half annoyed that she has to deal with other
people being worried.

Soon, I'll have to call her and tell her where I am. Listen to
her yell at me for leaving, even though I'll be able to hear in her
voice how proud she is that we left. She'll tell me that I better
not mess up my acceptance with NYU, even though she knows
I've already checked with the school. My mom will make sure
that both Ellis and I have filled out all the right paperwork,
even though she's already sent it to my email three times.

Because *I did not work this hard to let you forget about college*
—direct quote.

And I will.

But right now, these moments are only for Ellis and me. She's quiet this morning. Dark hair falls over her bare shoulder as she stares out at the beautiful Italian people who walk down the street outside our hostel. She scans the crowd and tucks her chin against her knees as she pulls them up to her chest.

"What's going on in your brain?" I ask and take a sip of espresso. Oddly enough, I miss drip coffee.

Ellis takes a deep breath, like she can sigh away the weight on her. "I was thinking about all of these people. Going to work, or school, or doing whatever it is they do with their lives. It makes me feel . . . I didn't expect everything to be so overwhelming."

I nod like I understand. I don't, but Ellis is like this. Trying to find ways to fit herself against the world she sees. Measuring herself against all the things she knows to be true and sorting through each version of it she has.

"You don't agree." She smiles. It feels like lightning against my skin.

I didn't expect to feel so overwhelmed by *her*. My hand closes on the table so I don't reach out and touch her. She makes me gluttonous. I hate that I spent so much time not touching her when I could have.

Her eyes light up like she can read my thoughts and takes a sip of my espresso.

"That's mine," I tell her half-heartedly.

Her head tilts to the side and she narrows her eyes playfully. I can't take a full breath. My lungs actually hurt looking at her. With my phone in my hand, I take a picture of her. Soft eyes and a bright smile. Vulnerable and open. It's a look she only has for me. One that only we share.

She takes another breath and stares out at the people walking past again. "It's . . . a lot."

"What?"

"All this. The places. The people. Everything. Don't you ever feel like you'll never get to do everything? See everything?"

Yes. "No."

She rolls her eyes.

"Sometimes I'm in awe of . . . how much life is out there." She ducks her head, shy. "I'm not explaining myself right."

But I know what she means. I feel that with her. In awe of her constantly. I am completely addicted to her.

I just.

The summer before our senior year, only weeks before she was sent to California, I was accepted to a weeklong writing program. They threw a mixer for all the students and their families. Professors and alumni stood around discussing their accomplishments and asking question after question. I remember standing in a crowd and talking with strangers about poetry and literature. The room felt too loud. There were too many people. Everything was too much.

And then.

All of a sudden, I saw Ellis. She stood off to the side, with a smile on her face, and somehow I didn't feel like I was drowning anymore.

She'd told me, *"You look lost."*

I made a joke, but the truth was, and is, I'm always lost without her.

I take another picture of her as she stares out the window and decide this is the one I will show people. I write a small caption and hit post.

A few seconds later—@duckertucker has commented on your photo: Nice caption loser. Stop using my model.

And then @Dixon123: Call Mom or you're dead.

I smile and for a small second, I miss them. And then it's gone.

I reread the caption and know I picked the right one.

And I am thinking
Of her.

ACKNOWLEDGMENTS

If you made it here, I'm assuming you've finished this book. You are holding my dreams in paper and ink and prose. I will never, ever not feel the gravity of that. My gratitude for you is ENDLESS.

An enormous thank-you to Sarah Landis. Your confidence in this book, and in me, makes my gratitude immeasurable. Thank you for always holding my hand and putting out the fire.

To my fabulous editor, Erica Sussman. Your love and belief in this story are a dream come true. You made this book better. You make me a better writer.

To Stephanie Guerden, thank you, thank you, thank you for pushing me, asking questions, and for the gifs. I am so lucky I get to work with you.

To the wonderful team: Mitch Thorpe, Shannon Cox, Alexandra Rakaczki, and Vanessa Nuttry, thank you for helping make all my dreams come true.

David—I dedicated this book to you because I'm obsessed

with you. Also, because you believed in me the whole time, even on days I didn't. I am so lucky to have found someone who loves me the exact right way.

To my children, Talon, Everlee (Bev), Coco, Marlowe. You are my first audience. My greatest joy is having you listen to my stories and watching you make up your own. I am only the writer I am because of you. Thank you for always saying I'm your favorite mom.

Mom. All my strength and bravery and determination comes from you. If a lesser person raised me, I would have given up on this dream a long time ago.

Daddy, you're reading this from heaven, but I know you're proud. Thank you for always encouraging me to read. Thank you for always believing the impossible for me. I wish you were here for this more than anything else. How dare you die and miss this. Absolutely ridiculous.

I have the most incredible family, and I am forever grateful for them. Minda and Chris, you make all your kids (including me) feel like we can do anything. To the brothers, pieces of each one of you are in the Albreys. Thanks for being the best brothers a girl could ever have. To the sisters, I'm unbelievably blessed to get to be creative alongside some of the most talented and generous and loving humans I've ever met. Grandma— strong women come from strong women. Thank you for raising the one who raised me. Beam—Thank you for all the belief and generosity that you have shown me with my writing. I am here because of those early seeds you planted.

Julie Juju Lint (and Katie)—Many nights you watched my kiddos so I could write. My tab is soooo big from twenty years of friendship.

Tianna Radford, Morgan Fischer, Lisa Walker, Jacki Jenkins, Christy Decelle, Lacey Ravera, Annette Reece. There is nothing like your first friends. Nothing like the people who watch you grow and change and become something different, and yet still remind you of the person you used to be. The people you don't have to explain your life to because they were there. I love you girls. I love the stories we tell and the way we laugh. I am who I am because of you.

And Lacey—Thank you for reading this book. Thank you for seeing me in it and understanding what it meant to me. Hottest, phattest bitches on Tonsai. Sorry about the time I sneezed in your mouth in Costa Rica.

Heather Petty—Thank you for reading early. Your black heart is my favorite. Maura Milan—Thank you for finding me at that party and making me feel important. Patricia Riley—my first reader who said she loved my book. Jenn Wolfe—I am so grateful for your enthusiasm and generosity. Sona Charaipotra—Thank you so much for your endless generosity and encouragement. And to my Clubhouse family: Melody, Taj, AJ, Inez, Hannah, Alex—Thank you for all the chats and pep talks and distractions. Harper Glenn—Thank you for your love and support and friendship. Patrice Caldwell—I will never ever be able to tell you how much I appreciated your advice. Akshaya Raman—crisis buddies for life. I think about the dinner we met at a lot, and, DAMN, I am proud of us! Truly. Alexandria Sturtz—Thank you for responding to a weirdo who just started DMing you. Thank you for supporting me, encouraging me, loving me. Your turn is coming.

Stephanie Brubaker—Your friendship is one of the best gifts I have ever been given. Every smart thing said in this book was probably something you said to me. I love you.

Lyndsay Wilkin, Joanna Rowland, Jenny Lundquist, Tamara Hayes—the best writers' group of friends in the business. Shannon Dittemore, you are the reason I am here. I love your generosity and your friendship and your brain. FOREVER.

Stephanie Garber, I feel like I never stop telling you how much I love and admire you as a person and a colleague. Thank you so much for always cheering me on and being such an outstanding example of genuine kindness in an industry that sometimes forgets to value those things. Isabel Ibañez—Thank you for that first retreat. Thank you for patiently waiting for me to realize you were right. I love you. Rachel Griffin—I am endlessly grateful to know someone so encouraging and wonderful and generous. Thanks for every pep talk and encouraging message. They keep me sane. Diya Mishra—I love that you get this book. You get the vibe. You get me. Honestly, I just can't wait for you to trash me in your acknowledgments. I deserve it. Adalyn "Addy" Grace—my twin sister. Thank you for always being so generous with me and believing in me and reading your sister's book, even though it doesn't have blood. Your RBF is strong and your heart is soft. Shelby Mahurin—thank you for always answering all my unending questions, and for your hilarious dark humor and your compassionate heart. Jordan Gray—I don't have sufficient words to describe how much your friendship, your insight, your own books, and your generous feedback have meant to me. I cannot wait to read my thank-you in the back of your book.

Sasha Peyton Smith—You are a gift. I love that you sent me an extensive google doc about SVT that kept me from writing (because, priorities).

Emily Wibberley and Austin Siegemund-Broka, Jenna Evans Welch, Rachel Lynn Solomon, Stacey Lee, Ashley Woodfolk, Elise Bryant, Robyn Schneider, Kami Garcia—thank you for reading early and saying such wonderful things about a book you didn't have to.

Courtney Summers—for saying "You're gonna be good at this" and for cheering for me always.

Victoria Van Vleet and Bill Povletich—The universe knew what it was doing when it sent you to sit next to me at that SCBWI.

D. J. DeSmyter—You are an amazing friend, and your support and encouragement is something that has always made me feel cooler than I am and smarter than I should be. Thank you for sitting on the floor with me talking about story and magic.

Axie Oh and Erin Rose—I love that you let me pretend to be cool enough to hang out with you on your writing dates. I love how kind and supportive and encouraging you both are to the people you love in your life.

Gretchen Schreiber—How to even put into words how much you mean? WELL, how about "You're so lovely, I'm so lovely, we're so lovely, lovely, lovely." I love you a Jimin-falling-off-chairs-laughing-so-hard-he-throws-himself-into-someone's-lap-champaign-drinking-Black-Swan-dancing-perfect-walking amount.

Susan Lee—You are one of the best things that has come out of publishing. Thank you for all the long chats and laughs and K-drama convos. Thank you for your friendship and love and gift packages of Korean snacks just when I need them.

Amy Sandvos—Your love is a gift. Your support and belief and encouragement, even on days where I didn't believe, mean more than you will ever know.

Mara Rutherford—my mentor and my friend. Thank you for always treating me like one of the cool kids, reading all my stories, encouraging me; your generous friendship is a GIFT.

Kate Pearsall—you knew. For both of us. You knew 2020 was it. Then it was on fire . . . but it was still "it." Love you, friend.

Kara Richard—I am so grateful that you're the same kind of weird I am. Thank you for unending fan fiction that reminded me of all my favorite parts of story. Borahae.

To the ACOBAF team—Alex, Ginger, Kelsey (who single-handedly organized a cover reveal for me), Meghan, and Chelci. I live for your conversations about the boys. Your fights give me life.

Joseline Diaz—Thank you for always offering to support me. Your blurb meant SO much to me.

Isabella Ogblumani—Thank you for reaching out to a stranger and asking to read.

Rick and Beth—So much of the Albreys' journey is about what family means. I'm so glad that I learned so much of that from you two. Love, Baby Mama #2.

Vanessa Del Rio and Natalie Faria—Thank you for . . . ★waves hands around★ literally all the things. Natalie Eiferd— Thank you for teaching me how to write.

To my BTS family: Diana Jeon Phang, Kara, Maddy S, Malory, Alexa, Gretchen, Alex, and Kalley. Thank you for always reminding me 1000 million trillion times about sales, appearances, and concerts. I am so glad I found you all.

To Joel, Ethan, Siah, Fin, and Roo. Joel, thank you for your magic coffee (that you make better than Adrienne) and for your support and cheerleading. And to the kids, thank you for all the hours of watching you grow and dream. Little pieces of you are scattered across all my stories. I love you.

I want to thank Namsan Tower and the people who leave their names on love locks. If places have energy, that place is filled with love and heartbreak and courage and inspiration. Those tiny little locks are imbued with hope and look out like sentinels over a city filled with people. I carried so much of that love home with me and put it into this book. So, thank you.

And absolutely no thanks to K-pop (specifically BTS). I WROTE THIS BOOK IN SPITE OF YOUR SIREN PULL TO THE ROCKY SHORES OF UNPRODUCTIVITY. But a big thank-you to ARMY (and many other fandoms). When writing felt like too much, you helped me laugh, swoon, and cry.

And finally to Adrienne Young.

This book doesn't even exist without you. I would never have made my dreams come true without your relentless hand-holding, aggressive encouragement, and general belief. It's the only reason you can hold this book in your hands and read these acknowledgments. You knew this was the one. You read every chapter as I wrote it and spent hours outlining and brainstorming and picking me up off the floor when I said things like "this book is so boring" and "nothing happens." And yes, yes, you were right. This book is the one. I'm big enough to say it. But I am absolutely not big enough to apologize for Harry Potter World. Here's to many more books that you can supervise. And acknowledgments where we pretend like we barely like each other. You are my best friend, my writing guidepost, my truth teller, and biggest fan. I love you so much that sometimes I hate it (and you).